For Lisa —
Readers are my favorite
kind of people!
Enjoy, Schuyler Kaufman
2006

Dear Mouse ...

MURDER, LOVE, AND MOVIE-MAKING IN THE CAROLINA MOUNTAINS

BY

schuyler kaufman

High Country Publishers, Ltd
Boone, North Carolina

High Country Publishers, Ltd.
197 New Market Center, #135
Boone, North Carolina 28607
http://www.highcountrypublishers.com

e-mail: editor@highcountrypublishers.com

Library of Congress Cataloguing-in-Publication data

Kaufman, Schuyler.
    Dear mouse . . . murder, love, and movie-making
in the Carolina mountains / by schuyler kaufman.
        p. cm.
    ISBN 0-9713045-2-1
    1. Motion picture actors and actresses—Fiction.
2. Fathers and daughters—Fiction. 3. Appalachian Re-
gion—Fiction. 4. Extortion—Fiction. I. Title.

PS3611.A84D4 2001
813'.6—dc21   2001032886

COVER PHOTOGRAPHS: RUSSELL KAUFMAN-PACE
COVER DESIGN: RUSSELL KAUFMAN-PACE

First printing February, 2002
10 9 8 7 6 5 4 3 2

NOTE:

All of my characters are fictional. None of them is meant to represent any real personality, living or dead, human or otherwise.

I made up Beller County, too. It lies about halfway between Watauga County and Avery County, near North Carolina's border with Tennessee. Places outside Beller County are quite real, though, and folks around those parts can probably tell you where they are.

Readers with current CPR certification will notice that CPR techniques used in my rescue scenes are outdated. Besides the plot points involved, some lag is inevitable, because real-life techniques are updated by the Red Cross each year.

"Barbie," as the name applies to the spectacularly proportioned fashion doll, is a registered trademark of Mattel Corporation.

A portion of the proceeds from the sale of every copy of *Dear Mouse . . .* will be donated to the Guardian ad Litem Program, to assist in their important work with children caught up in the complexities of the court system.

Dear Mouse ...

.Prologue.

HOTEL 1212: DAY ONE

Dear Mouse,
Coming out of treatment is like coming out of a womb. It's a whole, real world Out There, exciting, new, utterly untrustable. Not many of its people have the slightest interest in my sobriety. I have to learn how to live among them all over again.

I walked away from the treatment center. I'd sworn to myself I would. Nobody to pick me up. No limo. No photographers getting pictures of Matt Logan, Strongbow himself to the movie buffs, coming out of treatment with his face half-rebuilt.

Actually, the only people I could ask to pick me up would bring tequila—or vodka, if they can't deal with the worm. I don't want to go through all this again.

My watch said two o'clock: time enough to get to your school for a last good-bye. Sure, I'm not supposed to; I almost have the restraining order memorized. I didn't see why it ought to stop me. I had to talk with you one more time. I headed for the subway.

Five minutes before school was over, I waited in the alley across the street. I knew which gate the first graders come out, so I wasn't looking anywhere else. A bell rang somewhere inside the building, and a single finger tapped my shoulder. "You're in contempt of court," someone said.

I didn't want to take my eyes off the boil of children pouring down the steps. I might miss you.

"We can't bring Michaella out if you're here," he said.

I pulled my attention away from the schoolyard and turned.

A three-piece suit stood there, maybe an inch taller than I am, with a carefree, moustache-framed smile, and absolutely nothing else remarkable about him.

Beside him stood your mother.

She was beautiful, like a perfect, petite mannequin, and almost as warm. Her eyes were huge, luminous blue, made up like an Egyptian dancer's, in a face as pale as she could make it. Her hair clung close to her head, a shining black cap.

I activated what's left of the Famous Grin. "Uh—Hi. I guess you're wondering why I'm—"

He offered a friendly hand. "I'm your wife's lawyer."

"Mr. Wyndham," Nancy said. "To you, he has no first name."

I reminded myself to breathe, pitched my voice low and calm, tried not to stammer. "I only want to tell her—to say—"

"No." Tiny, delicately boned and combat-ready, Nancy poised on high heels like a game hen defending its only chick. "You could have killed her. You stay away from my child."

Anger came too easily, blocking my breath. I pushed words past it. "M-ickie's my child, too."

"Michaella," Nancy said. "She's Michaella. You're the only one who calls her Mickie."

The lawyer quieted her with a gesture. "Matt, if you didn't understand the order—"

"I understood it. I only want to tell her—"

"You're not to try to contact her. You are not to see her. You are to stay at least five hundred feet away from her. You can catch a glimpse of her from that traffic light down there, if you want. I'd say that's about five hundred feet away."

The light changed and a taxi's brakes shrieked. Windows of your school were blank as windows are in direct sunlight.

"The room she's in is on the other side of the building," Wyndham, Esquire said. "It doesn't have windows." As I turned back, he smiled, the only reasonable voice in all this chaos.

"Hey." He put a hand on my shoulder. "You're very lucky; you know that? If you weren't Matt Logan, you'd be in jail right now. We decided not to push for that. A little girl needs to be proud of her Daddy, even if he's out of her life. Let's not make your wife file a complaint for contempt of court."

I knew who was to blame, of course, and I couldn't do anything about it there. "Okay, Nance. You win this round. Look, will you p-please at least tell her—"

"No messages. Sorry," Wyndham said. "And if you have anything to say to my client, have your lawyer contact me."

"She's m—Nancy's still my wife—"

"Not for long, I'm afraid. Matt, please don't make us pull Michaella out of her school—"

"No!" I spun around to face your mother. "Nance, no—you can't do that! She loves this school—"

He stepped between us. "The child needs to be protected from harassment."

I moved off. "Okay. You've made your p-point. I wish—"

"Nobody here cares what you wish," Nancy said. He touched her arm and she was quiet. At least her lawyer behaves like a human being.

I picked up my bag, walked to the light, turned in time to see you come out. You ran to Wyndham, leaped into his arms, locked your legs around his waist, collected kisses from him.

I watched him as he put you and your mother into a cab and strode off down another street. I stayed where I was, watched the cab swerve into traffic and disappear. I don't know how long I stood staring at the place where you weren't. A single finger tapped my shoulder. "She's a very special little girl, you know," Wyndham said.

"Yeah. I only wanted to say Good-bye."

"I know," he said. "But New York has anti-stalking laws for just this reason. Maybe it would be better if you stay out of sight."

"I'm in compliance with the order."

"The order'll probably get tightened," he said. "Hey. You got a place to stay?"

None of his business.

"Some friend or something?"

None of my friends care for me, sober.

"Because Nancy's changed the lock on the apartment."

Surprise, surprise.

"Trust me, I know how you feel. We won't press charges, but don't do this again, will you?"

"I won't." I swung around to face him. "I won't, I p-promise. Look, t-tell Nancy she has my word—I'll leave her and Mickie alone. Please. Whatever Nancy wants from me is fine, but this isn't Mickie's fault. Don't let Nancy p-punish her." In treatment you don't bother to hide your feelings; everyone knows how you feel anyway. I haven't got back into the habit yet.

The lawyer smiled. "That isn't the issue here. It's my job to protect them. Both of them."

I don't mind his job. More power to him. What I mind is your mother's glitzy, vindictive smile. It says, "Now I know where to hit you." Mousy, it scares me out of my tree.

I got to the hotel the center referred me to, off Fiftieth Street near Broadway. It's small, sure, but the privacy is worth the rates they charge. A pair of alumni run it, so they weren't surprised when a zoned-out zombie checked in. I am not in any way unique.

The room is tiny on purpose. It's supposed to make us feel secure. I have a bed, a dresser, and a desk and chair. A little, padded stool lives under the bed. The maintenance program I'm in involves a lot of prayer. Me, I'm not a praying man. I feel silly making elaborate demands of a Power that I've always believed knows who I am and what I need already. My praying usually consists of "Why are you doing this to me?" or—more and more lately—"Thank You." The Serenity one happens, too, sometimes.

I unpacked the bag, phoned your Gammer and Gaffer to say I was Out. Mother said she'd tell Father, ended the call. I used up more than my share of her patience the second time I came home with alcohol on my breath. Her father died drunk.

I hung up and sat with my elbows on the desk and my eyes on the heels of my hands, and tried to think. Nothing. Not a single coherent thought existed in the universe. My brain had that tingly numbness you get in the Recovery Room, just before the anaesthetic wears off.

This was going to hurt.

I could stay and wallow in it, or I could let it hurt while I did something constructive. I have a life to put together. The sooner I confronted the real world, the sooner I could get started. I got up and went out for a newspaper.

It's odd, going into public with a face like this. Nobody

wanted to look at me long enough to wonder who I was. One glance at me, and people found the nearest theater poster very interesting. This must be what ghosts feel like. I walked fast, trying not to see them trying not to see me. It's easy to say we shouldn't regret the past, but Mousy—Never mind.

The corner newsstand displayed the *Probe* among all the other magazines and papers. That tabloid must be having a slow week; it's running a story about my getting Out. As usual, they have their facts wrong. It says I got Out last week and retired to Monte Carlo. It's just as well. There's a picture from last year, one of the better ones—the ideal Everyman.

Honey, I don't look anything like that now. I probably never will again. The plastic surgeon is an artist, but I'll never look any better than average. "Forgettable" is the best I can hope for, they tell me. I'm about a third of the way there: physical therapy and blunt stubbornness have overcome the limp. The nose is ruler-straight, and the jaw, just out of wires, is human if no longer heroic. But the boyish face with the Famous Grin is seamed with scars like a crazy quilt. One eye opens too wide; the other lid droops too low. Overall, this is the face of a great radio artist, on the way to becoming ordinary. I don't know if I'll ever get used to that. I left the *Probe*, got a daily paper, and headed back to the hotel.

Apartments For Rent is well stocked this time of year. I spread the paper across the desk, marked off ads. I don't need anything fancy, but it has to be within walking distance of the Acute Care Hospital at Central Park East. I start a year and a day's community service in the emergency room tomorrow, and I won't be driving any time soon.

I got to the bottom of the first column, started working up the next. So far, there were about half a dozen possibilities. I was doing pretty well, and then the pen ran out of ink. I scribbled a hole into the paper, threw down the pen. I did a few neck rolls to get out the kinks.

It went deeper than neck kinks and I knew it.

I got up and walked, rubbed my neck, tried to think.

No thinking could hold this back. I'd put it off too long. Against my will came the picture of your mother, vengeful, triumphant, her lawyer Wyndham barely keeping her civilized. And you, jumping into his arms, your legs around his waist, while he kissed and kissed and kissed you. I had just enough sense not to put my fist through something. One shattered hand is enough for this life. Your mother's lawyer's a decent guy, but he doesn't have to—never mind. It's probably my fault. Everything else is.

They tell you to remember the word HALT: never let yourself get too Hungry, Angry, Lonely, Tired. Great. What do you do when it's already happened?

There's the prayer for Serenity: "God grant me the serenity to accept the things I cannot change, the courage to change the things I can, and the wisdom to know the difference." I can't change this. I have to accept it. I can accept a year of face reconstruction; I can accept having my hand broken and reset so I can play my piano again. I have to accept losing you.

Geez, it hurts. Nothing ever hurt like this, not the crash, not surgery, not those hellish first weeks in treatment.

At least then I could cry. I cried for two weeks. The third week, I got so disgusted with myself that I stopped. I haven't put out a tear since. Not even now, when I need it.

I walked harder. In this room, that's five strides up, turn, five strides back. If I took shorter steps, I could make it six each way. I took deep breaths until I hyperventilated. I laced my fingers behind my neck and squeezed until it hurt.

When it's physical, there are painkillers. When it's mental, there's tequila.

Not.

Wrong.

You don't scream in hotels. There are people in other rooms to be considered.

Five strides up, turn, five back—and there was the stool. I aimed a kick at it, and stopped. What could it hurt? I dropped to my knees on the stool, dug my head into folded arms on the edge of the bed, and let 'er rip.

No tears. No words. No sound. Only pain.

I don't know how long I knelt there, trying to hold together. I was shivering when somebody knocked at my door. That meant I had to get up, do something about it. My knees hurt. I rubbed my dry eyes, breathed, tried to put on a civil face to answer the door.

The desk clerk had brought towels. "You try to go back to your family?"

I didn't need to be asked that.

"It's the roughest time you'll have," he said. "After this it gets easier. It does."

I nodded. "Thanks."

"Find a meeting and go to it." He handed me the linens and a much-copied list of meetings in the area. "Go tonight. You got to stop being sorry for yourself."

Right. As if everyone has gone through what I've gone through. They tell you to try to get to ninety meetings in ninety days after you get Out. At first I'd said, "No way." I closed the door, fished out my glasses to decipher the list. I think staying sober will be my full-time job for a while, Mouse.

Having something to do pushed the pain back somewhat. I had to plan to eat, shower, shave, think up something to wear— not that the bag had held any bewildering choice.

I think that meeting saved me tonight. Nobody understands an alcoholic like another alcoholic. You don't get pity, or lectures, or much poor-sweet-baby. But when you say you hurt, they know exactly what you mean.

Funny. One kid was putting in meeting time to get his license back. He'd caused an accident that injured several people. And I thought, "At least I'm the only person I damaged when I wrapped my car around the tree." Nobody knows why you weren't hurt, Mousy. You should have been smashed. I'm told I was too drunk to see that you were buckled in. It makes everything else bearable. All this and ten times more I can take, as long as you're okay.

I caught that boy staring at my face once or twice. Like most people, I had a container of coffee in front of me. I took my right hand from under the table and fooled with the cup, let him have a good look at the crooked bones and the scars. I could see him thinking, "At least I didn't mess myself up like *that*." If anything can keep me sober, it's the fear of hurting someone else. Maybe my scars will do the same for him.

Someone was advised to start a journal, write their feelings out. It sounded good to me. On my way back, I stopped and bought this clipboard, pad, and a couple of new pens. I can write anything here, and you won't ever see it. My head feels straighter already.

I may have inherited the alcoholism, Mousy, but I don't have to inherit the drinking. Not if I don't want to—hang on. Someone's at the door . . .

<><><>

. . . Mouselet, what can I say? What is there to say? "I'm sorry" doesn't mean anything. Not this time.

That was a process server, with two envelopes. One was a summons, of course. Your mother's filing for divorce. I don't know why she didn't do it a year ago.

The other envelope blew me apart. In it was a copy of the revised restraining order, forbidding me to come within sight of you, and a typewritten note.

They've taken you out of your school.

I should have left you alone. I should have left you alone, Mouse. I should have obeyed the order, not made trouble. Your mother's taking it out on you, and you can't do anything about it. I should have left you alone. Now you have to find new friends in a strange new school, in the middle of the year.

I won't do it again, Mousekin. I can't let your mother think I even want to communicate with you. Ever. I've done you enough harm. I wish I could see you one more time, just long enough to say, "I will love you forever"—but I won't try again. I won't. From now on, I have two ways to say I love you—paying your child support, and writing in this journal.

I'll write it here as often as I need to:
    I love you.
    I'm sorry.
    Good-bye.

Dear Mouse ...

PRODUCER: ANTON "TONY" PORNADA
ASSISTANT PRODUCER: DORA REDHAWK
CINEMATOGRAPHER: SERAPHINA "PHINA" POWIAK

CAST LIST:

MATT LOGAN	*AS*	JACK BADGER
HALLA McKEE		SARAH DRAKE
JULIEN DARCY		ANDREA QUAYLE
SCOTT PRATT		CHARLIE RANGER

AND INTRODUCING . . .

GABRIEL SPERANZO	*AS*	LITTLE GIDEON DRAKE

SET DOCTOR: PETER "DOC" JEFFERSON, M.D.
STUDIO RECEPTIONIST: YVAN WASHINGTON
WRANGLERS: "BABE:" TIM MADISON; "ZEBRA DUN:" BILL ASHE
DOLLY GRIP: DAKOTA SMYTHE
MR LOGAN'S STUNT DOUBLE: DAKOTA SMYTHE
MS DARCY'S BODY DOUBLE: CRYSTAL DAWN BELLER
MS DARCY'S ATTORNEY: OLIN BUNNEY
MR LOGAN'S ATTORNEYS: BREWSTER BEANE; GOLDE SILVER

"WE WOULD LIKE TO THANK OUR FAMILIES . . . "

KATHARINE TREVIDIC LOGAN	MR LOGAN'S MOTHER
MATTATHIAS PENN LOGAN	MR LOGAN'S FATHER
MERANDA LOGAN VON KOZAK	MR LOGAN'S SISTER
MICHAELLA "MOUSE" LOGAN	MR LOGAN'S DAUGHTER
ANASTASIA "NANCY" LOGAN	MR LOGAN'S EX
N. WYNDHAM, ESQ.	MR LOGAN'S EX'S ATTORNEY
DANNAL HARPER-McKEE	MS McKEE'S SON
ROLAND HARPER	MS McKEE'S EX
JANELLE HARPER	MS McKEE'S EX'S WIFE

LOCAL FAMILIES

TAMRA SPERANZO	GABRIEL'S MOM
KEN BELLER	CRYSTAL'S HUSBAND
RON BELLER	KEN'S DOUBLE FIRST COUSIN
SHARON BELLER	PROPRIETOR OF TARA

***BELLER MOUNTAIN REPUBLICAN* REPORTER:** LISA BELLER
LAW ENFORCEMENT PROVIDED BY:
INSP. MEGAN QUIN; LT. JONAS PIKE; DEP. DUANE SLOCUM; TABU

.1.

APRIL FOOL'S DAY: YEAR THREE
ON LOCATION: BELLER MOUNTAIN

Dear Mouse,
Everyone behaved nicely at this year's hearing. It says a lot for my lawyer's clout. The restraining order still stands, of course, still forbids me to see you. I've been sober for three years now, but so what? Your mother and Wyndham teamed up like heart and lungs, and I lost again.

I got back to work yesterday. Work keeps me sane. Sure, Beller County's out of the way. It costs less to shoot on location than in a studio. We're filming in the North Carolina Appalachians, surrounded by golf courses, ski areas, Christmas tree farms, and tobacco fields. The scenery is sensational, and the local people work hard and don't pitch tantrums. We've set up at a motel in Beller Mountain, the county seat.

The county movie commission rented us a studio, and Tony Pornada's script keeps on getting better. This is the first decent movie I've landed since before the wreck. Work is good.

One thing about low-budget projects, Mousy: I can have a hand in almost any phase of movie-making I want. It's been a long time since I've done more than recite lines, hit marks, and get photographed. It's like finding a whole, new way of doing what I've been doing for the last fifteen years.

Some doll broke into our motel room last night, hoping to make us "discover" her. She must have poked around in the room for several minutes before her heavy perfume woke me.

I sat up. "Good evening. Who are you?"

The girl shut a drawer and wheeled around. Recovering fast, she let her fur coat slip from naked shoulders as she—No.

[*Mousy, some things Daddy doesn't discuss with his little girl, even in his journal. It's late now, past your bedtime. Sweet dreams, wherever you are. Daddy misses you.*]

Moonlight and that new scent "In/Tense" filled the room. One of the old video cameras crouched on the dresser, its red light blinking. The girl floated toward me, her frosted nail polish glinting in the moonlight. "I'm Crystal Beller." Her voice was soft and childlike. She probably works hard on it. The coat slithered to the floor. "I came to make you happy."

Right. With those claws. I flicked on the light. The girl was tiny, like a sixth grader, exquisitely developed, expertly made up. This was a woman, fully grown and deliberately danger-ous. If stars were made her way, the world would be full of bad actresses' children. I cocked an eyebrow.

Tony rolled over in the other bed, growling. *Demon Dun*'s budget doesn't run to single rooms. "What to hell is this?" Tony hates waking at night. The girl snatched up her coat.

"Crystal Beller," I said. "She came to make us happy."

"My God's sake." He looked her over. "You're in the wrong room, Gorgeous. Matt here can't help you. I'm the director and I never listen to him. You're not my type."

She shook tawny curls, moving to his bed. "I can be any type you want me to be. I got experience. I sing four nights a week at Starling Resort—and I can give you the best—"

"Not tonight, Beautiful. Get an Inflate-a-Date."

"Oh, yeah?" She curled a pretty lip. "I got news for you—the *Probe*'s going to love this story. You got me in your motel and you raped me. In every grocery store in the U.S. of A."

"The *P-Probe*?" This wasn't funny. If my Mouse saw a story like that in the tabloids—

And Tony laughed. He fell back to the bed and cackled. "Nobody'd buy that, Baby." He pointed at the camera. Its red light winked. "We got all this on tape. What d'you think, Matt?

The TV show—what's its name—*Practical Jokes and Out-Takes*? Should we sell it to them?"

I gulped a breath. "Er—no—How about that *Funniest Bloopers* show? It pays better."

Crystal Beller wrapped her coat around her and left. As the door slammed on the spring chill, I leaped out of bed, grabbed the camera, pressed EJECT. Nothing happened.

"Hey, be careful, it's old." Tony said. "We're running the battery down to recharge it."

Dear God. "Tony, if we don't—the *Probe* would p-ublish anything—if she sells that to a tabloid—"

"She won't go near it. Stupid people can't stand being laughed at. Go back to sleep."

I didn't. That perfume of hers stuck around, nauseatingly. This morning, my journal in its manila envelope wasn't on the dresser, and the pants I pulled on had a broken zipper. Tony was already in the room next door, setting it up to have interviews for the part of Sarah the hag. This was the interview of a lifetime for some of these actresses. The least I could do was show up on time, and my phone trilled, somewhere under Tony's rewrites.

I dug it out. "This is Matt."

I could hear Tony's growl through the thin wall. "Matt? That first Sarah—what's her name? Halla McKee—is due here any minute. Where to hell is my bright particular star?"

"I haven't been particularly bright since *Strongbow IV*. I'm almost there. Look, did you say Halla? I know that name—"

Behind me, the doorknob rattled, and fresh "In/Tense" blew into the room. Last night's doll stood in the doorway, holding the plastic card she picks motel locks with, and my manila envelope. "Hey, Mr. Logan. You know that tape—the one y'all made of me last night?"

Damn. "Tony, I have company. I'll b-be there." I shut the phone, made myself breathe. I did not want to stammer before Crystal Beller. Acutely aware, suddenly, of the broken zipper, I stepped behind the chair. "Do you ever knock, wait till you're invited in?"

She stared through the vinyl, her smile lilting with fun, challenge, invitation. By daylight she is stunning. She lifted eyes the color and size of Olympic swimming pools. The sun backlit her skimpy dress. Nothing lay between it and a honey-gold salon suntan. She held up the envelope. "You want to, you know, toss for this? Trade that tape for your diary, and—me?"

If she touched me, I'd be in quarantine for life. "I don't want what you have, thanks."

Her eyes narrowed. "Sugar, I can get good money for this. You want to give me that tape, or—" She shook the envelope "—read this in the *Probe*? Or are you queer?"

Crystal Beller has the face of guileless innocence and the mind of a troll. I said, "We prefer the word 'gay'" (to all my friends who are gay—Sure, I lied. I can only plead self-defense, but I plead it desperately). I reached for the envelope. "That's mine. Give it back."

Crystal retreated to the doorway, my envelope held high. Someone nipped it out of her grasp from behind. "This is yours?" and my envelope flew spinning to my hands.

The first Sarah hopeful, Halla McKee, had arrived for her interview, dressed to impress and in the nick of time. The look was right—a bony, mobile face, an active body. Her eyes lit up with the relish of action, and Crystal attacked her, spitting obscenities. Glimmer-frosted nails slashed for eyes, fists struck at the breasts and face. Halla dodged, fending her off. "Hey! Crystal, you brat, watch it—this shirt's silk!"

I tossed my envelope to the dresser, stepped in to the rescue. "Halla, stop it!" I barked. "Don't hurt her!" Catching Halla from behind, I swung her out of the way of pink claws. "Get out!" I hissed at Crystal. "I won't let her hurt you! Quick!"

Halla picked up my cue like a pro, and struggled, kicking and flailing in my arms. Poor Crystal stood gawking as if she had the next line, and forgot it. "Go on," I panted. "I can't hold her much longer! Go!"

With a last, lost glance, Crystal leaped for her truck.

Halla struggled theatrically until Crystal's truck merged with highway traffic, then she relaxed against me. Her short curls, the color of dark sherry, brushed my moustache. She smelled clean, fresh; her body fitted solidly with mine.

We both spoke. "Are you okay?" We both nodded.

She pulled away, stepped back to the walkway. I clutched at my pants and slid behind the door, a bit embarrassed. Crystal had awakened a part of me that I'd thought was dead for the past three years, and my pants were unzipped. "I—Th-anks. How did you know—?"

"I've worked with Crystal before. She's pretty ruthless."

"She's—" I searched vainly for the word—"incredible—"

"Yeah." Halla's face is too freckled for prettiness. Her gaze never fell below my chin. Heaven bless her. "Crystal can look like anything you want her to be," she said. Turning away, she poked her silk shirttail into trim jeans. "See you." She headed next door for her interview.

"Give me five minutes—max." I could work with this one for the rest of my life. "I'll b-I'll be there—" Halla McKee was gone. I took a moment to watch her walk to the room next door, and found myself wondering if it was really Crystal who had awakened my interest.

Never mind. I shut the door, opened the packet. The letter on top caught my eye:

" *Dear Mouse,*
"Tonight I woke in cold horror from another dream about the wreck. I have no memory of that day, except in dreams. . . . Reality keeps me sober, now. . . ."

I lifted that page. The next was blank. All the other pages were blank. I held half a hundred blank pages, with one page of my journal stuffed in there to make the packet look real. My whole day was crammed with actresses like Halla McKee to interview, and some bimbo with the body and brain of an adolescent Barbie doll was out selling my personal life to a tabloid.

It was after six before I got time and privacy to call my lawyer in New York. Brewster Beane wasn't excited. "Easy does it, Matt. Who'd want your journal? You're not that famous. Stop worrying."

I don't pay him to stroke my ego, fortunately. "Look, can't you stop publication?"

"I'll warn Nancy to keep tabloids away from the child. Hey,

I got news. You've made your last alimony payment. Your ex-wife married her divorce lawyer yesterday."

"Nancy's married Wyndham?" I gave it a thought. Nancy deserves a good marriage. Wyndham never drank or raised his voice in his life. At the divorce hearing, I lost my temper, and he got a gun permit. "Sure, tell them congratulations," I said. "He's a great guy."

"If he wasn't your ex-wife's lawyer, you might even mean that. Matt, forget the tabloids. You're a free man, except for child support, and—anyway. We'll talk. Sleep tight."

I couldn't leave it—and I got it: Meranda! If anyone can handle tabloids, she can. Pit bulls avoid my sister because she's meaner and hangs on longer. It's why the network put her on the White House beat. I punched in my sister's cell number.

Meranda was not in a good mood. "Oh, for God's sake, Brat, are you drunk again?"

"No." I never expect civility from my sister. "Meranda, I need help," I said.

"That's Baroness von Kozak to you."

I could have disputed her claim to the title, but you don't bandy words with my sister unless you have a permanently un-resolved death wish. I said, "Huh?" The only wise response.

"Some charmer came up at my book-signing, prattling about getting *my brother*'s John Hancock on something. I thought it was you till I had a good look at him. You look like half the men on the planet. We had a deal: to the public, we are not related."

"I'd never tell anyone. Will you help me, or do I hang up?"

"You don't—ever—hang up on me. I can make you very sorry. Tell me your troubles."

I told her all about Crystal Beller. " . . . and if it's printed, Nancy can say I'm trying to get in touch with M-Mickie—"

"Reality check, Brat: your journal will never see light of day. Nobody's going to pay for maudlin drivel about Daddy's Little Darling. Take it from the Baroness—"

"Sure, *B-Baroness*. Only by m-marriage, and not anymore. You never were a b-bar-baroness anyway, because the mar-riage was an-annulled. Good-b-bye, Mer-randa." I hung up on her. My sister can get me to the stammering point faster than thought, always could. I hate stammering. She thinks it's funny.

And my journal was still gone. What a day.

Tony's assistant director knocked and poked her head around the door, her blue-black braids swinging like rope curtains on either side of her face. "Tony, I got Tara." If Tony ever went straight, Dora'd be his first love. She gave up smoking because he doesn't like the smell. "Everyone get packed," she said around the pen between her teeth. "We're moving. The budget can pay for a motel with bolt locks, people."

"It's why I keep you around," Tony said. "Matt, you ready to look at the interview tapes?"

.2.

NEW QUARTERS: TARA
(THE BARN DOOR BOLTED)

Dear Mouse,
It was an idea. The National Tabloid Rag and Bone Society, or whatever they call themselves, once named James Garner the Friendliest Celebrity of the Year, because he kept sending in stories about himself. How many lurid James Garner headlines have you ever read? I thought it might work for your Dad, Mouselet. After we moved, I took the page from the envelope, and found my way to Alpine Vista, Florida.

The *Probe*'s logo spreads across plate glass, as if they're proud of what they do. I put on my glasses, got into a needy bore character, ordered my skin not to crawl visibly, went in.

An expensive receptionist behind the desk cracked gum into her phone system. She dealt neatly with three phone calls at once before she teethed up at me, chewing. I pulled out the Famous Grin. "Hi, there. I'm Matt Logan. This page—"

"Ooh! Matt Logan! I love *Strongbow*! Ever since I was a little girl, I'd pretend I was Red Eva, and I'd gallop into battle at your side. It is so cool, the way you took a true historical figure, and followed the actual legend of the real Strongbow." She gave me a special, gum-filled smile, launched into the *Strongbow* plot with a true fan's disregard for time or convenience. "When you helped the MacMorrough fight off the Danes, he said you could have his greatest treasure, only it was his daughter, but her face was dirty from the battle, and she was six feet tall, and you thought she was a hag, but she grabbed that soldier's helmet and dipped it in the well, and washed her face, and she was beautiful! I loved that part! And you weren't just a mercenary, you were the Earl of Pembroke, all the time!"

"I—You're very kind. You know a lot about it."

"I wrote a paper about the Earl of Pembroke in high school. I got an A-minus on it." She reached for her phone system. "We got a thingie about you. You want to see it?" She used the phone and hung up as I brought out the page from my journal. "Ooh, no, is that the page we're missing?"

"I—yes—I'm offering—I'm making a new movie, *Demon Dun*, a horror-romance—You can add this page to the—"

"Ooh, I'm sorry, we can't. It's out. You want to see it?"

A folded paper was thrust in my face. I didn't want to believe it. There I smirk on the front page, Everyman with a hangover, a lousy picture taken with your mother six years ago. I look half-squiffed, probably was. Nancy looks brave and unhappy. Probably was. The headline wails: *"Strongbow Agony! Letters to Mouse!"* (CONTINUED TO THE CENTER SPREAD).

As I opened it, I heard a familiar sound. A camera clicked and buzzed as someone took serial close-up pictures. I hadn't fooled anyone. I ordered my face to stay still and let it happen. If you try to escape, these people get worse. Think of your Aunt Meranda. I don't know how I got away. I don't think I stopped moving until I arrived in our room at Tara, tonight.

<><><>

The *Probe* hit the stands today. Crystal'd got more pages of my journal than I thought. The article quotes bits dating back two months. Of course they've skewed most of the facts: my sister's an unnamed "dethroned princess"; I'm still a "big star"; your mother is identified as "Mouse"; she was in the car when I crashed. I collected every page of journal I've written since the night Crystal Beller broke in, stuffed them in the old manila envelope, and threw it into the dumpster.

I'm an idiot. Maybe an hour later, I sneaked back to the dumpster and climbed in to pick through flimsy plastic bundles of who-knows-what. The dumpster pealed around me like a gong. I straightened up, envelope in hand.

"Mr. Logan? What are you doing in there?" The owner of the motel peered over the edge of the Dumpster, mascara tangling around her hard eyes. Once a six-foot biker queen, she became a Southern belle after she won a lawsuit, bought this place and named it Tara. Her make-up is always perfect, her hair aggressively golden and curly, her dresses floaty and ruffly. Under the thin fabric, a skull is tattooed high on one breast. Once you know it's there, it's hard to look anywhere else. Her name's Sharon Beller. I only dare to call her Ma'am.

I offered the Famous Grin. "Hi, Ma'am. I—I threw this away. By mistake." Iron-faced, Ma'am let me clamber out.

Geez. Here I sit, writing again, beneath a white plastic column. Early moths make love to the "Vacancy" light. Behind me, Dora and Tony shuffle schedules in our room; before me, our camera operator springs on and off the retaining wall, hefting the hand-held camera like Styrofoam, shooting moonlight footage of one hundred seventy well-placed pounds of recreational gear. His name is Dakota Smythe, and Phina plans to talk Tony into hiring him as a dolly grip.

We've settled into our new home. This is Tara, the motel version.

.3.

THE STUDIO:
AFTER HOURS, FRIDAY

D ear Mouse,
      I thought I'd used up more than my share of bad luck
      last week. Guess not. Nothing went right for me today.
No, that's not entirely true. You're safe and that's good.

But Mouseling—Hang on, I'll start with this morning. I'd
stepped out into slippery rain, when the room phone rang. I was
running short on time, but I stepped back in and picked up anyway: "This is Matt."

"Mr. Logan?" The night clerk was going off duty. "Some
girl called for you at four-thirty this morning. She sounded kind
of young. I didn't think you wanted to be woke up—"

Quite right. "Thanks. Give me the number; maybe I can
call her back." I scribbled it down, pocketed the paper. The
code was in-state, at least. I don't have many fans, Mousy; the
last *Strongbow* movie came out before I married your mother.
I've done some TV since, and a few films, mostly fizzles. I like
live theater best, but who goes to that nowadays? Some fans
aren't very considerate, but I can't afford to alienate even them.

I got to the studio ten minutes later than I wanted to. The
syndicate that owns Starling Resort also runs the county movie
commission. They bought an old tobacco warehouse and con-
verted it into a studio, hoping to attract film projects to the
area. I've worked in worse places. The roof doesn't leak, the

floor won't flood, the place is cavernous. It's fireproof inside and out. We could shoot a barn burning in here, and have room left over for a flash flood.

The tobacco aroma drives Dora crazy. She started smoking in elementary school, and quitting's been hellish for her. She's bitten the ends off all of her pens. There's always a new one between her first two fingers. As far as I know, she hasn't cheated, and she refuses to get a patch.

This morning, my make-up didn't go on right. I do my own make-up, so I could only blame myself for it. At last, I slathered it on anyhow, didn't bother to trim my moustache—my role as Badger isn't glamourous. During tests for Andrea the heroine, I had to focus on every move. Actors break their hearts over auditions like this. The least I can do is give what I have.

When lunch time finally came, I played with the idea of retooling the make-up, and my intercom chimed. "Uh—" Tony's done a deal with Appalachian State University in Boone. Most of our support staff are students on internships. They call nobody Mister off campus, but I seem to be too old for them to come out with an actual first name. Most of them call me Uh. "I got a detective here, asking for you."

I thought of Crystal Beller's break-in. "I'm on my way."

A man in razor-creased pants paced the front office. He stopped to glare at me. "Hello, sir." The words were a greeting. The tone was chronic dislike. This was not about Crystal.

I gathered I ought to know the face. A fuzzy memory, from the old days— "Pike. That's it, Sergeant Pike." When I was drinking, tough guys used to beat up Strongbow a lot. Pike was one of the detectives despatched by the NYPD to find out who hit me. I always pretended I didn't know. I added, "*Detective* Sergeant Pike. Why aren't you in New York?"

His folded arms did not invite a handshake. "Lieutenant Pike, retired. I live here. The Sheriff asked me to help them out on this. You got an empty office, sir?"

An office down the hall was unused, not empty: a desk, chairs, dust. Pike took charge. "Sit down, sir." Pike calls everyone Sir or Ma'am so he doesn't have to learn names. "We'll be here a while." As I sat, he leaned over me. "Where is she?"

"Where is who?"

Pike slapped his hand flat on the desk. I jumped like a gun-shy rabbit. He always does that. It used to play merry hell on my hangovers. "Don't act dumb, sir, you're no good at it. You know what I'm talking about."

I shook my head. His face hardened. I said, "Hang on. Hang about. Pretend I don't have a clue and tell me what's going on. Every 'she' in my life is where she belongs, as far as—" and my diaphragm turned over. "Dear God, it's Mouse—my lit-little g-girl?" I forced myself to breathe, my fists jammed into the pockets of Badger's jacket. "How did you lose her?"

"I got a golf date," he said. "The longer this takes—"

I gritted teeth. "*Tell me.*"

"Tssht. Her parents put her on a red-eye to Orlando—"

"Her parents? I'm one of her parents."

"The Wyndhams. Last night they put her on a plane in New York to visit her grandmother in Orlando, while they went out of town. She wasn't on the plane in Florida this morning."

"Atlanta—No, Charlotte! They stop over in Charlotte—"

"Yeah, you should be a detective. Her grandmother claims her no-'count father took her. That'd be you, sir. Where is she?"

"I haven't—" Hang on. Some girl, sounding kind of young—I shook my head, looked him in the eye, shrugged. "I've had no contact with my daughter since I wrecked my car."

I outstared him, accepted his card, saw him to the front office. "I'll call you if I hear from her." I flashed the Famous Grin, ushered him out. Then I wheeled around, tore up the hall to my dressing room. My jacket hung where I'd put it. I dug into the pocket. The phone number was there.

I got hold of it, and Pike loomed over me. As I startled, he reached for the paper. I snapped a fist around it, held it up between our faces. It's a big fist, scarred, with one bone that never healed straight after three resettings. Pike should have been impressed, except he knows the only fights I've ever won were choreographed. He held out a hand.

My jaw jutted sideways. I locked on to his eyes. "I want you to tell me if you find her."

"Sir, you know the court order—" He reached for my fist.

I kept it tight. "Just that she's safe, that's all."

"You look like a moron."

"Probably. A Yes or a No. Please."

It took him a moment. He sighed. "I'll let you know."

I uncurled my fingers with the paper between them.

He nipped it away. "What is this?"

"The night clerk at our motel said a girl tried to call me early this morning. She didn't say—"

Pike vanished. I fisted, pounded the doorjamb. Not hard; I've just started playing ragtime again. I told myself I'm a working man, and dragged myself out to the set.

Halfway across the studio floor, I met Dora. Clipboard in hand, a chewed-up pen between two fingers, she looked me over. "Matt, what's wrong?"

Was it so obvious? "My d-daughter's missing. They think she r-an away to find me. Look, would you ask Tony if I could have f-ifteen minutes? I have to get myself tog-together."

No problem. Tony has a knack for appreciating unclaimed treasures like Dora. She swings those black braids over her shoulders and things happen. In my dressing room, I sat down in my old make-up shirt to redo the face. I was almost finished when someone tapped at the door. "Come in."

"Uh—It's locked?" It was the guy whose new job is actors' hair. Dora thinks having hair done is soothing.

I unlocked my door. "Look, Badger doesn't do anything special with his hair. Just put it in order, would you?"

He moved around me awkwardly, thinking carefully whenever he changed position. The hair got fluffed in time. He stood back, critical and satisfied. "There, how's that?"

"Good," I said. "Heroic. Have you read the script?"

"Well—no—Should I have?"

"Maybe. Badger's no hero. He's a cold-blooded brat, whose thoughtlessness triggers the demon's curse."

He studied my reflection a moment. His eyes said Aha! and he swooped at my face with some implement. I flinched away. He did, too. "Oh, man, I'm sorry! Everyone knows you dread anything near your face."

Word gets around on a film set. "Okay, d-on't—don't worry

about it. Let's—let's try out what you had in mind."

It worked. The make-up needs a change of some kind, the hat won't sit right, but by gum, the hair works. I used it for focus, walked out to the floor in operating condition again. Work kept my mind occupied until the camera operator straightened her square back for the last time. She nodded, Tony yelled, "Cut!" and the last test for the role of Andrea was printed. Dakota, the new dolly grip, bent splendid shoulders to the task of shifting camera equipment, and the lights flicked out, set by set. I headed to my dressing room.

I had glop smeared over my make-up when my intercom chimed. It was the front desk. "Uh—I was supposed to tell you, 'She's safe.' Does that sound right?"

"Yeah. Thanks." I unglopped my face, locked my door, dug in to write. You must be on your way back to your mother by now, Mousy. Please, honey, no matter how much I want to see you, running away is dangerous. Think it through, next time.

So, the Andrea tests are finished. Time to clean up and get out of here. I'd better call and let your Gammer and Gaffer know that you're safe, at least.

Ah, geez, Mouse. I was *that* close to talking with you.

.4.

BLUE RIDGE PARKWAY:
RECOVERY: (LIFE GOES ON)

Dear Mouselet,

It's amazing how things work out. I thought I was in for a two or three-day tailspin at least, after your escapade. I've been going to meetings every night, trying to stay sane. Fortunately, at least ten meetings a week are held at the Beller Mountain Community Center, and a dozen others happen between here and Blowing Rock.

Then, when I got back from work this afternoon, I had a letter from Shannon. Shannon's a Beller Mountain girl about your age. She wrote to me on paper torn from a school notebook, and asked if she could keep on writing—but it'll be simpler to attach her letter. You probably have to read a Southern dialect into this:

Dear Mr. Matt Logan,

You can not know me. But you can call me 'Shannon,' which is my faverate name in the whole world. I am ten years old. I am in fourth grade. My Father has been gone for a long time. First, my Mother said, 'He was dead.' Then she said, 'He does not love me.' It makes me very sad. Then, my best friend, you can call her Tanya, that is her faverate name, found where you wrote letters to Mouse in the Probe. It said, 'You love her, but you are not allowed to tell her.' Well I thought, 'Maybe, my Father is like you. Maybe, he can not talk to me. So, maybe, I

*can pretend to write letters to him.' I hope you do not mind if
I send them to you. If you do, you can throw it away. The paper
says, 'You have a little girl.' I am not like her in some ways,
for instence, my hair. Her's might be red. Like your's. Mine is
brown. I am not tall, but short. But my gymnastics coach says,
'I have good power,' because I can run fast and jump high.
But, I am no good on the balence beam. I fell off three times, in
the meet. I kind of love school. I get to go out of class on
Mondays, Tuesdays, and Fridays, for Enrichment. We do: Photography, Astronomy, and we write stories. My Stepfather says,
'I am too young.' But I like writing. Well that is all for now.*
    Your Friend,
    'Shannon.'

Mouse, it's great, like hearing from you. Sure, you two are
different. Any bright child is different from any other bright
child, but some things ten-year-old girls have in common. I have
more energy now, because I don't have to wonder about you so
much. It's fun to think I could see her anywhere in this town,
and never know I'm looking at her. I may come to depend on
her letters to me as I depend on mine to you.

    Shannon thinks my hair is red, so her family must be doing
their job. My hair was dyed red for *Strongbow*. I wouldn't want
a child to see many of my other efforts.

    Demon Dun may be one I can be proud of, though, Mousy.
The tests for Sarah the hag are going faster than we predicted.
Nobody we've seen stands out, yet. We use the arrival scene—
Badger, with Andrea on his arm, turns up at Sarah's horse ranch
after four years, to pick up the car he left with Sarah. She slaps
him, "for coming back." The car has been sold, and Sarah spent
the money on her prize stallion Demon Dun, and on little Gideon,
a son that Badger didn't know he had. Fun stuff.

    Tony's called Halla McKee back after her interview. She's
scheduled to test tomorrow. Mousy, I'm looking forward to
this test like a starstruck amateur. I like Halla. I like the
way she jumped in when Crystal Beller tried to blackmail
me. I liked her quick responses during her interview. I like
her expressive, bony face and the energetic grace of her

movement. I like the way our bodies fit so comfortably together. I know I've seen her before. I wish I knew where.

Today, in the middle of the afternoon, our camera operator
began to kvetch: this was wrong; that wasn't right; she hated
everything. Tony knows the signs. "Take five, people. Phina,
my God's sake, what?" They huddled up, as Phina's dolly grip
stretched his spectacular back.

When the huddle broke up, Tony called a meeting, and gath-
ered us around a monitor to look at audition and rehearsal tapes.
Phina records everything. "It's not much," Tony apologized.
"It's subtle, but it's driving Phina nuts. Dora and I see it, too.
Check this out. You remember Halla McKee's interview?"

Of course I remembered Halla McKee's interview. My face
sneaked into a smile without consulting me. Every exchange
between us showed Halla and me behaving like interlocking
parts, working in tandem. I settled in and enjoyed.

"See that?" Tony said. "That, my angels, is chemistry. Now,
look." He ran my test with Julien Darcy, the soap diva who got the
role of Andrea. It's a great screen test. "You see it? Badger has to
end up with Andrea. Has to. I can't have neo-romantics coming
out of the theaters saying Badger should go back to Sarah."

I kept my voice low, gathering myself for a fight. "Look,
what are you saying? You won't want to use Halla McKee?"

Tony blew out his cheeks, flicked the question away. "We
haven't seen all the Sarahs, but you know what we got. Shut up
and let me think." After a long scowl, he heaved himself off his
seat. "If McKee gets here tonight, I suppose we could call and
ask her to come in early, tomorrow. Dora—"

My head lifted up. "Gets here? Doesn't she live here?"

They exchanged looks. On-screen, Halla laughed at me
again. Dora said, "He's right. Her agent's in Wilmington, but
she lives right here in town. This area has quite an arts community since the Starling Resort Syndicate set up this studio."

Tony zapped the machine off. His face had Executive Deci-
sion written all over it. "Listen up. Here's what we do." We
listened up like a class of trainees. "I want you—" he pointed at
me— "to get with the Darcy. Get her to work like that." He
pointed at the blank screen. "Think you can?"

"I don't know," I admitted. "If it's technique, I can. If it's genetic, I'll have a problem."

"If it's genetic, *I'll* have a problem. Dora, it looks like it'll be a long night again. Sorry."

She flipped a blue-black rope of hair behind her shoulders. "We'll sort it out. Don't forget who's coming tomorrow."

"Oh, my God's sake, I can't deal with a Star tomorrow!"

"Hang about—" I acted a laugh. The money people wanted to replace me with a bigger name when I was cast in this project. "What Star? Am I missing something?"

Tony was busy scowling. "Yeah, he called this afternoon. He wants to talk to you. Dora, what if we tried—"

Dora gave me the name. It didn't help. This guy and I are the same type. Height, build, coloring—we could be brothers. Since the wreck, there's a more-than-artistic resemblance to our noses and jawlines. The surgeon who put my face back together did the same for him once. I'd be a great stand-in for him. He'd be a great replacement for me.

Don't get me wrong, Mouselet, I like the guy. In the old days, before I met your mother, we occasionally showed up at the same parties. But this is my project. I like it. It has a good plot, solid characters. I need it. Acting is insecure work.

Tony and Dora were too busy, and Phina doesn't believe in actors. I drove away from the studio, trying to worry about useful things, like how do you tell a charming and talented actress her work has to improve? What will an outsider think of *Demon Dun*? How will Halla like working with me?

Right. I wasn't thinking about work. I thought about Halla McKee, and how easy she is to be with, how her angular face lights up when she smiles, the way her eyes and her hair match exactly, how we connect like mind readers. Nobody would ever call her pretty, so how come I keep thinking she's beautiful?

I do some of my best thinking while I drive. The Blue Ridge Parkway runs by, not far from Tara. We've contracted to shoot some exteriors at the Cone Mansion, near Blowing Rock. Several miles up the Parkway, I found an overlook at Beller Gap, got out to watch the sunset. I stayed until it was dark, and something magical happened. As shadows took over and color faded,

tiny pinpoints of light pricked to life all over the hills they like to
call mountains in these parts. And I thought again, "I have to
show that to my Mouse."

I miss you, Mousekin. It hasn't become any easier over the
past three years. I've been ignoring messages from your mother
for two days now. I don't feel like hearing a harangue about
your adventure. I don't feel like hearing from her at all.

In the gathering dark, I switched on my dome light, took
out glasses, pen and clipboard, settled in to write this. Good
night, sweetheart. Daddy loves you, more than I can say. Tomorrow will be here soon. Tomorrow I get to work with Halla
McKee. That'll be fun. At her interview, we laughed almost
more than we talked.

Remember what I used to tell you, the night before your
birthday? The sooner to bed, the sooner tomorrow. Maybe I can
talk Tony into cutting out the shower scene, tomorrow. Tomorrow, things will start going my way, at last.

.5.

YESTERDAY'S DISASTER

Dear Mouse,
[You are beautiful, exactly like your mother. Only your eyes
are my own. Knowing where you are, I have a hard time think-
ing about anything else. It's been a hellish two days since I
wrote to you out on the Parkway. Yesterday morning, I slid
open my closet door and Crystal—No.

[Mousy, look, I'd better leave you for later, when no-
body will see this. This isn't something I'd write to a little girl
from now on. I love you, Mousekin]

[Note: This starts well over twenty-four hours ago. I'll try to
be as accurate as I can]

My family made me stop singing in the shower when my voice changed, but yesterday morning, I felt like caroling from the time I woke up till I got in to work. I put on the jeans I wore in *Thundercars 500*—tailor-made, comfortable and close-fitting. I took some time considering the color of my shirt. I even stopped at Tara's restaurant and ate breakfast.

I tried returning Nancy's calls. Her service said the newly-weds were still out of town, so that was all right. I headed to the studio with a fairly clear conscience.

Each of us has a title and a personal chair, now. Tony's the Producer-Director; Dora's his Assistant Director; Phina, of

course, is Director of Photography and never uses her chair. A
bit player finagled chair and title: Doc Jefferson, a local sports
medicine specialist with cinematic fantasies, is our Set Doctor.
By virtue of investing some *Strongbow* money in this project, I
have become an Associate Producer. Geez.

Halla McKee hadn't arrived by the time I did. I was twenty
minutes early. Tony was there, of course. I think he's starting to
live there. I reported to him, out on the studio floor. Tony was in
a bear of a mood. He's not psychokinetic, but I had to suppress
an instinct to duck whenever he looked at me. Dora tiptoed
around, her braids trailing submissively down her back. She bit
down hard on her pen whenever she came within ten feet of
him. Phina's huge dark eyes glared from behind her cameras.
Square-built and feisty, she put out a force field that bounced
me off several yards. I retreated to the front office, to ask Yvan
what was going on.

Our receptionist Yvan is an Entertainment Management
major on an internship. Her tuition comes from commercials
she did years ago. She's sworn she'd never get in front of a
camera again, which is why Tony hired her. Since her last weight
loss commercial, she's fifty pounds heavier, three shades darker,
and proud of both.

Yvan was subjecting her desk to its daily search. She gets
in an hour before anyone but Tony, knows everything before
anyone but Dora. I closed the door to the studio. "Look, I know
I should have asked you first. What's going on out there?"

"Not what, who," she said. "I got a message for you. Isn't
Anastasia Russo your ex-wife? The petite swimsuit model? She's
in town, you know."

"No, Nancy's out of town on her honeymoon. She just married—what, in this town? Here? Why?"

Yvan picked up the whole telephone, examined its bottom,
squared it on the blotter. "Her and her new husband's been at
Starling Resort two days, trying to get ahold of you. They're
coming in today. Whatever it is, they want it bad. You want to
not be here when they come?"

"No, I'll see them. Thanks. Is that why Tony's raging?"

Yvan sputtered scorn. "I wish. He's ill at the girl."

"Girl? You mean Halla?"

She pulled her head out of a drawer. "No, a girl. Halla McKee's thirty-to-forty. This one's my age, give or take ten years. You want to know who the star is? Just ask her."

I felt a freezing draft. "Not Crystal Beller—a pretty strawberry blonde, looks like an overprocessed teenager?"

Yvan cast a suspicious eye over the contents of the center drawer. "She called Tony last night, told him all about himself, and came in to take us over this morning."

Whoopee. All my favorite people the same day we get A Star on the set. Why'd he pick that day of all days? I hitched a hip to a corner of the desk. "When did Crystal come in?"

Yvan's training us not to sit on her desk. "Excuse me," she commanded. I pulled myself off. Finding nothing wrong with the desk, she soothed its feelings with a massage of spray polish, taking extra care where I'd sat. "Crystal sashayed in a couple minutes before you got here. That's all the time she needed."

"What does she want now?" I appealed to the Cosmos.

"Get discovered and be a star, seems like," Yvan said. "I don't know anything."

"Birds'll come and make a nest on your nose, Lady. You know everything."

Gratified, Yvan swung her beaded dreadlocks. "I'm not Pinocchio. Don't you have to get make-up on or something?"

I had to talk with Tony. By all the signs he blamed me for Crystal. I headed for the set, and Halla McKee walked in. If I had a tail, it would have wagged. "Halla!"

Yvan dissolved the spray can into empty air. "Halla McKee?" She picked up the phone.

"Mr. Pornada asked me to come early." Halla reported, and looked at me. Her polite smile warmed to a beam that tightened down the corners of her mouth and flashed a system of subtle, lopsided dimples. "Hey, Matt." Around here, people say *Hey* instead of *Hi*.

Basking in her smile, I groped for something to say.

Yvan put the phone down. "Tony's expecting you, Ms. McKee. Your agent's here, too."

"My agent? He's in Wilmington."

Yvan picked up a business card, reached it to her. "This isn't your agent?"

Halla gave the card a sneer, dropped it on Yvan's desk like a slimy thing. "No. She must be here for someone else."

"Well, she said she was your agent," Yvan said. "Maybe she's working for one of the kids. She said she'd be here for their audition, later. Tony's out on the floor. This way." She opened the door to the studio, and Julien swept in.

Julien Darcy got written out of a soap opera last year. She's a distractingly pretty blonde, all pro, loves her work. She'd do that mindless and unmotivated shower scene herself if she had the chest for it. The *Beller Mountain Republican* claims Julien as their darling. They run pieces about "Hollywood Among Us." A little of that goes a long way with me, but Julien loves it. She's settled at Chetola Resort, an arch-rival of Starling Resort, about half an hour away in Blowing Rock.

Julien's momentum carried her into a stumble that flung her against me. I steadied her as she spoke. "Oh, Matt, thank you for coming in early! Can we go over this scene a bit?"

Halla looked back from the door to the studio, shrugged one shoulder, wheeled around to follow Yvan. I stood blinking in their backwash, still holding on to Julien.

Julien aimed us toward her dressing room. I steered away. "No, let's use the porch set. It's available. Phina won't need it till we're made up."

Julien missed half a beat, nodded brightly. We had twenty minutes, but Julien knows how to concentrate. When she was called for Make-up and we had to stop, she found a hold on my shirt. "Matt? I—Okay. I can't find my motivation. If you could help me tonight? I can rent a meeting room at Chetola."

"No. Look, I've got an A-number-one coffee maker at Tara. We can work till ten, then we'll quit. Mornings come early around here. If you're not a morning person—"

"I'm not, not at all," she twinkled. She's a twinkly person—twinkly eyes, a cute nose, twinkly personality. She has a trick of tilting her head back to look up at me. Makes me feel six feet tall. "That's why I never used my doctorate in education. I'm not Cinderella till midnight. See you tonight, okay?"

"Sure, great. Look, if I run late, ask the clerk to let you in. You shouldn't suffer if I'm late." She fluttered fingers to her lips and then at me, and danced off.

Tony has a broom closet office at one corner of the studio. He finished dealing with Halla before he noticed my existence. She slipped out to Make-up, and he turned on me.

"Look, Tony, about Crystal Beller—" I began.

"I don't want to hear it," he snapped. Then he sighed. "No, it's not your fault. You got it worse than I did. I don't want to talk about it, all right?" He made a move away.

In our family we don't get physical. Father always insisted on communication with words. Physical I had to learn in theater classes and I don't use it much in real life. But I needed to make Tony hear, and he was not in the mood to listen. I wedged myself into the doorway, straight-armed the jamb. He looked out to the studio, took on a why-me glare. I spoke fast. "Tony, look. I don't know what Crystal thinks she has on you—"

His glare blasted me. "Why not? You gave it to her."

"What?"

"She told me you and I are having an affair. You know what my wife can do with that in court? You got a clue?"

"I—what—?" I thought, hard. Damn. "No, I let her think I'm gay. She took it from there. But it was a lie, Tony; I'll testify to that, anywhere, any time. I know it's a lie. I told it."

"It's not a lie. I am—"

"So what? I lied, and I'll say so. Tony, call your lawyer, control damage. *Don't try to buy Crystal Beller off.*"

"Will you get out of my way?" Tony demanded. "I've taken care of it. She'll be gone by noon; all she wanted was a job. She's doubling Andrea's body in the shower scene."

"No! Tony, I will not get into a shower stall with that—I wish you'd cut that scene."

"And cut half our backing? Phina's dolly grip's doubling you. Are you happy?"

"Flattered. It's not the point. That type doesn't go away, Tony. Crystal Beller's like an unwanted boomerang. She'll take what you offer, come back, and trash you. Listen to me, Tony!"

His eyes shifted over my shoulder. "You have visitors."

I released the doorjamb. Tony shoved past me and out. Nancy and Wyndham breathed down my neck. That's what I get for ignoring messages. "I heard you two got married. Congratulations. Excuse me." I made a move past them. I don't mind Wyndham, but Nancy can shred me with a look. I didn't need to be shredded yesterday.

"Matt—" It was maybe the first civil word Nancy's said to me since the divorce. She slid a tiny hand up to my face. It used to melt me into compliance.

I jerked back. "If you want to watch, you can stay out of the way in the Canteen. I have work to do."

Wyndham put an arm around her. His moustache framed the cute smile that charms judges and juries alike. "Do what you have to. We'll be fine, trust me. At least I can look civilized, and keep the Vickers under my jacket."

"Not on these premises, you can't. We don't allow firearms. Sorry. You'll have to get rid of it."

"Let's not clash over this, Matt. The county sheriff's office issued me the emergency permit. It's perfectly legal."

"Look. Sorry." I tried to quell the resentment I've amassed since the hearing. Wyndham's a nice guy, but his job description doesn't include befriending me. "Look, I promise I won't try to kill you or Nancy here. We can't allow weapons in the studio."

"Well—" Wyndham glanced at Nancy and nodded. "You probably won't try anything here. I'll put the gun away, we'll come back at a better time."

"Sure. Next year might be good."

He laughed and steered his wife away. I watched them leave, hauled my mind to where it belonged. Halfway to my dressing room, "In/Tense" rolled over me like a storm front.

The blonde wig made Crystal look a lot like Julien, but underneath, it was all Crystal. Her long terry robe fell dangerously loose at the chest, stretched tight on the hips. I didn't bother to be polite. "Get out of my way and stay out of it," I snarled. "You sold my journal to the tabloids."

"I didn't have no choice, that reporter gave me five hundred dollars." Her silvery voice wheedled. "Y'all got me mad, you and Tony." She reached for me.

I stepped away. "Too bad. Don't expect an apology."

Her eyes hardened, but she was looking over my shoulder. She flashed a quick grin like a gymnast, skipped prettily off. Fresh prey. I don't know whom she was stalking. It didn't matter then. I headed for my dressing room, trying to wrinkle "In/Tense" out of my nose.

Badger wears tight black jeans, a cowboy shirt, leather jacket, and bolo tie, and repellent, shiny-black cowboy boots with stiletto toes that curve up like Persian slippers. I warmed up, put on the pants and boots, then climbed into my XXX-large, stained and stretched make-up shirt. Nobody fools with my face without an advanced medical degree. Anyone can instruct me in special techniques, but I do my own make-up or I don't do the show.

The hat still didn't work. I pulled it off for the third time. It tilts to shade where my eyebrow doesn't quite come together over a scar. I twitched that eyebrow, leaned in to the mirror. That was it. I dug out a tin of moustache wax I'd experimented with once, waxed the eyebrow hairs to tangle away from the scar, and tilted the hat the other way.

That was Badger: rake, scoundrel, full-time spoiled brat. I decided the scar happened when he cheated on the wrong girl, slung on Badger's leather jacket, put away the shirt, straightened the bunk, headed for the set. Halla came out of the dressing room next to mine. "Hal!"

She turned, sent me a wave and an absent smile, didn't stop till we got to the porch set.

Someone handed me Badger's folding jackknife. Someone else came at my face with reaching fingers. I fended the fingers off, tucked the knife into my back pocket. The person reached again while my hands were occupied. I reared back. Another reach, and I caught wrists, looked into young, wide eyes. "No. Please. I'll do whatever needs doing. What is it?"

"Your eyebrow. It's all messed up."

"I want it that way. It's part of the character."

"But I'm Make-up—"

"It's okay. I'm in the union, too. Please. Stay off my face." Make-up backed off, and I gave myself a second to calm down.

Halla was there, ready to work. Right. So was I.

Halla had an open grin for Julien and a crackling eagerness for everyone else. Me she occasionally skimmed with her eyes, her warm, lopsided smile fading. Maybe she was preparing for the scene. I hope she was preparing for the scene. Tony called "Places" before I had time to figure it out. His idea is to see how efficiently the actresses take direction.

Behind the camera, Phina was as kvetchy as Tony. She insisted on opening the scene with Andrea's full skirt spread precisely across the porch swing. Julien's a pro, but no living being could stay still enough to keep that skirt from moving before the camera rolled. Three interns held its hem, then let go and scuttled out of the picture when the scene started.

"Marker—" The clapper dropped on a board that showed what take of what scene we were shooting:

"TEST: H. MCKEE. SCENE: SBA-164. TAKE: 1."

There is something about that moment, that split second before you start certain scenes. It doesn't happen often, and it doesn't guarantee a good take. But once you've felt that rush, the world does not hold enough money to lure you away. It happened to me, now. I was Ready.

"—and—Action!"

Julien, as Andrea, snuggled to my arm. As Badger, I lied to her, disengaged my arm, approached the door.

Knock, knock.

The door opened. I unfurled the Famous Grin.

There stood the strongest, maddest, meanest woman I have ever faced. I don't know what happened to the Grin. Her cold eyes locked on mine. Her shoulder twisted down and back, and Sarah hauled off with a roundhouse wallop fit to send Badger tush over teakettle into next week.

So I fell down the steps.

I staggered down the first two, hit ground at the bottom and rolled. Sarah followed Badger across the porch to the top step, hands on hips, light of battle in her eye. Julien had the sense to back Andrea out of the way.

And Tony yelled, "Cut!" He tore over to me: "That'll be all, Ms. McKee—Matt, my God sake, are you all right?"

I was fine. Halla's fist had missed my face by inches. I picked myself up grinning. I haven't done a fall that good since the TV movie about the quadriplegic hang glider.

It took me time to explain things to Tony. Halla was on her way out before I convinced him. "Halla, wait," I called.

She stopped, looked back. What a face. Unremarkable, forgettable, but what she's thinking might as well be written across her forehead. She knew she'd blown it. All she wanted was privacy to get over it in. She tried to look civil.

"Come back," I said. "We're doing it again."

She's had cruel jokes played on her before. She hesitated, looked around. Tony was stepping back to the camera. Phina bent over an eyepiece, measuring or something. I beckoned impatiently. "Come on, Hal, we're wasting time."

She turned professional, leaped briskly up the steps. She moves with a gung-ho grace that's fun to watch. Tony called, "Ms. McKee, just do the slap, okay? You don't want to knock him down the steps."

Halla nodded, watched me pick up Badger's hat. Checking that Tony was out of earshot, she caught my eye. "I may not, but *Sarah* wants to take your damned head off." And she marched back behind the door.

She was right. Halla put an edge of pain on Sarah's fury that defined the character. Sarah's capitulation at the end would take on new dimensions with it. I wanted the wallop.

We did the bit with the slap, and it worked. Halla gave and gave and gave and kept on giving. I put out shovelfuls to keep up, and she took that and came back with more. I haven't worked so hard for a test in years. It wasn't enough.

Tony yelled "Cut! Print that," and I jumped down the steps to do some fast talking. Hal's test was already costing more than it should.

Tony saw me coming. "Damn you, Matt. Again, please, people?" We've worked on this project long enough to read each other's minds.

The lights were reset almost before Tony'd called for them. We did the scene again, with Halla's wallop and my fall. It sang. It was IT. It was exactly right. Tony didn't yell. Like a real director, he said, ". . . and—cut. Print that one, too, please?"

I shook myself back to reality, tried to think of something to say. I couldn't. I nodded. Halla gave a tiny, "so-there" nod back and threw me a polite smile to show no hard feelings. I don't mind hard feelings. What I can't stand is no feelings. She thanked the crew without looking at me again.

Julien and Halla worked together like sisters—viciously competitive, mutually contemptuous, tuned directly to each other's minds. Hal and I thought in tandem without trying. Julien's and my work session in the morning paid off. Altogether, we'd put out a pair of printable takes in thirty-five minutes. It wasn't yet eight o'clock.

Make-up came at me with a tissue to blot my face. I did my own blotting, put on the jacket against a chill. Tony purred. "You are a trio of cherubim and I adore you. Break. Matt, Julie, I need you back here at eight-thirty. Ms. McKee—may I call you Halla?—I want to talk to your agent. Can you come back at eleven? I need you to read against the kids, for little Gideon."

Halla nodded. "But my agent isn't here. If you talk to—"

"I'll use a telephone. The signal goes all the way to Wilmington. Take the same room you had this morning. Watch it, the latch sticks. Dora, will you set up and do that godforsaken shower scene so we can kick Ms. Beller out of here? Please? For Uncle Anton?"

Dora brightened. She's been hoping to direct something. She didn't know Crystal yet.

It's not that Halla has any greater talent than the others. The last actress we tested showed near-genius, with a pure, classic beauty. It's attitude. None of the others connect like Halla. She is Sarah. Nobody else comes close.

◇◇◇

Dora materialized as Tony and I were seeing off the last Sarah candidate. "God, I need a smoke. Let's get together and choke Crystal Beller."

"Not if I have to touch her," I said.

Tony went to the point. "Is the shower scene done?"

"Hardly," Dora grated. "Ten takes, she blew them all. Do we really need that scene?"

"No," I said.

"I need to pay the—" He looked at Dora—"strumpet."

"Slut." Dora scanned me with a glance. "What did you do with your hat and tie?"

"They're on the porch set. Nobody'll steal them, Dora."

Tony looked around. "What did you do with the Beller?"

"Called lunch break. I had to remind her to put her robe back on. Matt's double will probably undo that." She glanced at Phina, communing with a light meter on the porch set, and lowered her voice. "Dakota's a dolt. I bet that tramp Crystal has him for lunch. Don't forget who's coming today."

"I don't care if Jenghiz Khan's coming," Tony exploded. "He wants to talk to Matt, not run an inspection, my God's sake. We got a show to produce—" They went to his office.

Phina straightened up, square jaw tight, and stalked off toward the shower set. She and the splendid Dakota have been sharing quarters since we came to this location. Crystal Beller's a nasty bit of work. Whatever Phina might be capable of doing to her, Crystal probably deserves it.

When Halla got back, Tony sent her to Wardrobe and Make-up. I started across the floor to meet her, but an expensively suited brunette beat me to it. Halla stiffened; all her light and strength shut down. She barely moved her mouth to answer some greeting, squeezed out just enough civility to repel two advances and point to the kids' set. The woman left. Halla all but steamed at the ears. The wanna-be agent, apparently.

Halla glanced around, took a deep breath, stretched, shook herself. As I approached, she gave me a passing nod, then headed to where she was supposed to be. Halla is one of us, now. I wish I knew what was going on with her. We'd been getting along so well, but now that we're working together, suddenly we're civil strangers. I can't figure out what I've done wrong. Baffled, I got ready for the kids' audition.

Auditioning the children for Little Gideon, Sarah's weird kid, took less than an hour. Gabby Speranzo is destined to rule the universe by the time he graduates from elementary school. All the children were good, of course, but Gabby rocked, with all of us. As soon as the readings were over, the suited brunette moved in on Gabby's mother.

Tony called lunch break. Yvan caught me on my way to my dressing room. "Uh—you got a mess of visitors. Look who's on the porch set."

I looked. The Star was sitting in my chair. People clustered around him, catching his ready laugh like a cold. A terry-robed back pushed through to present herself. He appreciated the view, moved to someone else. Geez. I put a year's work into this project, but I knew the money people want a big name to play Badger. Halla would be pleased, I thought—if they didn't replace her too.

A single finger tapped my shoulder. Joy. The Wyndhams. I gathered breath. "Look, I'm busy. If I need to know anything, call my lawyer. Brewster Beane. You've met him."

Wyndham offered a hand. "Hey, we're family now. Can't we get along without lawyers?"

"No." I kept my hands in my pockets. "You trashed me in court, took away my child—"

Nancy joined battle. "She could have been killed—You were too drunk to drive—"

"Three years ago! For crying out loud, I've been s-ober ever s-since. Why can't you—Nev-n-ever mind." I turned away. This fight never gets won. Anger, like alcohol, is for other people who can handle it. "Somebody important's waiting for me."

"Here, look at this." Wyndham pulled out a small frame.

Dear God, Mouse is so beautiful.

It's this year's school photo, and she is laughing in it. I can almost hear her. Her skin glows golden, her eyes grey as glass, her hair in long, tight, smoky-brown curls, her permanent teeth all in. I remember her with two teeth missing on the bottom, the top ones strung like seed pearls almost too small for her mouth. She's like her mother. Beautiful.

Nancy said, "We wanted you to—see how she's grown?" Nancy talks in dashes and question marks.

I asked, "Why?" but led the way to my dressing room.

Wyndham said, "You've been good, support payments always on time, never short—"

What did they think, that I'd cheat my own kid?

"—and the mature way you handled that *Probe* mess."

Nancy said, "Lieutenant Pike said you cooperated—when she got lost in the Charlotte Airport? Lieutenant Pike found her in the V.I.P. Lounge. She'd gone straight to it."

Wyndham chuckled. "We didn't find out she was missing till we got in to the Resort and there they were. Imagine our surprise. Nancy and I are proud of you. You've grown up."

My hand stiffened on the dressing room door latch. I let go. "I really don't have time—"

Nancy said, "She's taking gymnastics?"

"Gymnastics?" The Star would probably be busy for a while.

"For two years, now. Her perfect little body flies through the air like there's no gravity—trust me, she's amazing."

I spared a thought for poor Shannon, falling off the balance beam three times in one meet, and we were in my dressing room. Nancy sat cross-legged on the bunk, stretchy trousers behaving beautifully, shoes shed to the floor.

Wyndham headed for my make-up chair. I got petty. "Ah— nobody's allowed to sit in that chair. Sorry."

He sprang out of it, landed on the bunk beside Nancy, and didn't miss a beat. "We think she's another Yanescu."

"Not Yanescu." Nancy shifted sideways to make room for him. "Magda Yanescu smiles."

"Why won't she smile?" Wyndham had left Mouse's picture on my table. I picked it up. "Does she need braces?"

"No, her teeth are coming in perfectly. Must get it from your side of the family." Wyndham hugged Nancy. She laughed.

"What's that about not smiling? She's smiling here—"

"She's going through a difficult stage—that age?"

I said, "She was ten, February eighth. Ten's not that—"

"You remember her birthday?" Wyndham said. "Great!"

I turned my wrist, but Badger doesn't wear a watch. Mine lay on the table. I pretended not to look at it, elaborately. That worked. I got a tidbit.

Nancy said, "She's on the TAG-Team at school?"

"TAG-Team?"

"Talented / Academically-Gifted?—and the Honor Roll."

It was hard to keep my eyes off the picture. "What was that about not smiling?"

"Growing up without a Daddy isn't easy." Wyndham consulted Nancy, apparently got what he wanted. "Now that we're married, we can put some stability in her life. Here. Look. Let me get your John Hancock on this." He passed over a sheaf of papers. "It gives me the authority to sign if Michaella needs professional help. It'll simplify everything, trust me. Here—"

I took the papers he handed me, dug for my glasses.

He shoved a pen to my hand. "Sign right down here."

I moved away, strung on glasses, flipped pages. He said, "It's a lot of legalese. You don't have to read all the—"

"Adoption Release. Why do I have to sign this?"

"We're a family now," Nancy said. "We're planning—next month?—to move down to Florida."

"Move down to Hell." I ripped the pages in half, handed the pieces to Wyndham. On the table, Mouse laughed up at me. "You asked my sister about this at her book-signing."

"We know how you feel, Matt, but think," he said. "Aren't you being a bit selfish? Why hang on to the past? We can all win, here. I adopt her. You get rid of support payments, free and clear, make a new beginning, start a family. That blonde you were acting with? I bet she'd like to know you better."

"Julien? She's taken."

Nancy said, "Matt, you need to let go? Nigel adores Michaella. The three of us?—we need to be a family."

"She's a very special little girl," Wyndham struck in. "Trust me, when I married Nancy, I married Michaella, too. You release her, and I don't see any reason why you shouldn't see her once again, maybe. She's still here, since Lieutenant Pike rescued her the other day."

I shouldn't have ignored those messages. I stood. "Look, let-let me call Brewster Beane—"

"No." Nancy leaped to her feet to stab three exquisitely manicured fingers at my chest. "No lawyers. Sign the release?" She stabbed. "Maybe we'll let you see her—Talk lawyer—?" another stab. "You'll never get another—"

I pushed the fingers aside, pitched my voice flat. "Poke me

like that again, and we'll talk lawyer in a big way. I don't sign
anything without Brewster Beane. I may give her up if she tells
me, in person, that she wants me to. Maybe."

"Sweetie," Wyndham said. She sat abruptly, and their eyes
met. He moved his head at the door. Nancy pushed toes into her
shoes. "Um—is there a ladies' room?"

"You can use my—"

"No, I need a real ladies' room."

Wyndham watched her go, smiling after her. "She'll get
over it, trust me."

The ladies' room is at the end of the hall. I showed her and
held the door for him. "You can wait for her out there."

He sat down. "No, she'll be a while. I have to tell you, she
wants this as much as I do, but you don't need to decide right
away. Let's talk about—"

My jaw pushed out to the side. "We don't have anything to
talk about. Look, someone's waiting for me—"

"Of course, of course. Take all the time you want. Mean-
while, I could use something to drink. You have a lunch room,
some place where I could find ginger ale? Hey. Nancy's pretty
excited by this whole movie scene. Maybe we could stick around
and watch a bit, like you said. She'll enjoy that."

Nancy married me during *Strongbow IV*'s publicity campaign;
she knows all about movie "glamour." Never mind. At least I
don't have to worry about how he treats her. The only reason not
to like him is that he's so damned good at his job. I said, "Sure. You
can see the studio from the Canteen."

He looked around. "Canteen? Where?"

"Around that corner. Come on, I'll show you." I locked my
door, saw him to a table in the Canteen next to a window looking out on the studio, and then I walked off. Don't ask how I
thought Nancy was supposed to find him. I had a problem of
my own: I'd seen my doppelganger sitting in my chair.

◇◇◇

When I got to the porch set, the lights were out. My chair stood
empty. Crystal, coming across the studio, adjusted her robe to
show more chest, and glided past the darkened porch set without seeing me. Her smile was mysterious, wet and sweet. Her

eyes were narrowed, hard and diamond bright. She headed for
the dressing rooms.

It took me some time to find my visitor. I checked around
the floor, stopped by the hall to the dressing rooms, when I
heard a familiar voice raised in mock protest. A group of people
laughed. Across the studio from the dressing rooms, the kitchen
set was under construction. The Star sat in Phina's chair among
a knot of fans, scrawling autographs, working the crowd.

My powers of reason came flooding back. If the money
people had railroaded Tony into replacing me, he'd never let me
find out this way, and it isn't in this guy to come near a set until
whoever he's replacing is long gone. When I reached him, the
hand I held out was cordial.

"It's about time." He gripped my hand and used it to unfold
himself from Phina's chair. The crowd around him broke up
and wandered off.

"What's a great star like you doing on a set like this?" I
demanded. "Weren't you in Vienna being Interpol?"

"That was Venice, and it fell through, because the wrong
person lost money at Monte Carlo over Easter."

Stories like that put ice down any actor's spine. "Geez.
Shows it can happen to the best of us. I'm sorry."

"I'm not. It was The Production From Hell. Everyone wants
to work with her until they work with her, and then no one
wants to work with her. Nobody ever works with her twice,
ever notice that? Listen, how did you like doing *Romeo and
Juliet* last season? Guess what that guy's directing next year."

He so rarely has a bad word for anybody that I needed a
minute to catch up, but I knew this one. "*Macbeth*. Don't bother.
He wants nothing but hairy muscles this season."

"That's Little Stratford. I mean a movie, next year."

"I have no idea—why are you pushing Shakespeare? You
don't do classics."

Halla came out of Tony's office and went to her dressing
room. The latch stuck. She shook the handle, banged it twice.

He watched her a moment, renewed his assault. "Come on,
get your mind off your co-star—who is she? She looks familiar—
and think."

Yvan passed by on some errand. Halla stopped her, got pointed toward the ladies' room, and was gone. Like a game-show host with a dull guest, he asked, carefully, "What Shakespeare comedy would I come six thousand miles out of my way to yap at you about?"

Obediently, I bent my brain. What Shakespeare comedy— "You're out of your mind. *The Comedy of Errors* at our age? Tunics and sandals?"

"I'll never outgrow tunics. You promised."

"I was drunk!"

"So was I."

"You're never drunk."

This guy is the easiest laugher in the business. I've seen him come unglued over the one about the chicken crossing the road, an actress's kvetch about her weight, a Japanese pun on a German noun declension. But he's a Star and I'm a has-been because he keeps at things. "We agreed—whose party was that?—if we ever heard of a decent production of *Errors* we'd go out for the Dromio twins. They're doing it as sci-fi—aliens, wire work, you know, zero-gravity stunts—"

"Ooo." Dora and Tony bore down on us, arguing over something on Dora's clipboard. I headed us toward the Canteen. Coffee is in the Canteen.

He pushed on. "How do you feel about special effects?"

"Hate 'em," I lied.

"Me, too. And blue-screen stuff, way-out weaponry—"

"Ooo."

"Gotcha."

"Hang on." I shoveled sugar. "Why can't you do both the twins yourself?"

"That's too much like work. No, seriously, he wants different actors for all the twins. Shakespeare used pairs of actors— he wants pairs of actors."

"But that doesn't make sense—in a sci-fi format?"

"Who cares about making sense? Come on, I really want this, and I can't do it without you."

"But nobody plans a production of *Errors* without lining up all the twins first. The twins are probably cast already."

"They are, now. If you say yes. Don't spill your coffee."

A timely warning; I was gawking. "Yes—sure." I'd thought he was there to replace me, and there he was recruiting me. I've always had to audition for my roles, like everyone else.

As I adjusted my ideas, he said, "Tell me about your co-star." I gulped coffee, led him to a table. The Canteen was suddenly no longer empty. People were drifting in, pretending they didn't know a Star was there. Nancy sat alone at a table in the corner nursing a Perrier and some carrot sticks.

"Hal—Halla McKee," I said. We found her here—"

"No kidding. Halla? I always hoped she'd turn up again."

As if on cue, Halla came in with Gabby. Apparently, Tony'd let them loose. Gabby looked as if he'd just had a nap, big-eyed, with one side of his face rosier than the other. They were talking trash like a pair of prize fighters: "I'll get a great-big straw and suck up a zillion marshmallows," and: "Oh, yeah? I'll eat a zillion and one, and a googol more!"

No worry about the chemistry between those two. Gabby's mother slipped in and effaced herself in a corner, her mouth set, her eyes grim. Tigress protecting her young.

I could feel my whole face loosening into a smile. Halla's eyes slid past us, paused to wonder why she was being nodded at by a Star. She lifted her chin our way, and settled at a distant table with Gabby. She showed no sign that she'd even noticed my presence. My urge to smile dried up.

"Whoa," he said. "What'd you do to her?"

"If I ever find out, I'll let you know."

He watched them. "She looks like the same one."

"The same what?"

A single finger tapped my shoulder. "Hey—ah, I hate to interrupt, Matt, but did you know your dressing room door's wide open?" Wyndham's eyes shone; I'd swear he was wearing a fine sheen of sweat. Nancy was excited by movie glamour? Nancy's Perrier bottle stood empty and abandoned on the corner table; the excited one was right here. He held out a hand, eager as any fan meeting a Star. "Hi, Nigel Wyndham. I married Matt's ex-wife. How are you doing?"

I interrupted him. "What?—Who opened my door?"

"Beats me. A pretty blonde in a bathrobe ran out of it to the ladies' room, several minutes ago. We thought you ought to know." The crowd around us hooted softly.

Julien spoke up. "That little redneck Crystal Beller, I bet. She isn't really a blonde, more of a washed-out redhead, but she's wearing a blonde wig, to look like me. She's my stand-in. Yvan said you were in there, Matt, fighting with her."

"Crystal got into my room? Geez. I locked my door—" I lurched away, then remembered that I had a guest. "Look. Do you mind—"

"Go away," he ordered. "I want to talk with people who appreciate me." There were plenty of them, practically lining up in hopes of getting him to notice them.

I headed for my room. The door opened easily, but my room was empty—no Crystal, no nothing.

Wyndham was stepping on my heels. "Where have you been, the last half hour?"

"The Canteen. I got—sidetracked. Where's Nancy?"

He pointed with his thumb. "Ladies' room—again. I kind of think I'm not her favorite person right now."

"We're about to clear the area. Maybe you'd better—"

"Yeah. Good idea." He went down the hall, knocked on the ladies' room door. Crystal came out, turned to ease the door closed. She looked okay, but I want to know which guy she'd hunted down. He must have boxed her ears nicely. The robe was closed, the blonde wig fanned softly before her tanned face. Halla was right. Crystal can look like anything you want her to be, anything at all. Even a lady.

Wyndham said, "Hi, sweetie, is my wife still in there?"

She nodded, slipped back in. The woman's a chameleon. I relocked my door. I don't, usually, but Crystal was loose in the studio, and she has no grasp on the concept of privacy. I met Nancy and her husband as they came up the hall. "I'll walk you two to the door."

Halla had come out of the Canteen. Her latch stuck again, and she had to use violence to subdue it. As he passed her, Wyndham put an arm around his bride. "An ugly woman is a useless thing, trust me," he sang.

Nancy laughed eagerly. Faint wisps of Crystal's perfume had floated out of the ladies' room after her, clinging to her hair and clothes like cigarette smoke. I hope Wyndham doesn't mind heavy scents, because Nancy wouldn't smell it.

I was ready to be rid of them and they were ready to go. Nancy's heels stabbed the carpet in quick little steps. In the lobby, he stuck out a hand. Not a fast learner. "These people don't come back," I told Yvan. "Tell Security."

"Right away, Mr. Logan." She reached for the phone, staring darkly at the Wyndhams.

"What?" Wyndham protested. Nancy glared.

I held the outside door open. "Have a nice day." They left without another word.

Yvan put the phone down. "We don't have any security."

"And you improvised like a pro. Do you want candy or flowers? Tony underpays you."

"I'd rather have a tire iron." Yvan cleared her throat. "Uh—you know you'll want to keep your voice down, entertaining ladies in your dressing room."

"What? I haven't been in my dressing room—"

"Crystal wasn't in there bragging that you couldn't love a real woman, and you didn't say she didn't know what she was talking about, it wasn't but ten minutes ago?"

I thought about fighting my way through this thicket of negatives, shook my head. "I wasn't in there. Who was it?"

Yvan ran a thumb along the desk, checked it for dust. "You, it sounded like. Your drama school voice, your Yankee accent. Crystal likes secrets. If she gets yours—"

"She's already done her worst to me," I said. "She won't get another chance if I can prevent it."

Yvan shrugged. "What it sounded like, Crystal was saying she wasn't no baby, and you—"

"You were listening?"

Her look said my next remark was likely to be stupider than that, so I'd better not make it. I suddenly, conveniently, remembered that I was still in make-up, and a shower stall existed in my dressing room. Wyndham probably left Mouse's picture there, too. I stretched my legs.

◇◇◇

Mouse's picture lay on the table where Wyndham left it. I took it up and stared. I don't know how long I sat there with her. I was still in Badger's jacket and getting warm. I sloughed out of it, slid open the closet door to hang it up.

A pretty hand with frosted nails flopped out onto the rug. My first thought was, "Geez, doesn't she ever stop?" The hand twitched once and lay still. I tossed my jacket to the rumpled bunk, stooped to look.

I almost gagged. There was no robe or wig; it was just Crystal. Badger's bolo tie was knotted around her neck, two ends sticking out of swelling flesh. Her face make-up looked lurid over her purpling color. Her body make-up was streaked and smeared. It takes a lot to smear body make-up.

I rolled her out to the open floor, damning myself for not renewing my CPR certification after I'd stopped working at Park East Hospital. Badger's folding knife was still in my hip pocket from the tests. I had to coax the knife deep into that crease and cut the tie without cutting Crystal. I got to work, bellowed for help.

Nobody heard me. They were all in the Canteen, being dazzled by a Star. You don't cuss somebody who's doing you the favor of your career. Crystal's color worsened; she swelled like a balloon. It pushed her tongue—never mind. I ordered myself to stop seeing it, kept working, kept yelling.

Someone came to my door as the tie broke apart. "Matt, why are you—Good heavens." Halla dived for the phone.

"Call 911—she's been strangled," I snapped. "Do you have current CPR?"

She shook her head, pushing three times at the buttons. "Not for two years or so, but I know the moves. Ambulance," she told the phone.

"It'll have to do," I said grimly. "I'm starting rescue breathing." She nodded, relayed that into the phone. For the moment she shoved aside whatever wall she'd put up between us.

There was no way to get a breath past that tongue. I tilted the head back and tried the nostrils. It worked. The chest inflated with each breath. I pushed fingertips into where Crystal used to have a neck, focused on feeling an artery push back. "No pulse—beginning CPR."

Halla told the 911 operator. I found the right spot, laced my hands together, and pumped: "One-and-two-and-three—"

I'd done two cycles when Halla dropped to her knees beside me. "Want me to breathe?"

I nodded, keeping my count: "—and-fourteen-and-fifteen-and-*breathe!*"

CPR induced an artificial circulation that brought the swelling down somewhat. Halla got a breath past the tongue, buried fingers into the neck. "No pulse."

I began the next cycle. "One-and-two-and-three—" Halla tilted the head back, ready for another breath.

"—fourteen-and-fifteen-and—*breathe!*"

Halla bent down and took a mouth and faceful of stomach contents. I rolled Crystal onto her side while Halla dragged the bandanna from around her neck to clear out the mouth. She wiped her own face as I rolled Crystal back. Without a pause she was there to breathe for Crystal again.

We went on.

I didn't count time or cycles or anything but what I had to. I only let myself think of blood rushing through Crystal's heart, letting her live. "—fourteen-and fifteen-and—"

A blue-sleeved arm came into view, edged me out. The medics from the Beller County 911 Complex had arrived. I sat back on my heels. Halla was replaced with an air bag. She went dead pale, swallowed hard. Halla was in trouble.

I wrapped an arm around her, brought her to the sink, turned on both taps. Not a second too soon. I held her forehead, while Halla's lunch went down the drain.

I keep paper cups by my sink. Once Halla was empty, I filled one with water. "Swish, don't drink. No swallowing."

She obeyed, spat.

"Again." She did.

I poured mouthwash. "Swish."

She rebelled. "I hate that kind!"

"I know. Come on."

She did as she was told. "Sadist."

"Inhuman. Come on, again."

She pulled against my arm. I held on. "Hal, you don't know what diseases she's carrying. Come on!" She nodded, swished, spat. I ran more water. "Now you can drink."

She took the cup and drank.

I'd tried not to cut Crystal when I cut the tie. It wasn't possible. I washed my hands and wet a clean washcloth.

Crystal and her attendants were between us and the door. They'd hooked Crystal up to something that beeped. I drew Halla to the bunk. "Here, sit, let's stay out of the way."

We sat and I applied the washcloth. She made a feeble protest. "It's getting me all wet."

"We won't do any more work today."

Halla took the washcloth from me and cleaned herself up. When she was finished, I threw it into the sink, where she didn't have to smell it. She turned her face to my shoulder to keep from seeing what the medics were doing.

They'd defibrillated, throwing electric jolts through Crystal's heart, trying to get it started. People crowded at the door. I heard Tony harrying them into the Canteen. Doc battled through them. "Let me in there. I'm a doctor."

Halla muttered, "I've never done CPR on a real person before. I forgot about using a protective barrier."

"You did fine. More than fine. You were magnificent."

"Have you—?"

I was glad to get my mind away, back to Park East. After doing my community service there, I stayed on another year because I liked it. "Five times. This was my sixth."

They defibrillated again. Crystal's body lay inert, like wet clay. It wasn't fun to see. I looked down at Halla's short curls. There was grey threaded among them. Hair will do something about that when we start shooting. Never mind, it'll grow out.

The beep became a high, steady whistle. A sudden silence. Doc muttered, "Shit. She's gone."

One of the medics said, "No—we have to keep trying." They did, hopelessly.

Halla heaved, pushed her face against me. I said, "I know. I know, dear. They don't always make it, you know."

"I thought—" Her body went rigid under my arm.

"Yeah. So did I." I'd always tried to be Superman for Nancy. It had never worked. I held on to Halla. "I really thought we'd do it, this time."

Halla's arms snaked around my waist and squeezed. It's what I get for not being Superman. Poor old Superman.

We held each other and Halla cried. If I kept my mind on Halla, I didn't have to think about what was happening to Crystal. I made soothing noises while people did things to the body. Minutes ago it was Crystal Beller, throbbing with life, proud of her sensuality. Now it was The Body. Halla shuddered, swore into my shoulder.

I murmured, "Sh-sh—I know. It's all right." What was all right I don't know and can't guess. I kept talking, trying to keep our minds off what was happening to Crystal. "It looks as though we're in for a real-life whodunit. The Sheriff's Office seems to know its job—"

"Logan. Mattathias the Clam Logan." The voice was bitter disgust. The pants had creases like a razor's edge.

Halla sat up and glared. I tightened my hold on her. "Lieutenant Pike. I thought you were retired."

"Yeah, well, now I've been deputized. The Sheriff called me off the tenth green of the prettiest—Tshht. He found out who your sister is."

Great. Meranda scares everyone, from the President on down to the Beller County Sheriff. Pike jerked a thumb over his shoulder. "Into the lunch room, sir. You've destroyed enough evidence. And where did you learn your CPR?"

"It's been a year or two."

Halla stared at him, her eyes huge and haunted. "Shit." She looked toward the group of people still working over Crystal. "Ah, shit. Did we—is she dead because we—?"

"That's for the medical examiner to find out," Pike said. "Come on, we got to clear this area."

I murmured at Halla again. She balked at skirting Crystal, so a deputy took her other arm and we coaxed her out. Police lines were setting up all around. My dressing room would be sealed off, and Mouse's picture lay on my table.

"Leave it!" Pike ordered. "Don't touch anything—sir?"

I was locked on to that photograph. I didn't have a choice, but I could not walk away from my Mouse.

"Move it, sir. Everything in here stays in here."

Halla slid a hand across my back, not understanding, but on my side. I tried to explain. "It's my daughter. Her mother brought it today. Can't I take it with me—?"

"Get out. You'll get it back later."

Halla said, "Come on, Matt. He'll give it back. I'll *make* him give it back."

That brought me around. Of course I had to leave it. Of course they'd give it back. I let Halla get me away. We got each other to the Canteen. Everyone was there, except my famous "double." He'd left before anyone knew anything was wrong. If he'd stayed, I don't think they'd know it yet.

As we came in, people set up a cheer. Some clapped, a few stood up, applauding. Halla shrank back, her eyes filling again. I gathered her in, faced the crowd. "We lost her."

Someone screamed, somebody else burst into tears. Julien came at me, opened-armed. I had to look after Halla. I don't know what happened to Julien.

Deputies went through the crowd, getting names and addresses, asking questions. I settled Halla to a seat in a back corner. She was in control again. I sat with her, dug the heels of my hands into my eyes to think.

I've done enough thrillers to be fairly sure that Hal and I were in for it. So was anyone else who was outside the Canteen at the wrong time. Crystal was found in my closet, with my tie around her neck. I probably head the suspect list.

Whoever finds the body doesn't have an alibi. Maybe I ought to sign the adoption release. Maybe I should let go, as Nancy said, put a distance between Mouse and this mess.

No. Maybe it's childish fantasy, but no. Shannon says in her letter that she still loves her father. Maybe Mouse does, too. I'll wait. I rubbed my eyes and turned to Halla. She was still with me, gave me a smile's ghost. "Do you know what you've done to your make-up?"

"I don't think they'll let us clean up. Am I hideous?"

"Not bad. Tell people you bumped into a door in the dark."
Geez, it was good to have her with me.

A detective came to our table, being professionally civil.
"Mattathias Trevidic Logan," I answered, and gave my addresses
here and in New York. "I have places in London and L.A., too, if
you need them."

She got all that. "Can you tell me where you were between
1:30 and 2:30 today?"

"I found her. I could probably place the time for you, too."
I was invited to make a statement for the Sheriff's Office at the
County 911 Complex at my earliest convenience—like now.

Halla got a bad start. "Halla McKee—"

"Is that your legal name?"

"Um—" She shrugged one shoulder. "No, it's Hallelujah. I
don't have a middle name and I've never been married."

"Address?"

Halla gave it.

"Can you tell me where you were when—?"

"I left the Canteen soon after Matt did, and went to my
dressing room. When I heard him calling, I went to see what it
was about." Halla was invited to the Sheriff's Office, too.

◇◇◇

There's no use going through my interview blow-by-blow. They
recorded it. They call it an interview. I call it an all-out third-
degree grilling, but I'm not in the club.

Right. There were no blows. They're not allowed to touch
you. But anything else they can do to make you crazy, upset
you, scare you—and me, I'm easy to scare—they do it all.

Sgt. Pike—I beg his pardon. Lt. Pike did it all. A rather
pretty inspector from the Sheriff's Office worked with him. Good
cop, bad cop. I've played this scene before. All you have to do
is tell the truth, right?

They took me through my story, from when I left the Canteen until the medics came. That was easy. They got me to tell it
again. Again, easy. I reasonably assumed (I thought it was a
reasonable assumption) that they didn't get it all.

Then the bomb broke. "What was the fight about, sir?"

"What fight?"

"Simple question. You were overheard in a violent quarrel with Crystal Beller. What was it about?"

"This morning? It was a line or two each. She said—"

Pike slammed his hand flat on the table in front of me. Every nerve cell I had short-circuited. "You were heard fighting with her in your dressing room, less than half an hour before she was discovered. Tell us what it was about."

"In my dressing room? But I didn't see her in my—"

The inspector broke in. "Lieutenant, quit. Matt, if it's irrelevant, we can forget it. But we need to know."

"But I wasn't in there—"

Pike said, "People heard you, sir. Several independent reports place you in that dressing room, at that time. What did you fight with her about?"

"I didn't—there wasn't any fight—not then."

"Matt, you can tell us," his partner crooned.

They worked together the way Hal and I had over Crystal, but police are trained to work that way, and Hal and I just did it. In an hour my brain was jelly, not a coherent thought in my universe. They kept on.

For the I-don't-know-how-many-eth time, Pike asked, "So, who's the little darlin' you were fighting over, sir?"

"I wasn't in there," I insisted for the I-don't-know-how-many-and-first time. Of course that made no impression.

"You quarreled with Crystal Beller—"

"No! And if I wanted to kill her, I'd shoot her. That way I wouldn't have to touch her."

"Why not touch her, Matt?" the other one said. Quin's her name. She told me her first name: Heather, or Ashley, or Robin, or something. As far as I'm concerned, it's Inspector.

"I told you," I said. "She doesn't care what she goes to bed with, or rolls in the hay, or whatever. I value my health."

Pike poised for an attack, then subsided as Quin moved in. "Give him time, Lieutenant. So she was promiscuous?"

I rubbed my temples, dug the heels of my hands into my eyes. "Didn't you get that?" Of course they'd got that.

"Do you have a headache, Matt?" Inspector Quin said.

"I'm developing one. Does it matter?"

"Why, sure, it matters. Lieutenant, do you care to get him something?" Pike left.

Quin sat down, too close beside me. "Woo-ee. He's got a temper. I tell you what, I don't even want to see him really riled. Matt, how do you know Crystal was promiscuous?"

I hitched my chair away. "It's hard to miss. She'll go with anyone if she wants something. She'd trade sex for—"

"Not random, then. She used sex?"

"Yes, I told you."

Someone came to the door with a clipboard. Quin pushed it back. "I can't read this now. Put it on my desk." She sat, hitched her chair closer to mine. "Did she try it with you?"

I leaned away. "Of course she tried it with me. She tries it with everything in pants."

"What did she try and get from you?"

"A job in *Demon Dun*, of course, but I didn't do it."

"Didn't do what, Matt?" Quin laid a hand to my arm.

I pulled away. "I didn't sleep with Crystal. I told you, I don't want whatever she's got."

"So, you got jealous, and you two had a fight—"

That was almost funny. "Nobody with sense gets jealous of Crystal Beller. She doesn't even pretend. She's like the moon, she belongs to everyone. And I didn't fight with her."

"Did you love her?"

"No, I can't stand her, nobody can."

Pike came back in with water and foil-wrapped tablets. Some signal passed between them, and they both watched me swallow and drink. Quin took the plastic cup and handed it to Pike. "Did you need more water, Matt?"

"No. Thank you."

Pike moved in. "So, you came out of the lunch room, looking for Ms. Beller. Anyone see you?"

It was getting old. "Wyndham was with me. See, they were in the Canteen, and he—"

"They? You said Mrs. Wyndham was in the ladies' room."

"Well, yeah, she *went* to the ladies' room—"

"So was she in the Canteen or not?"

"I guess—Wyndham said they'd been wondering—Hang

about. You mean Nancy killed Crystal? Nancy wouldn't hurt a
spider. Why would Nance kill Crystal? She went into the ladies' room to pull herself together—"

"I'm asking you. Why'd you say *they* were in the Canteen?
You allergic to the truth?" Pike leaned over me. "What little
darlin' were you fighting about, sir?"

"I don't have one—I didn't fight with Crystal—"

Quin said, "Lieutenant, you don't need to do that. Matt,
who did Crystal mean when she said you got a little darlin'?"

That's how it went. People heard Crystal in a quarrel in my
dressing room. I deny being there. I deny having a little darlin'.
I can't tell how much time passed between seeing Crystal at the
ladies' room door, and finding her in my closet.

So I'm the top suspect. Or Nancy.

No, not Nancy. No way. Nancy couldn't hurt anyone, at
least not physically. Nancy's right out of it.

Crystal's robe and wig were found in a heap on the floor of
the ladies' room. "What were you searching for when you
stripped her, sir?" Pike said. "Did you get a kick out of it?"

"I didn't!" My "I didn'ts" were making no sense. "She was
like that when I found her—strangled with my tie—in my
closet—" It was beginning to sound like a confession. I tried to
think. "Look, I started CPR as soon as I could, as soon as I cut
the tie off her. I tried to revive her, for crying out loud."

"CPR's deadly if you do it wrong." Quin remarked.

"She—I—No! Geez, I haven't been certified for over—
but—" Dear God, I know the technique; I'd done it before. I
tried to think. "I must have—didn't I—?" If I'd done the CPR
wrong, Crystal was dead because of me.

"You didn't like her, did you, sir?" Pike said.

"No—but I wouldn't—I'd never—I thought— I did it the
way I was trained—" The harder I tried to remember the less I
remembered. Why fight these people? If I fouled up the rescue,
it wouldn't matter who tied my tie around her neck. I got Pike
into focus. "Can we be sure?"

"Medical examiner's on it. You won't get away with it."

"How long?" I said. "How long before we know?"

"Any minute. You want to call your lawyer?"

What could Brewster do about this? "I'll wait, thanks."

Quin didn't let up. "How did you first meet her, Matt?"

I couldn't make the medical examiner work any faster. I pictured the night Crystal broke into our motel room, rewound the tape in my head and let it all out. I didn't have to think. It rolled out of my mouth while my mind tried to make sense of the possibility that I killed the person I was trying to save. It took minutes to tell the story: "—and the *Probe* came out the next week. Legally, I'd defused it, but—" I wound down.

"So she blackmailed you?" Quin prompted.

"She tried—"

"And double-crossed you," she said.

"I guess—"

"And you fought with her," Pike said.

"No, I was too mad at her."

"She was a manipulative, ruthless little tart, sir, she pulled your last string. I'd be mad. It's understandable. Hell, sir, she kept yapping at you, you had to shut her up. It was an accident, a tragic mistake. You didn't mean to kill her," Pike said. "Is that how it was? Sir!"

I wasn't with him. "I thought I was saving her."

He slammed his hand onto the table before me. I blinked. "Look at me!" I did. "Why'd you undress her? What were you searching for?"

"No, she was already undressed." I kept trying to remember. "I cut the tie off—I tried not to cut her, but it was so tight, she was so swollen. And—" I concentrated, dredged at memory— "I got it cut, and Halla came in and called 911, and I couldn't get a breath around the tongue, I had to go through the nostrils, and that worked. I felt for a p-p-ulse—" Panic welled up, blocking memory and breath. I moved my hand, tried to get the fingers to remember. They didn't. I shook my head. "But I c-couldn't *not* start CPR—she was—"

Pike said, "Tssht. Actor. Tears my goddam heart out."

Someone was at the door. The medical examiner's report. It had to be the medical examiner's report. Quin took in some papers, lifted one to read the next. I stood up to see.

"Siddown!" Pike barked. I sat down, craned my neck. Quin

gave the report to Pike, pointed. He read, swore, took the papers for himself and reread the bit Quin showed him.

I couldn't see. "What's it s-say? Was it the C-CPR?"

Pike banged the report down, fetched a patient sigh. "Sir. You've been lying to us all along. Haven't you?"

"No." The report lay open, just out of reach.

His hand slapped the table before me. "Haven't you!"

I shook my head, barely hearing him. I had trouble making out the details of his hand in front of me, but the report in the middle of the table came right into focus.

"No, you don't lie to protect yourself. It was the McKee woman. The one you schmoozed with when I came in."

That got my attention. "Hal? No. Halla? She left the Canteen after I did, she called Rescue, she helped me with the— what did the medical examiner say?"

"She was loose on the set, she's a strong woman, she and the victim were rivals—"

"No, you've got it wrong. Halla's even less likely than Nancy. Look, was it the CPR?" The report was neatly typed and spaced in paragraphs, with headings and everything.

"Shit. You'd go to the Chair telling the same lousy little lie you started with. Get out."

I sat still, focused on the report. Without much squinting I could make out the type. A little concentration, and I had it: "Circulation was minimal to nonexistent at least three minutes before rescue efforts were initiated . . . " I sagged like a dropped puppet. The relief hurt as much as the uncertainty.

For a moment. Then the brain shifted gears. "Hang on, that's too long. It wasn't three minutes—I know it couldn't have been three minutes before I found her."

"What are you—shit." Pike snatched up the report. "Get the hell out!" I stood. My legs were stiff.

"Don't leave the county," Quin said. "We might could use you again." Heartwarming.

I left, pushed through the doors next to the fire station. It wasn't that easy, of course. I had to sign things, retrieve stuff. They kept Badger's jackknife. It's evidence, apparently.

<><><>

I hauled myself back to Tara. The others must have gone to supper. I still had a co-star to work with. I dragged off bits of Badger's costume, with nothing but a shower on my mind, and my phone trilled, from somewhere underneath Tony's electronic mess. I dug it out, flipped it open. "This is Matt."

Brewster Beane didn't mince words. "Did you kill her?"

Geez. "No, I didn't. I—guess I should have called you."

"I guess you should have called me. Thank God for freedom of the press. The whole nation's heard about your little murder. You're no superstar, but that article in the *Probe* won't die. You want a good lawyer down there?"

"It might—Do you know any?"

"Do I know any. I've already talked to her. Got a pen?"

This lawyer's name sounds comically like a stripper's— Golde Silver—but Brewster swore that she's the best. "Keep in touch, though. I'm still here," he said. "You might want to call your family. Your mother tells me your father's worrying."

I did, then treated myself to a shower and a change. With a shot of new energy, I hiked around to the front desk for messages. There was one phone message for me, from a number I never heard of. Everything in me perked up, and a phone behind the desk burbled. Ma'am handed the phone to me across the "Sharon Beller, Proprietor" sign.

I all but snatched the phone. "This is Matt."

"Matt? Matt Logan?" It wasn't Mouse, it was Halla McKee. Who knew I'd be disappointed to hear from Halla McKee? "Uh—hello. What's up?"

"It's not what's up, it's what's down. I had to pick my son up in Lenoir, and I think my carburetor flooded, halfway up the mountain. I'm stuck, most the people I could call aren't home, or they're sick and tired of my car troubles, and I'm sorry to bother you, but I've got to get Dannal to his father by seven, and it's six-thirty now—"

"Where are you?"

"Thank you! I'm so sorry! It's really simple—"

It was. All I had to do was drive through Blowing Rock, shift into neutral when I passed the Green Park Inn, and stop when I saw a yellow station wagon with the hood up.

Halla's car languished in an old lumber road halfway down the mountain, the kind of spot that makes city people like me think a landscaping genius devoted a lifetime to creating it. Newly leafed trees filtered hazy sunlight, a warm breeze whispered odes to spring, a creek tumbled noisily under the road. There was no sign of Halla.

I thought of using the phone in the car, kicked myself for not making a note of the number she'd called from. Beneath the water's rush, I heard a peal of young laughter. At the bottom of the eight-foot gully, Halla stood knee-deep in wild flowers with an eager-faced boy about my daughter's age. They were playing some game. Halla lifted her face with the laugh still on it, and something clicked in my brain. I'd seen her sometimes at the Beller Mountain Community Center. I hunkered on the bank. "Practicing acceptance?"

"Matt! How long have you been here? I shouldn't keep you waiting—" She scrambled up the bank. Her young made it to the top with a grin like his mother's and no visible effort. His eagerness clouded as he saw how I've changed since the *Strongbow* movies. By the time we had his feet packed into the back seat of my undersized rental car, though, he overran his mother's apologies with his own concerns.

"Mr. Logan—"

"That's Matt."

"Not to my son," Halla said. "Until he works or plays with you on exactly the same level, he's to call you Mr. Logan. Sorry." Her face was pale and drawn.

I remembered that she'd had to interview at the 911 Complex, too. "Are you okay?"

She nodded. "Fine," she said. "I have to get my car towed all the way up to Blowing Rock, and pay for repairs before the end of the month. Other than that, I'm peachy."

"Anyway," her son rolled on, "Did you really play that keyboard thing in *Strongbow*, or was it faked? I bet Dawn-Regina Black it was you."

"You win. That keyboard thing was an ancient instrument called virginals, an ancestor of the harpsichord. They tuned it to the modern scale. I might have played it in the twelfth-century mode, but it wouldn't sound right nowadays."

He fisted air. "Yesss! Do you ever play Billy Joel?"

"Sure. Not on the virginals. You like Billy Joel?"

"Yeah, 'Root Beer Rag' rules! I got the music." He waved a book over Halla's shoulder.

She said, "Pa didn't want you trying Joel, Danny."

"No, that's not Pa, that's Janelle. She wants to groom me for the religious market. She says it's wide open. She wants to get me on WATA."

Halla's jaw clenched. "Janelle is Dannal's stepmother."

"Does religious music—er—rule?" I asked.

He shrugged one shoulder. "Piece of cake, it's all harmonic, but I'd go on tour."

"Which would get you out of school."

"Yeah, and then I couldn't play basketball."

Halla twisted in her seat to look at him. "I thought Pa told you not to play basketball. His hands," she explained.

"Ma, I told him, if I can't play basketball, I won't play piano. I try out for the team next year. Tarheels *rule*!"

Halla pointed. "Turn right after that burned-out church."

Dannal's father is Roland Harper. I can't say I ever heard of Roland Harper. That shocked both Dannal and Halla. Janelle produced Roland's album— "and not long after that, they were married," Halla added.

Roland's house hangs over the edge of the mountain, looking down on two states. He's easily recognized, once you've seen Dannal. They're both the brooding, Byronic type, but Dannal's brooding brow keeps getting broken up with his mother's grin.

As we crunched to a stop, Roland and his wife were waiting. Another revelation. Halla's wanna-be "agent" is married to her son's father.

Dannal scrambled out. His father bent to Halla's window. "God, Luie, car trouble again? You're going to have to buy a new car. No arguments."

"I'm sorry, Roland, I can't afford a new car."

"I said, no arguments."

The wife stopped Dannal on his way to the house. "Dan, you left your book in the car."

"It's mine," I said.

Roland looked through Halla's window at me. "Thanks for coming to Luie's rescue like this. She's no use with—wait a minute. You're—don't tell me—Oh God—Mark Hamill!"

"No, but I have been paid to look like him."

His wife was more perceptive. "You're Matt Logan!"

"I knew you were somebody!" Roland reached past Halla's face to shake hands. "Sorry Luie took you out of your way like this. Roland Harper. Call me Roland."

I got us away. Halla sat with her arms folded tightly around her, her face turned away. "Where can I take you?"

"The Community Center, if it's not out of your way. I need a meeting. I'm sorry you had to come all this way—"

"I'm tired of apologies. You'd do the same for me."

"Of course, but that's not the point—"

"It's the point. I've been rescued when I deserved it a lot less than you do, by people I never saw again. I owe, on a largish scale." I parked at the Center, reached into the back seat for my baseball cap, tugged it well down in front. "I'll take you home later, if you want."

Halla said, "You know you're about invisible under that?"

"If I want to be. I prefer to control my visibility when I'm really being me."

After the meeting, I drifted out to the verandah with every-body else. Halla's rich chuckle floated over the lilac-scented air, the talk, and the cigarette smoke. A molasses-voiced six-footer named Bradford moved out of the way, and Halla lifted her chin at me with a grin. It was good to see her head high again. Bradford knocked dottle out of his pipe. "Do you mind talking about your work?" he demanded.

"Not if you don't mind talking about yours."

"I'm a hospital chaplain, and I profess philosophy to the young owners of the world at the college over there." He waved his pipe vaguely between Boone and Banner Elk. "I was on that tour to Little Stratford last year. Your Mercutio—"

"It was brilliant," Halla cut in. "When I stood up after your death scene, I had a stitch in my side from laughing too hard or crying too hard, one."

"Do you think Willie Shakespeare wrote all that crap?" Bradford said.

Halla jumped in. "It had to be a theater man. It was *not* the Earl of Oxford, or any of the University men—"

"Begone, Hallalujah. I want a professional's opinion. Who was the real Shakespeare? Bacon? Oxford? Raleigh?"

I shrugged. "Who knows? I only memorize the lines."

The resulting explosion was everything I hoped for. It lasted over an hour and several cups of coffee at a nearby all-nightery, and involved half the talkers from the verandah. On the way back Hal and I kept at it, the subject taking several swerves that ended with *Demon Dun*.

"See, you'd never cast a gorgeous starlet as Sarah."

"A couple of our Sarah finalists were stunners. Find another example," I said.

"But Sarah's ugly, it says so in the script," Halla said. "I don't mean why doesn't Sarah end up with Badger—who'd want to?—but there's a feeling that she doesn't deserve to, specifically because she's ugly."

"It doesn't say that, Hal; you're reading your own opinion into it. Badger has to end up with Andrea. Tony wrote a horror romance, not protest literature."

She pounced. "That's it! That is my exact point! Why is it a romance if Badger and pretty Andrea end up together, and protest literature if he and Sarah do?"

"The world thinks that way. You can't change it."

"That's a cop-out. You can't blame 'the world.'"

"It is not a cop-out. Look—" We were approaching the parking lot at Tara. I pulled in. Halla lives in an apartment complex about a mile farther down the road, practically straight up. I said, "Let's go in and annihilate each other over a decent cup of coffee."

She shook her head, smiling. "Not in there. I'm grateful that you picked me up, but—"

"What do you mean—oh." The penny dropped. "No—no, that's not it. I just want to finish this discussion. Hal, look. What do I gain if I have to talk you into what you don't want, or trick you, or force you? I have to work with you."

She frowned. "Well—I guess I could hurt you if I had to."
She let herself out of the car and beat me to the door. I reached
around her to unlock the room. Something moved on the chair.

Julien. I had completely forgotten Julien.

She uncurled long, tightly jeaned legs. "Hello."

"Who's a silly presumptuous little girl?" Halla muttered.

I scrambled for balance. "Julien! Geez, I'm sorry—You
remember Halla McKee? She's the new Sarah, and—"

Halla came forward, a friendly smile ready. "Hey, Julien.
It'll be great working with you. You all are busy, so I'll get
gone." She moved to the door. "See you in the morning."

"Hang on, you can't walk," I said. "It's dark, I can—"

"No, you can't. You've neglected Julien long enough. I can
get around here, I live here, you know."

Halla was gone. Julien was there. I had some abject grovel-
ing to do. "Geez, Julien, I'm really sorry—I didn't expect you—
The murder must have been traumatic for you."

"Oh, no, I didn't know the—you know. She was just my
body double. I'm okay." She sounded as if she meant it. "But,
do you still want to work? Let's do the hayloft scene first, up to
when the fire breaks out, and then the scene under the apple
tree. I have it all planned out. The ladder comes up here—"

I don't believe my luck. There can't be two women in two
million who'd have handled that situation as well as Julien and
Halla had. I took a moment to change channels. "I—hang on.
Hang about. We can't block the scene."

"It's not blocking. We need to act it out."

"No, Jule. 'Acting it out' is blocking. That's Tony's job.
What we have to figure out is where we've come from, why
we're together. That's our job. We make Tony's work real."

"How real can it be if we don't get up and act?"

"How real can it be if we get up and act before we know
who we are? Do you like coffee?" I faced the coffee maker.

Julien greeted the aroma with a coo. "Oh! Hawaiian! That's
so hard to get where I come from."

"Yeah, I'm an alcoholic. I can't be a wine connoisseur, so I
connaisse coffee instead. Cream? Sugar?"

"Oh, you can't ruin nectar like this with adulterants. It should be savored—" She watched me heap sugar into my cup. "But you don't act like an alcoholic."

"Well, I am. I stopped drinking three years ago."

"Oh! Congratulations! So you *used* to be an alcoholic."

Alcoholism is nothing to be ashamed of, but I can't say it's any great achievement, either. "I'll always be alcoholic. It's like being diabetic." I stirred my coffee, took a sip. Perfect. "Right." I cleared cassettes off the table, dragged it to the middle of the floor. "Come on, Jule, sit. We'll act after Tony blocks the scene. Look, how did Andrea and Badger meet?"

She scanned a mental array. "That's not in the script."

"Right, it's not. You never took scene study classes?"

"Oh, yes, but I don't believe in that. I believe that motivation comes from *doing*."

"Jule, look. How would you snuggle up to Badger if you'd only known him for two months? No—just think. Then think how you'd do it if you'd known him for two years."

She thought. In a breath she had it. "Oh! If we met in a bar, we'd act different than if we met—okay—in church."

"Right." I beamed. "So let's fill in the gaps. How did Badger and Andrea meet?"

We worked till midnight, then I made her quit, sent her away. She's right about having her energy at night. She was ready to stay till dawn. I hope her fiancé's a night owl. I could hardly keep my eyes open.

.6.

TODAY: FOR THE SHERIFF

All of that happened yesterday. Today was easier, marginally. Tony slept in, so I went around to the office for mail. Ma'am was ready for me. She's ready for most things. "Hey, Mr. Logan. Tough day yesterday?"

"You could say that."

She handed me sorted packets of mail. "That's yours. Looks like you got a fan letter. Everybody's jumping on the murder."

"Everybody?" Two bills, a statement from my agent, junk mail. The "fan letter" was from Shannon. I chucked it between the bills. I don't know why I hid it, unless it's because Shannon seems so afraid of being found out.

"It's on all the news," Ma'am said. "NBC says you did it, CBS says you'll get off because you're famous, ABC says you'll get nailed because you're famous. Fox says you're innocent. CNN won't say. They'll get it together tonight."

"What do you say?"

"Did you do it?" She was serious. Nothing surprises her, everything interests her. Ma'am is a born concierge.

"No." I remembered the whole CPR procedure, now. I'd done it correctly. I took a free breath. "No, I didn't."

"That's good. Can't have that around here."

"Ma'am? Has 'Gee Whiz' ever been in your vocabulary?"

An unexpectedly charming smile: "I don't think so, Mr. Logan. Have a nice day."

I opened Shannon's letter as soon as I got in, treated myself to a dose of normality. It's a rambling letter, hits several
topics, apparently in the order she thought of them. She seems
to have discovered ampersands. She writes stories for her enrichment class, and she sent me a sad one. All the nice characters end up dead. The bad guys go to jail, "*& so it was alright.*"

She mentions names: "*I like names that are sort of Irish,
like Kelly, Erin, & Colleen. My very faverate is Shannon. I
hate baby names that repeat, like Gigi & Lulu & Nana. A
girl in my class is called Jojo. Isn't that gross! But most of
all I hate & detest Mimi. My Stepfather calls me Mimi. He
thinks everybody should like baby stuff.*"

This isn't entirely true. He's teaching her how to play chess:
"*I never want to beat him. He likes to win, & so I do not check
him untill he can get out of it easy.*" When I taught Mouse, she
must have been the right age to learn, because she picked it up
in no time. She's a lot more ruthless than Shannon; she took my
queen the third time we played. I like to think it was because I
was drinking instead of thinking, but I have a nasty suspicion
it's because she was shrewder than I thought.

I have a feeling Shannon's stepfather must have a hard time
with her: "*My Stepfather does not know that I write to you. He
only wants me to love him. He takes me to the Starling Head,
he says, 'To look at the sunset,' but really, he wants to bond
with me. I hate bonding.*" Evidently the man is trying to be a
good parent. Maybe he should back off, stop trying so hard.
Maybe I don't have a lot of room to talk.

Shannon signed her letter: "*I love you, Pretend Daddy.*"

Pretend Daddy.

Ah, geez. I'd better go on.

I had a polite phone call inviting me to the Sheriff's Office this
morning. Tony was unimpressed. "They want me, too. I ducked
out on the Star to check out the shower scene. Dora thinks she
got a usable take when Crystal and Dakota were thinking about
something else, so she called it quits. Nobody saw me, and that
little tart was blackmailing me. The police think I did it."

"No, they think I did. I spent all yesterday afternoon saying
I didn't. I may sign a confession for the change."

"Me, too. And Dora. And Phina."

"What?"

"Yeah, Dora found me, and we worked on the kitchen set—
I don't know—twenty minutes. Not in sight of each other. Phina
never went in. You know how she is about actors. One of her
precious cameras had an anxiety attack or something, and
Crystal'd been diddling with Dakota."

"You were out there? Why didn't you come when I was
calling for help? I howled."

"We thought you were practicing. We rehearse the Badger-
yelling-at-Sarah-in-the-kitchen scene tomorrow."

"I don't practice that way. I was tearing my voice out. I
was calling for help, for crying out loud."

"What do I know? You're an actor. You can't ever tell when
actors mean it."

"Who's talking?" I said. "Good luck with the Sheriff."

"Wait. Dora and I figured out our party line. We don't
want to trash the dead in the media. Listen. 'Crystal Beller was
a'—where to hell did I put that—here it is." He pawed through
rewrites and electronics, found a piece of scribbled-over paper
and read from it. "'Crystal Beller was a highly motivated and
dedicated artist, committed heart and soul to working on
this film.' How's that? Phina put in the bit about the heart
and soul."

"Phina did? Geez. Sure, it sounds fine to me. Motivated,
dedicated, committed—got it."

"Good," he said. "Do me a favor, meet me at the Studio
when you get done. I don't like all those local cops running
around my sets."

"Sure. See you there."

Yesterday they confiscated everything I had in my pockets.
It wasn't much: Badger's knife, a luck piece I carry, my keys,
my belt. If I'd been wearing a watch or shoelaces, they'd have
got them, too. They gave most of it back, of course, but I don't
like letting go of personal things, even temporarily.

Today I'd be comfortable: loose-fitting khakis—no belt,
they'd take that—T-shirt, moccasins, windbreaker. I stuck cash
into my pocket. They'd confiscate it, but cash isn't personal. I

left everything else at home. For all I knew, this was it, and I was going to be arrested for murder.

I was all but out the door before I remembered that Brewster had recommended an attorney. I might as well call her, if I'm about to get arrested for murder.

I only had to say my name once, and she was in my ear. "Good for you, you called *before* you talked to the cops. I like that in a client."

"Well, not exactly," I admitted. "I had an interview yesterday at the 911 Complex—"

"Yeah, that's normal," Golde Silver said. "Mr. Beane tells me you didn't do it."

"I didn't, but I don't expect anyone to believe me."

"Mr. Beane does. Meet me there, " she said. "Megan Quin's the investigating officer?"

"Yeah—with Lieutenant Pike—"

"Good. Meggy's scared of me. See you there."

I'm not sure I can blame Inspector Quin.

Golde Silver is built along the lines of a tennis ball. As I hiked across the parking lot of the 911 Complex, she bounced out of an illegally parked pickup truck. I am prepared to swear that it bounces, too. "Come on, Meggy knows to wait for us," she said. "They have a special soundproof room where they let me talk to clients."

It was actually an oversized interview room with a carpet, ashtrays, and a soda machine, besides the table and two chairs. We sat, and she arranged pens, legal pads and things around her. I organized the facts from yesterday in my head, and prepared to reel them out.

She said, "What did you think of Crystal Beller?"

"I—What—?"

"You didn't expect that, did you? You got to be ready for questions you don't expect. What did you think of her?"

I consulted the ceiling. "She's a highly motivated—"

Striking like a cobra, Golde Silver pointed a sculptured nail at my nose. "Don't you lie to me, Matt Logan. I will not have a client lie to me. You tell me what you really thought, or you fire me, I don't mind which."

Geez. The walls suddenly seemed too close.

"And don't try and evade, either."

"I haven't even—"

"You're about to," she said. "Trust me or fire me, one."

"Look. Crystal must have a family. If they—"

"What, you've been Brewster Beane's client all these years and you never heard of lawyer-client privilege? What was Crystal like? Skin the truth and tell me."

Right. I skinned the truth. "Crystal's a heartless bimbo addicted to blackmail, whose death will probably slow the spread of venereal disease in this county by fifty percent."

"Woo-ee." Golde Silver sat back and mimed wiping her brow. "You talk like that, you and I'll get along just fine."

We got along well enough. At last, she gathered her overused legal pad and pens. "Good, I believe you. Come on, let's go in and see what Meggy wants out of us."

We walked past interview rooms to an office roughly the size of a telephone booth. Maybe not that big. It was stuffed with a desk, two chairs, a file cabinet, paperwork. Inspector Quin received us with the kind of charm that belongs to steamy plantations and frosty mint juleps. "Hey, Matt, you all right? Golde, sit down. Let me get another chair."

Quin used her phone, put it down with a smile as if she had all the time in the world. I can't say she gave any sign that my lawyer worried her in any way. "They'll bring one—here it is—thank you." She waited graciously while the chair was tucked among the other furniture, and the uniform who brought it withdrew. "We want to record this, do you mind?"

I sat and braced myself. "No. Go ahead."

She coaxed something from a drawer, laid it on the desk. A clipboard. My clipboard. This clipboard, with about a week's worth of journal on it. The pen was still on the clamp. It was all a bit disarranged. Maybe I shouldn't have been shocked, but I was. "You've read my journal."

"Yes, we've read it."

"But it's personal—private—"

My lawyer spoke up. "You got the paperwork for that?"

"It was on the scene," Quin said.

Golde Silver raised almost invisible brows at me. I nodded. She gestured. "Go on."

"There's no such thing as personal privacy in a homicide case, Matt," Quin said. "You need to get used to it."

"But this has nothing to do with it—"

"That's fine." She spoke kindly, but I think she shares Pike's opinion of me. "Then we can give it back to you."

I didn't believe her.

She said, "Matt, tell me about Mouse."

A harmless question. "She has nothing to do with—"

"Good. We got enough paperwork. Who is Mouse, really? She's not really your ex-wife, is she?"

I didn't want my Mouse in this mess, not even her name in it. Of course Quin had to ask. I got stuck. I tried again, stuck again. The third time I tried, I got as far as "M—" and I could not come out with it.

"You can answer that," Golde Silver said.

I held up a hand. My voice worked long enough to say, "May I—have a mo-moment?"

"Go ahead."

I stood, took a three-step tour of the office. The wall was a mosaic of framed things: training certificates from the Atlanta Police Academy, citations for valor, photographs. I stopped to look at one picture at eye-level—a place of honor, evidently. It showed Quin, proud in a handsome uniform, holding the leash of a German Shepherd. The dog had a medal ribboned around its neck. A plaque was riveted to the picture's wooden frame. I leaned back to read it: "Cabot," with dates. The dog died when it was seven years old. I lost Mouse when she was seven years old. The difference is that Mouse is alive and safe, with her mother and her mother's husband. They both love her. What was I feeling so sorry for myself about?

It was simple enough to say. "Mouse is my daughter. M-Michaella—Russo—Logan." Odd. I don't think I've said her full name out loud in over three years.

"Is this her?" Quin turned over the picture. I reached for it, pulled back. She said, "You're fine. You can take it."

I treated myself to a good look, tucked it into a pocket.

"That's—that's my daughter."

"You think the world of her, don't you?" Quin said.

"Yeah."

"Would you kill for her?"

Golde Silver bounced to attention. "Don't answer that!"

"Yes," I answered. "Without a blink."

Golde Silver let herself back into her chair. Quin flicked a nicely manicured finger at the clipboard. "And Crystal took and sold this to the tabloids?"

"Yes."

"Are you going to keep on writing?" Quin said.

No privacy. "It's a hab—a ha-abit. I dep-pend on it."

"Good. I want it as soon as you write it. We'll copy it and give it right on back to you."

Golde Silver exploded. "Now, hold on there—How dumb are we, today? You ever hear of the Fifth Amendment, girl?"

"I sure have. Matt, it's your constitutional right not to incriminate yourself. Are you saying you didn't kill Crystal?"

"That's what we're saying," Golde Silver said.

"You want to prove it?"

I considered a flat refusal. Futile, but I considered it.

Quin tilted back in her swivel chair, caught at the file cabinet when the chair didn't catch itself. I bet it hasn't caught itself in years. "Did you have fun here, yesterday?"

"No. Are you threatening me?"

"Meggy—" Golde Silver warned.

Quin shrugged. "Threatening, blackmailing—whatever."

"And you'll use this against me in court," I said.

"Not if we get it before you've heard your rights. You can let me read your diary, or I can have you come in and talk to me. I just thought writing might be more convenient."

"I don't know what you care to call this, I call it intimidation," Golde Silver said. "What do you want it for?"

"Insight." Quin brought her chair up straight. "Details. Matt's writing's full of them, all about these movie folks, like a story. I don't know how these people work, how they think. Maybe some kind of thing they do looks highly suspicious to me, but I'm just a simple country girl. Maybe that kind of thing's perfectly normal for people like Matt to do. Give me insight on my suspects, I'll think kindly of you forever."

"You sure will," Golde Silver scoffed. "And if he accidentally writes about smoking something that never came out of a tobacco field—"

"I don't do that," I said.

"See? He don't do that," Quin said.

"Matt, I want to talk to you. Outside." Golde Silver bounced out of her chair and led the way down the hall. What she meant by "outside" was the parking lot, beside her mud-dappled truck. "Now, I need the absolute, gospel truth," she said. "If these people saw your diary, is there anything in it—spitting on the sidewalk, gunrunning—you know what I mean—that could get you arrested? Anything at all?"

"No," I said. "I can't afford another addiction. I don't have time for the other stuff."

"What about women?"

I thought of Halla, evaporating and leaving me with Julien last night, and shook my head. "Not at the moment."

"Men? Boys? Kids? Billy goats?" She planted hands on hips. "What are you, a saint?"

Amused, I spread my hands. "A loser. Sorry."

"You'd better be right, because I'm going to advise you to write your diary, only you give it to me, not to Meggy or anyone else. I'll go over it, and get it typed out for them."

"What—why can't we have it put up on the billboard, on the road coming into town? Geez, how many people have to read my life? No."

"Now, now, take it easy. If you keep going in for questioning, how many people are going to read the transcripts? This way, there'll be me—and you know you want me to see anything they see—the typist—and he doesn't care—and Meggy and her pals, who'll see everything, anyway. Anybody else sees it, someone'll get the pants sued off them."

"Do you know what it was like, seeing my journal smeared all over that tabloid?"

"Take your time. You don't have to do this, but it'll accomplish two things." She counted pointy fingers. "It'll get them off your tail, as far as coming in for questioning, and we can tell the media you're cooperating, submitting written statements. And can you think of a better way not to have anything you say misinterpreted? So that's three things."

"I—I guess you're right, but—no. I know it's irrational, but what I write is—no." I made a move toward the doors. "I'm sorry, but I won't do it."

She opened the one marked Use Other Door. "You want two women begging you?"

"I don't care who begs me. Look. I could lie, I could conveniently forget important bits, right? So why bother? I'd rather be misinterpreted, if you don't mind."

She stood in my way. "What if I do mind?"

I should have known she wouldn't make it easy. "Nobody reads my journal. I'm sorry."

"Oh, quit. Hiring a lawyer means never having to say you're sorry. Let's tell Meggy."

As we came back to Quin's burrow, Golde Silver shook her head. "You want that journal, you'll need a warrant."

I said, "I'm sorry—I don't see why it's such a big deal. I only write about myself."

Quin leaned forward. "Matt, you notice things. You don't even have to pay attention to them, like Crystal's nails, or like— tell me. What was she wearing the night she broke in?"

"I don't know, it was dark—hang on." I sat down, called up the picture of Crystal's manicure glimmering in the moonlight. "Fur coat, high heels, 'In/Tense.' Nothing else but make-up. You want that kind of thing? When do I eat?"

"We don't need you to do anything special, just write. You got plenty of material. It's not evidence. It gives us a way to start thinking, a reason to ask questions—"

"A way to make someone else's interview tougher."

Beside me, Golde Silver said, "Easy, now—"

Quin's charming face hardened. Really hard. "You want to protect your friends or do you want to stop a killer? Someone killed Crystal, Matt."

There was a right answer to that, and a true one. Out of blank air came the memory of willing that heart to beat, pumping all I had into turning it back to life. Then the high, steady whistle of failure: "*Shit. She's gone.*"

Whoever killed Crystal is probably someone I know, maybe someone I like. But a murderer you like is still a murderer. I slid the clipboard off the desk. "Look, if I write about something that has to do with the case, you can read it. But my journal— no. I can—if it would help, I can write about yesterday—"

Quin softened, even smiled. I wasn't fooled. This wasn't much, and I'd made her work for it. "Can you do it now? You can use the interview room."

"What makes you think I'm not going to leave things out, or lie? I'm your top suspect."

Quin's smile got real, even mischievous. "Don't flatter yourself. What you leave out and lie about tells us more than what you write. Think I don't know the difference? Try and lie, you'll be doing us a favor. You study on that a spell."

Golde Silver said, "You don't want me to get it typed up, and leave out the personal things?"

"No, thanks. If they get it at all, they get everything." I started to get up. "May I have my glasses?"

"Do you not have an extra pair?"

"Not with me."

Quin used her phone, hung up. "They'll bring them."

I stood up to look at Cabot, its eyes large and bright, ears pricked as high as a dog's ears can go. One of them bent inward a trifle. The uniformed Quin looked as if it was hard to keep her face from splitting into a grin. One of her buttons had caught the camera flash and burned a star into the film.

"Finest dog Meggy ever handled," Golde Silver said.

"And my last." I hadn't heard Quin come up behind me. She moves like a velvet panther. I stepped aside. She flicked a fingernail over the dog's skewed ear. "He was with me five years, saved my life three times. That last time . . . "

I nodded.

"I swore I'd spike that bastard," Quin said in her soft Southern drawl. "I transferred to Investigations, but the killer died in a chase, I never did get him. No matter how hard I try, I never will get the killer I want. I'm still trying."

"What was the photographer doing? The dog liked it."

Quin didn't answer right away. She was years away, being Sgt. Quin of K-9 Division, on top of the world with her fabulous dog. "Squeaky toy," she said. "Brand-new. Cabot was on a mission about squeaky toys; he chewed the squeakers out."

"That was one dedicated dog," Golde Silver said. "He only worked for the Sheriff on the side."

A uniform came to the door bringing a plastic bag with my life in it—wallet, glasses, two pens—stuff you never think about until it's taken away. Quin had to leave Cabot and come back, too. She had a paper for me to sign, saying I got it all. I distributed everything into my pockets, took up the clipboard.

Golde Silver—I can't seem to separate the two names. She isn't Golde, or Ms. Silver, she's Golde Silver—brought me to the room where we spoke today, and left me here to write all this. Two days of chaos has taken some time put on paper, but writing lends some form of order to my head.

As soon as the door closed on her, I took out Mouse's picture. The backing has bits you can pull out to make it stand up. I stood it in front of me, leaned chin on fist, and stared at the face I haven't seen sober in—in 'way too long .

Dear Mouse,

I have to forget you are here, less than three miles away. In New York three miles make a galaxy, with thousands, maybe millions of people between us. Here, there's almost nobody. It's ruining my concentration.

Wyndham says if I sign that release, maybe they'll let me see you. There is nothing I want more than that, Mousy, but I can't trust their maybe. They don't want Brewster Beane in this. What does that tell you? Maybe if you said you want me to sign it, from your own mouth to my own ear, I'd consider it. Maybe).

[Inspector Quin,
I didn't mention a fight with Crystal Beller in this, because I didn't have one; and the only "little darlin'" I have would be my daughter. Sorry—MTL].

.7.

SHERIFF'S OFFICE AGAIN:
POST TESTS

When I walked out at last, my clipboard under my arm, my worldly possessions in my possession again, the universe was balanced on an odd but somewhat steadier keel. I turned a corner, and my doppelganger accosted me, lit from behind, its face hidden in shadow. The apparition bared its teeth and called me by my name.

I stopped dead. "What are you doing here?"

Maybe he isn't completely "doppel." His name still shows up on celebrity birthday lists. "Just the guy I wanted to see," he said. "They were asking about you in there. I told them you were a nice, quiet, well-bred boy with no women friends. That was okay, wasn't it?"

"Ah, geez. Look, I'm sorry you got mixed up in this—"

"Are you kidding?" he said. "They wanted to talk to me in the privacy of my own hotel room, but I made them take me down to the station. I wanted to see what it's really like."

"You wanted—" What could I say? This guy has no sense of self-preservation. Curiosity took over. "And?"

"Big letdown. No rubber hoses, no bright lights—"

"They handle things with psychology now. If you deny anything, it means you did it."

"That lets me out. I couldn't deny or confirm a single thing they asked me about. Do policepeople check their watches every time they sneeze? They just booted me out, no handcuffs, no nothing. *Big* let-down. The squad car was okay—unmarked, no siren, but—"

"They didn't let you take your own car?"

"I refused to. Come on, I may never get another chance; I had to see what they're like. It was great inside—mobile computer, weapons, satellite gizmos, you name it, but the outside—bor-ring."

"So you need a ride back?"

"A ride back? Oh, yeah. D'you mind?" His head lifted up. He tossed a smile past my shoulder. "Hi! Halla? Halla!"

Halla stalked by, her face set and grim. She turned, pulling her face into resolute civility. "Hello—" Suddenly she smiled, like the sun coming out. "Matt! Did your keys get sealed off?"

"Hal—Halla." Everything in me loosened up. "Do you need a ride, too?"

There was a second of silence, then, "Thanks, no, my car's fixed." Halla's car troubles must be a sore point with her. I can't seem to get it right when I'm around her. Her jaw set and the grimness took over. "I came to see about getting my stuff back, and found out that some tabloid called here asking about Dannal. I want to know who's responsible. Does *Demon Dun* have a public relations department?"

"It's not that kind of project, but you might want to talk with Dora. She's probably at the Studio. Look—I understand you two are old friends."

She turned to offer a hand. "Old friends? Aren't you—"

"Let me be incognito for a day. I'm tired of being *him*." He took the hand. "I used to be a regular of yours at the Chugg'n'Mugg."

Halla thought, got past a bad patch, lit up. "You paid my gas bill one Halloween!" Behind her face I could see that memories were filing by, not all of them good. She gave him a polite smile. "Um—will you excuse me? I have to—"

He stepped aside. "Good luck. Let me know if you find out who sold your kid to the media. I know an eight-hundred-pound gorilla named Biff, see, we'd find a secluded spot—"

Her lopsided dimples flashed in and out. "Thanks. I might take you up on that."

He watched her walk across the parking lot to her lemon-colored car. "That's her. I hoped she'd turn up again."

I led the way to my undersized rental, watched him buckle the belt. "Turn up again?"

"Yeah, Halla put herself through drama school, checking coats in this night spot I liked when I was starting out—"

"Hal was in school when you were getting jobs?"

"She started late, but she's good, I saw her in a few showcases. Everyone at Chugg'n'Mugg had a Halla story. You know how it is when you're looking for jobs, everyone knows everyone else, no one knows anyone with clout—"

I put the key into the ignition. "What's your Halla story? You paid her gas bill?"

"Yeah." He scrolled through memory banks, found one he liked. "Halloween night. She dressed up as a French mime and didn't say a word all night, so you couldn't get near her booth for all the guys crowding around, buying her drinks and trying to make her talk. I'd done a bit on this TV show called—" He assessed my face. "No, I won't give you the satisfaction. It was—" He shoved his eyebrows upward. "Anyway, it aired that day, and this girl went crazy."

"Who, Hal?"

"No, some girl who recognized me from that bit, and she was really nice; but a couple of stingers, and—" He made a claw and clutched space. "I couldn't peel her off. Nobody's bottomless, though, so when she had to go I blazed a trail to the door, but she was out before I could get my coat. I said, 'Omigod, she'll see me,' so Halla pulled me in, and threw her black cape over me. The girl asked, and I didn't hear the answer; Halla wasn't on audio, but, pooff!" He flicked a piece of air, and his laugh rolled out. "My huntress left with one of the doormen. I tipped Halla big that night."

A light rain spat at the windshield. I started the wipers. "That's not all, is it? What happened?"

He frowned through the streaks left by the windshield wipers. "Nothing good. That night, she left with this stud, you know the type: never goes home alone, and never with the same girl twice. She walked out with him like she was the queen of the world. Next night he came in, picked out another sucker, and she watched them all night; it hurt to look at her. I don't know, something about her face. After that, she came in drunk, lost her job, and—that was the last I saw of her."

We stopped at a crossroad near the foot of a rugged bluff. Above a valley opposite us, hillsides folded around fog-filled glens. Grandfather Mountain's knobby profile brooded far off behind the mist. "I'm glad she's on her feet again." He twisted to face me, direct as a child. "What about you?"

He had a right to ask. He'd made a pretty show of begging yesterday, but he's doing me a stupendous favor. I cleared my throat. "I'm fine. Three years sober."

He waited. I followed carved wooden signs around a hair-pin turn up to Starling Resort. Once on the straight drive, I reminded myself to breathe. "My—I'm divorced, now."

He nodded. "I heard. I'm sorry."

I pulled the car to the main entrance at the Resort. "My ex-wife has custody. I don't see my d—you know."

"At all?" His eyes grew round and huge, like a marionette's. He's crazy about his own offspring. "I heard about it, but I didn't believe a court would—man. If I can—"

"It's okay," I lied. Someone eager and deferential was open-ing his door. "I'd better—"

"Yeah, sure. Thanks for the ride." He got out, greeted the door opener with the professional charm that keeps his fans loyal for life. I doubt that the door-opener even saw me.

◇◇◇

Pike had shown up at the Studio just before I arrived. Yvan warned me as I came in. Great. More questions. I curbed an impulse to hoist a hip onto the corner of the desk. My training is coming along nicely. "Yvan. Did you tell the police about hear-ing a quarrel in my dressing room?"

Buddha statues should take serenity lessons from Yvan. "And what you said about she'd done her worst to you and she won't get another chance if you can prevent it."

"I appreciate the warning. Look. I don't know a lot about real-life murder. In movies, people who know too much tend to get killed off in the first hour. I want you to—"

"Uh—You worry about yourself. I read murder mysteries

all the time. You won't catch me running down a dark hall to
meet you all alone at midnight in a silken nightie."

Which was all there was to say about that. I escaped.

Everybody else was there. We'd all gravitated to the studio.
Julien stepped away from me with a soft squeak, and nearly
missed falling against the actor who plays Sarah's husky fore-
man Charlie. Scotty looked smug. I tried to look jealous. Phina
fooled with a camera. Even I could tell she wasn't doing anything to it. Dora's braids curtained her and her clipboard. She
chewed frantically on a pen. Tony buttonholed Halla, explained
Sarah to her. She paid diligent attention.

Yellow plastic tape draped around the porch set and my
dressing room, with county employees still working inside the
areas. Pike materialized out of my room, swung a leg over the
tape. I braced myself. "Tony, we may need your office—"

"Sir—" Pike gestured to the Canteen.

Tony interrupted his lecture to point. "Can't you use the
empty office over there? We had it cleaned and everything."

Pike pushed his head that way, and I followed him. The
unused office is across from Tony's. Pike shoved a chair at me,
and sat on the desk. Yvan wasn't there to object. He pulled out a
micro recorder, looked me over. "Oh, for God's sake. I'm not allowed to hurt you." He held up the recorder, switched it on.
"Mind if I record this?"

Little wheels went round and round inside the thing. My
brain rebelled, my breath stuck. "No, please!" I squeaked. "Don't
hit me again! What d'you want me to *say*?" When I act, I can't
even fake a stammer.

Pike turned off the recorder. "We could go to the station
and record this on video."

"No, I—that—th-at won't be n-necessary." I stopped long
enough to force myself to breathe. "Sorry, I was being silly. But
I didn't have a fight with Crystal. I have no—"

He switched the recorder on. "Mind if I record this?"

My ears reddish and well pinned back, I said, "Go ahead. I
wish I had fought with her. Should I make something up? I can,
if it would help."

"No. The truth would help. I want to know—"

"I can't give you what I don't have." I dredged up yesterday. "This fight happened when?"

He made a grab at his temper. "Sir—"

"I didn't have my watch—hang on." My watch had been on my table. I thought. "It was two when the Wyndhams went home. I'd shown him to the Canteen. She was in the—Hang on." I sat up straight. "Nance was in the ladies' room with Crystal, but she must have gone back to the Canteen. Wyndham said they both were wondering where I'd been—"

"Sir, you want to let me do my own job? The Wyndhams left before the murder. I got other questions—"

"Oh." I was not covering myself with glory. "Right." I put my memory in gear. "Right. I had someone waiting—"

"We talked to that guy," Pike said. "He doesn't know the time of day. You left Mr. Wyndham in the Canteen, went to your room, the girl met you—"

"No, I went out to find—"

"Yeah? Then how'd she get into your dressing room?"

"Uninvited. Probably with a plastic card. That's what she used on our motel room—"

"Sure, she did," he said. "You saw what she was wearing. Where'd she keep her credit cards?"

"I have no idea. I wasn't with her. I don't like her."

"Yeah, you keep saying that. So, you left the Canteen, and nobody saw you wandering around the sets till you spent the rest of the afternoon with a movie star who barely knows daytime from prime time. And you expect us to believe you." He heaved a martyred sigh. "Okay, forget it. Let me ask you this: Ms. Beller had sex with at least two men, less than three hours before she died. Any idea who? M.E. says the second one was rough—consensual, but rough."

That was no shock, considering Crystal, but—gaah. "I can't guess. Any guy who likes girls and doesn't care where they've been—" Dakota came to mind, the splendid idiot.

"Like who?"

"I can't—what if I name somebody and I'm wrong?"

"Then we forget him. Sir, if this killer hits again, the psychologists can give us a profile, and that'll help us." He leaned

over me. "But the second victim will still be dead. Who's it
going to be? Ms. McKee? You want to perform CPR on
Halla McKee? If you're not too late? You were too late for
Crystal Beller, sir."

"Cut it out!" I erupted from the chair, paced around, rubbed
my face, tried to get a grip.

Pike waited. Of course he was right. Obviously he was right.
I gritted teeth. "Crystal did a nude scene—I doubt that we'll be
using it—but she worked with my body double—"

"Your what?"

"Like a stunt double, only—"

"What, he dubs in your muscles?" Pike was on duty, so he
wasn't allowed to think it was funny.

"Yeah, because I don't have any. So—"

"So you think she might have frolicked with your muscle
man. Okay, so who else? You? There's evidence that she had
one of her romps on the bed in your dressing room."

I wondered if Dora could flip her braids, get me a new
room. "Not with me. You have no idea how repellent she is."

"Would you care to prove it? Give us samples?"

(*There's no such thing as personal privacy in homicide.
You need to get used to it*). It means nothing to the County
lab—a number, a specimen for testing. I swallowed revulsion.
"If it would help."

Instantly dry, brisk, businesslike, Pike said, "It would help."
He found a paper, rattled it. "According to the medical examiner, somebody, probably not her sex partner, slapped Ms. Beller
around within an hour before she died. Did you—?"

"I didn't fight with her. I don't hit."

"Yeah, I've seen your face after a brawl. Did you notice
bruises on her yesterday?"

"No." I frowned. "No, her make-up was pretty heavy."

Pike sharpened. "Wasn't she being—what'd you call it?"

"Body double, for Julien. Crystal was wearing body make-
up, but her face make-up was her own."

"You don't show the doubles' faces, do you? What was she
wearing make-up for?"

"Do I know? Women do it so they can all look alike. Some

actresses won't even get in front of a camera without perfume—hang on. That's weird."

Pike held still. "What's weird?"

"Hang about." I sat down, elbows on knees, eyes on the heels of my hands, coaxed at a piece of memory. "Crystal used this heavy scent that came out at the beginning of the year—'In/Tense.' She must have wallowed in it yesterday morning; I couldn't get the smell out of my nose. She was in my dressing room; the place should have been reeking with it, but—I even did CPR on her, and I didn't notice any—"

Pike relaxed. "Great. What was she doing all day?"

"What was she—oh. Shower scene."

"Do you use real water for those things?" he said.

So much for the great revelation. "And shaving cream."

"Shaving cream?"

"It stays sudsy longer," I said.

"God, what a way to make a living. What'd she mean, you can't love a real woman?"

I didn't bother with the rolling eyeballs or heavy sighs. "She wasn't saying it to me. My guess is that the 'real woman' was herself. For the record, the only person who could qualify as a 'little darling' of mine would be my d-d-aughter—" No. I ordered my mind out of that rut, cast around for something else to think about. Working with Halla came to mind, the way our bodies fit— "I'm sorry, what—?"

"You seem to know a lot about this fight you never had."

"Yvan told me. She knows everything. I never fought with Crystal. I don't like her."

"You only fight with people you like?" Pike shifted his weight. "Where's your sister?"

I blinked, trying to keep up. "Meranda? I don't know. Air Force One, last I heard. No, she's on her way to Sri Lanka for an election or a massacre or something. Why do you ask—?"

"Did you know she went to see her last week?"

"Crystal went to see Meranda?"

"Other way around," Pike said. "Why would your sister want to see Crystal Beller, just before she was murdered?"

"She did? I couldn't possibly say. They hardly lived in the

same universe. Probably Meranda didn't know Crystal was planning to get strangled. Why don't you ask her?"

"Like you said, she's on her way to get massacred. Never mind. Send Ms. McKee in."

"Hang on—Meranda came here? It makes no sense—"

He spoke very distinctly. "Send Ms. McKee in here. It's very simple." He switched off the recorder. "Sir, get rid of the idea that I have some kind of vendetta against you. You're not that special. I just don't like you. Now, will you get Ms. McKee for me so I can do my job?"

I dragged myself out. These interviews are worse than a whole day on one grief scene. But—What could Meranda want with an oversexed, starstruck tartlet?

As I emerged from the office, Julien's faultless enunciation floated across the studio. "Oh, you all know the way Matt Logan looks at me. And she was my body double—dressed to look exactly like me. If he came creeping up behind me—" I cleared my throat, cutting her off.

Everyone was standing in the same places they were in when I'd left. All conversation died out as Julien turned a pretty carnation pink. Silently, they watched me approach Halla. "Lieutenant Pike wants to talk with you."

She nodded, no problem. When she was gone, I got a shock. Halla was the only person there willing to meet my eyes, and it was an effort for her.

What fun.

There's not much to say when people don't want you around. I brought out the first coherent thought I found. "Tony, let's do a table-read."

"What? Why a table-read?"

"You've written today off anyway. Let's read through the script. That way everyone'll know the plot."

It was something to do. We all trooped into the Canteen, got to work to make it happen. Tony made a speech about how committed Crystal was to working on this film, and such a dedicated artist could only want us to keep on—and all that. It gave us the excuse to do what we all wanted to do anyway—work on our movie. Coffee was created, snack machines dispensed junk, we made ourselves comfortable.

Halla came in, flounced to a seat. "I sure wish whoever slapped Crystal would fess up and be saved. My one regret is that I never got the chance."

Julien gasped. "Halla, she's dead!"

Halla flushed. "I'm sorry. That was in bad taste. But am I the only one who admits I didn't like Crystal? They want to talk with—um—Ms. Powiak? I don't know last names—"

Phina nearly knocked her chair over as she slammed out. Dakota wasn't there. "I think I know who slapped Crystal," Julien commented. Into the silence she added sweetly, "I never really knew her, myself."

"What are we doing?" Halla asked. We were glad to talk about anything else. She heard all about what we were doing.

They've edited the auditions to show everyone's best takes. Tony set up Phina's monitor, and Gabby banged through the door, dragging his mother behind him. "I told ya," he told her.

We all froze as if we'd been caught cheating.

"I know," his mother said to the Canteen in general. "I ought've kept him away. But when we drove by, and he saw y'all's cars out there, he had to—"

"No, great," Tony said, almost as heartily as if he meant it. "Come on in, Pal." A superfluous invitation. Gabby scrambled to a place beside Halla. His mother found an obscure cranny and camped there to keep an eye on her child.

We opened scripts, burrowed into the reading, playing audition scenes on video whenever we came to them. With all of us working together, *Demon Dun* took over our minds, displacing the presence of the County out on the studio floor. It was good to forget we were homicide suspects for an hour or two.

Occasionally someone finished with Pike and came back to call out someone else. It never occurred to anyone that we could refuse to answer questions if we wanted to. Scotty came back steaming. "I don't care who hit her," he said. "Whoever boinked that little—"

"Scotty, look! Gabby's here!" Julien intervened. Gabby sponged it up. Scotty clamped his mouth shut, jerked to a seat.

"See, that's another reason to get a lawyer," Julien said. "It makes them think twice. The police aren't bothering me."

That's when I recalled that I have a lawyer, too. Damn.

Scotty was too upset to care who got hit next. "Oh, yeah? Guess who's in there now."

"What do you mean?"

"Olin Bunney of Bunney, Bunney, Bunney and Hutter—I think I said all the Bunneys. He just came in. It's your turn."

Julien half-rose, groped air. "But I don't understand."

"Isn't Olin Bunney the one you hired?"

"Yes, but—"

"Well, go on in and tell your lawyer to tell the nice policeman you didn't slap Crystal around, so they won't throw you into jail for murdering her."

"But, I thought the camera operator—"

"No, I didn't," Phina grated. "I slugged Dakota."

As our minds boggled, Gabby cried out, "Mom?"

Out of nowhere, she was with him. "Oh, my God. Honey, it's all right, I'm fine." She looked around. "Do they not know who hit Crystal Beller?"

Headshakes all round. "They think it was the murderer," someone said.

Gabby's mother stood straight, an undersized Sherman tank, her arm around Gabby. "No, it wasn't. It was me."

Dead silence.

She glanced down at her child, squared thin shoulders. "I lost track of Gabby, yesterday. When I found him, he was standing at her dressing room door. It was open, and she was—"

"Buck-nekkid," Gabby relished.

"Gabby, be quiet—Crystal up and slapped him. I went ahead and gave Crystal what she gave my boy. I know for a fact she had a man in there hiding. She's not poor Beller, she's trash-Beller. I hope I hurt her," she trumpeted.

"Brava, you," Halla said. "Exactly what I'd have done."

"I might could go in there and tell them," she offered. Julien accepted, and they left.

We all relaxed, looked at each other. "Good. That's one mystery solved," Dora said. "Can we go on now?"

"I thought Crystal was supposed to use the extras' room,"

Phina said. "Who gave her a dressing room?"

"Nobody. She took over mine," I said. "What I want to know is who her man was."

A fast chill. "It doesn't matter," Dora said. "The police will take DNA samples, and they'll identify him, and that'll be the end of this mess. Thank God it's not my job. Can't we go on?"

We could. Suddenly it was a party. We started clowning with the script, finding new ways to read lines, hamming it up. Tony wallowed in it. The sillier we got, the better he liked it. He sprayed endearments all over the room. We were his genii, his seraphim, his immortals.

Julien and I came close to a food fight while we read the fiery love scene in the hayloft. Scotty and Halla narrowly missed a sex scene when Charlie explained to Sarah how the curse worked on the horse they called Demon Dun. The scene in which Andrea sees little Gideon's powers for the first time giggled like a knock-knock joke contest.

We took a break when everybody's mugs dried up at the same time. Gabby's mother brewed new coffee while we read. She became our hero. We learned she has a name that isn't Mom or Gabby's Mother. She's Tamra Speranzo, married happily to her first husband, living in a trailer park just this side of Blowing Rock. Tamra still erases herself against the wall, but we've stopped forgetting she's there.

We buckled down again. Silliness brought ideas. Ideas became visions, visions jelled to created reality. Some new faces slipped into the Canteen when we were too busy to notice. I know Hal and I were followed as we walked out, and I doubt that we were the only ones.

Collective consciousness can be a powerful force. We came to the quarrel scene that ends with Sarah's fall. Tony, crackling like a bonfire, described the action between our lines. Nobody remembered we were sitting around tables in the Canteen, cherishing coffee mugs. Halla and I fought venomously in dust and hot sun, while the overtrained, demon-possessed horse shifted restlessly, excited by the violence in our voices.

When the Dun threw Sarah, she landed with a thrump we could all but hear. A horrified silence. Badger, hardly daring to face it, croaked, "Sarah?" Tony added, "and—cut."

The silence held a long moment. Coming back to the worka-day world was a wrench and a relief. And we were only a third of the way through *Demon Dun*.

Nobody knew what to say. Someone let out a "Powerful stuff, Tony," but that hardly counts as something to say.

Tamra came out of hiding. "Well, I read it to Gabby, and it don't stand to reason. How come Sarah can't get Badger?"

Tony turned on me. "Matt, damn it—!"

"Geez. Tony, I'm sorry. I wasn't—"

He turned to Halla. "Halla, you got to stop—Aw, hell!" He stood scowling, with no idea of whom to yell at.

I said, "Badger ends up with Andrea, because she—" and I bogged down.

"Sarah doesn't get Badger because Sarah doesn't want Badger," Halla said.

Tamra held her ground. "You ought to let Badger try and get her, and her spit in his eye."

"Ooo." Halla and I connected. The possibilities fizzed between us, seductive and dizzying.

"But why should Andrea take Sarah's leftovers?" Julien complained.

"Why indeed?" Halla said. "She'd turn him off if he tries to come back to her after that."

"No! Shut up!" Tony yanked us out of dreamland. "Just—everyone—shut—up. I wrote this the way it should go, and I demand your permission to direct it the way I know how. If anybody has any objections, let's hear them right now, then you can go out and make your own goddamn movie however you want. Understood? Any takers?" Halla stepped back a pace.

Tony let the silence drag on a long, effective moment. Then, more quietly: "Good. Now. Let's read this script."

We got to work, but it wasn't the same. It was work.

In the end, Sarah stands with Gideon among the ashes of her ruined horse ranch, alive but destitute. She says to Andrea, "There's your wedding present. A useful man. Take him and get out of here," and Badger and Andrea drive off into the sunset with a flip tag line or two. A polite moment before everybody applauded, stretched, moved around to get tables into standard position and take care of dirty coffee mugs. We were all ready to go home.

Halla came up to me in the confusion. "Matt? Should I apologize to Tony? Or something? I honestly didn't intend—"

"No." I herded her into a corner. She wore that whipped look she'd had when we drove away from Roland's house. I can't stand to see her look that way. "Hal, listen to me. Are you listening?"

She thought, shook herself, came back to me. "What?"

"Leave Tony alone. I mean it, stay out of sight. He'll get over it, he always does. But—are you listening?"

Another nod. She was with me.

"Let's give him space the size of Wyoming to think. I like the idea of being blown off twice in one film. Let him stew."

Halla was virtually crawling around inside my brain. Her eyes deepened, brightened, turned down. "It's yours. Thanks." She lifted her head to where it belonged. "At least the murder's solved. We can get to work again. See you tomorrow."

I watched her walk away. Every muscle knew exactly what it was doing. I told myself, "That's one person I don't ever want to lose out of my life."

A detective appeared at my shoulder. "Mr. Logan? Will you come down to the Sheriff's Office? We need you to give us a specimen, and there's something else we need you to do."

"But I was there this morning. Isn't the murder solved?"

"No way, sir. If you can do it right now?"

As I stood goggling, Julien sang out, "Oh, my God, are you arresting Matt?" The whole room slued around like toys on one gear. I held my wrists up, wide apart. "Look, everyone! No handcuffs! That means I'm not under arrest, right?"

Besides samples the County wanted a polygraph test.

"Lie detector?"

"Polygraph," they corrected firmly.

"I think I'd better—do you mind if I call my lawyer?"

No problem. They gave me a phone and privacy. She was right there; I hardly had time to enjoy the hold music.

I said, "I have a confession to make. Lieutenant Pike was

at the studio when I got there this morning, and I talked with him—I know I should have called you—"

"You're going to do this a lot, aren't you?" Golde Silver sighed. "Mr. Beane warned me. Anyone wants to talk with you, you talk first, confess later. Now, don't you worry about it, just try not to get chatty with them again—or with anybody else, you hear me? If you didn't do it—and you didn't, right?"

"Right."

"Then there's no physical evidence against you. They can't hold you on a confession alone. I love that, it's a delectable rule. Is that why you called, to confess?"

"No—they want me to take a polygraph test."

"Then take the thing. Now, you listen to me, and listen good. Follow directions to the letter. Take your time answering each question. Tell the absolute, gospel truth; they don't give a damn about anything except the murder. Then get back to me. I have to know everything you do."

So I did a polygraph test. Golde Silver showed up by the time it was over, took me here to the interview room so I could write this out. Geez. I ought to charge her by the hour.

.8.

BELLER COUNTY HOSPITAL EMERGENCY ROOM: FOR INSPECTOR QUIN

It was late afternoon by the time I walked away from the Sheriff's office. Technically, I was not under arrest. I could walk out any time I wanted to, but they made sure I knew that my best interests lay in cooperation. Physically I was fine, but mentally I staggered away.

Outside the glass doors by the fire station, a small crowd craned necks, waved microphones and cameras. I ground to a stop. I haven't faced a crowd that size in years. Two weeks ago, I couldn't have paid most of them to look at me. Now no amount of money would get them off my back.

A few familiar faces jostled among younger reporters. Microphones thrust out at me. My arm shot up to shield my face. The cameras pushed hard. I couldn't make out any clear questions. I am so tired of questions. I hitched myself onto the concrete wall, sought eyes, pantomimed speaking. It worked. They started taking turns.

"Is it true you had to take a lie detector test?"

"Polygraph," I corrected. "There's a difference—"

"*Beller Mountain Republican*—what's the difference?"

"I have no idea." I emitted the Famous Grin, shifted to an easier position, pointed to a local reporter who was getting pushed out of the crowd. "I didn't hear what you said—?"

"What was the result of the lie det—polygraph?"

"They'll have to analyze it. That'll take a day or so. It's probably inconclusive; they always are on the news. See, they have a black box, only here it's sort of greyish, but in the movies it's black, and there are electrodes on Velcro straps—"

"Mr. Logan—*Mountain Times*—What's your bail?"

"You can't get bail for first-degree murder; even I know that. I wasn't arrested."

"Have you seen Michaella?"

"First they tell you to answer every question with Yes. That's a lot harder than it sounds—"

"Why do you think it'll be inconclusive? Did you lie?"

"They usually come back inconclusive. Boring, but true."

"Did you know Mouse is at Starling Resort right now?"

Snagged, I froze up a split second, gave myself orders, swung to someone else. "I'm sorry, what were you saying?"

"Were you having an affair with Crystal Beller, Matt?"

"No. She was a dedicated artist—"

Behind me the doors opened and I heard a little cry. Julien emerged with her lawyer. He tried to bundle her through the crowd, shooting off "No comments" like firecrackers. Someone local shouted, "Look! It's Julien Darcy—Ms. Darcy—!"

Like well-drilled piranhas after fresh meat, the press corps wheeled off, left me flat. Olin Bunney did his best to protect his client, but two things worked against him: Julien is irresistibly photogenic, and she kept making herself hard to protect.

I slid off the wall, nipped around the corner in shameless retreat. A back I knew was going down the ramp. "Hal!" I called. "Wait up!"

She stopped, turned, waited. I ran down, took her by the shoulders. She grabbed my arms. "Matt!"

We both said, "Are you all right?" We both nodded.

"I used to think it would be interesting to be in a real, live murder case, but it's getting to be a shrieking bore," she said. "It's not like reading a book. I can't put a bookmark in and go to sleep."

I rubbed her arms once or twice. "I know. Let's go clean up, put on something comfortable, and go somewhere to eat."

She let go of me, stepped back, glancing at the crowd around Julien. "No, I'm exhausted. I'll just go home and—"

"Hal, don't do that. Please!"

She shrugged one shoulder. "Don't do what?"

"Don't go away from me like that."

"I haven't gone anywhere," she said.

I was not in the mood for cross talk. "No. Listen to me. We were good friends last night when I picked you up, we argued in perfect harmony, we worked like Siamese twins over Crystal, but in between, you've been a polite stranger. Why?"

Her eyes shifted away, far away over my shoulder. She spoke with her mouth tight on the words. "I've had a relationship taken apart by another woman. It hurts. I won't do that to anyone else." She let me have it straight. "If you must have fun on the side, find some other bimbo."

I blinked. "What relationship? I haven't had one since the divorce. I haven't been interested," I added frankly.

"Oh, come on. What do you call Julien?"

I was lost. "Julien?"

"Yes, Julien. That pretty girl who has access to your motel room when you're not there."

"You think I'm seeing Julien? She's a good actress, she's fun to work with, but—"

"For one thing, when we got back to your room, there she was at ten-thirty last night—"

"I know. I had Ma'am let her in. Poor girl, when I got your call, I forgot about her—" Halla's look of disgust brought me up short. "No, listen. She wanted to go over scenes we're doing this week, but the murder happened. When I picked you up, I forgot I'd promised her. I don't—oh, geez—" as a memory flitted in and found a space.

"Oh, geez—what?"

"After you left, she wanted to block the scenes. Act them out, she called it. I wouldn't; I gave her a lecture on not doing your own blocking without the director's express orders—Oh, geez."

"And those scenes were—let me guess—"

"The hayloft and under the apple tree," we both said.

"But if she thinks you—"

"Matt!" Something pretty hurled to my chest, broke into stormy tears. "Oh, thank God I found you! Oh, Matt, nothing like this ever happened to me—oh, Matt, hold me!" Cameras out of nowhere clicked and buzzed and flashed like strobe lights. Halla bit a lip and walked away.

I held Julien off. How can such a smart girl have such lousy timing? Her pretty blue eyes opened up at me like rain-drenched flowers. I asked her, "Were you interviewed in there, too?" shoving my jaw at the station.

"What? Oh, no! I'm not as famous as you. They just wanted my fingerprints. Yesterday, they made me give a statement right there in front of everybody in the Canteen, but when they wanted to fingerprint me, I said I'd have to get a lawyer first. Today, Olin brought me here—Oh, Matt, I knew you were here, and so I came to you. It was so terrible! Oh, Matt!"

"Did you know Crystal?" I said.

"That little redneck? You're the one who fought with her. She was only my stand-in."

"I did not fight with—Geez. She was murdered, Jule."

"Matt, no—you can't know it was murder."

"People don't generally knot strings that tightly around their own necks," I said.

"Oh, Matt, don't, it's so gross." She moved in, found a hold. "Oh, Matt, I need you." Photographers lapped it up.

I made her look at me. "Jule, I have another commitment. You're a great actress and I like you a lot, but outside of work, I will always have another commitment. Why don't you go home and call your fiancé?"

"No, I broke our engagement when I came up here. He's too possessive. I can't be dragged back by his insecurity."

"Then find Scotty. He'll listen to you." Scotty is a stalwart hunk with shoulders. If I have any luck at all, he likes girls.

Julien's eyes filled. She heaved a great sob, wheeled around and ran off, with the press corps in hot pursuit. I hope she'll be over it by the time we get rolling again. We do not need a star in an emotional tailspin.

I escaped to my car, where it huddled in the lot. As I reached it, a head popped up over the roof. "Mr. Logan?"

Great. The reporter from the local Press. "Hullo. Have you got lost?"

"I feel like you have as much right to publicity as Julien. Are you two in love?"

"What are you, new at this, or are you being creative?"

This person is almost invisible—tall, thin, with pale hazel eyes, pale skin, pale brownish hair, like a monochrome photograph. "Well, I—"

"You want an exclusive?"

"Would you?" she brightened.

"What's your name?"

"Lisa. Lisa Beller. *Beller Mountain Republican.*"

"Ah, geez. Were you related to Crystal?"

"Our husbands' daddies are double first cousins. Bellers've been here since before the Pilgrims; they're all related. There's rich Bellers and poor Bellers and trash-Bellers and all kind of Bellers. You'd think they don't have much to do with each other, till you get one of them mad. Then—whew."

"Hang on—Crystal was married?"

"You wouldn't know it, would you? Can I ask you—?"

"I'll answer three questions for you if you'll answer one for me: what is a double first cousin?"

She snatched at the deal before I could change my mind. "Like Ken and Ron Beller, their daddies were brothers that married the Cody sisters. Ken and Ron and them's trash-Bellers, they work up to Starling Resort. There's stories about trash-Bellers: they mostly steal from people that's rich and hateful, so nobody wants to tell on them. But mean—whew! Okay." Lisa Beller took a quick breath and fired off her first question. "Did Crystal break into your motel room the night before her audition?"

I handed her a gentle laugh. "By mistake. For the record, she only took off her coat. She stayed less than thirty seconds and was very embarrassed when she left. Her husband doesn't have anything to be jealous about—"

"They're separated. Ken, he knows everything that goes on at the Resort. He found out who gave Crystal her fur coat, and—you know? He's a carpenter on your movie, too, him and Ron. Why won't you talk about Mouse?"

"I'm not allowed to, by court order. Third question."

"Then, why won't you talk about your little girl?"

"Good-bye, Lisa Beller."

"Wait, were you in love with Crystal?"

I might as well get used to that one. Directly into her color-less eyes I pronounced, "I haven't been romantically involved with anyone since the day my wife told me to move out. Crystal's beautiful, but Crystal isn't Nancy. There's no one like Nancy. That's four questions."

"Wait, why do you keep on evading questions about—"

"Have a nice day, Lisa." I nipped into the car, pulled out of the parking lot without a backward look.

Signaling, I turned, drove about a hundred yards before I remembered Tara lay in the other direction. I was headed for Starling Resort. I stood on the brakes, made a U-turn, slogged back. With luck, Tony'd be out and I'd have the room to myself. As I pushed open the door, all I could think of was my bed.

My bed was stacked with various bits of electronic equip-ment. The video monitor was cranked up to full power. Tony, Dora and Phina bent over it, faces intent and grim, looking at some other guy's Badger audition. They saw me and their jaws dropped to their toes. "Matt! Julien said they arrested you."

"O ye of little faith."

"It's the Sheriff we have no faith in," Dora said. "How'd you get away?"

"It was just a polygraph, for crying out loud. Can I get through? I need a shower."

They made room. I grabbed some clean sweats and headed for the shower. When I got out, my bed was swept clear of debris. I rolled onto it, decided to write this down, decided to call Halla, and faded out.

The sun slanted through the window when Tony woke me. "Matt. Telephone."

"I'm busy."

"It's Halla McKee."

Right. I sat up, took the phone. "This is Matt . . . "

"Matt? I'm at my friend Rose's house. The press have my

place staked out. I can't get through them. My cats—"

"They should be gone by now—the press, not the cats. I don't want to hurt your self-esteem or anything, but you're not nearly famous enough for them to miss dinner for an exclusive on you. Next year, after *Demon Dun* opens . . . "

She chuckled. "I think you're good for me. Keep my head from swelling. See you."

"Hang on—wasn't I disgraced back there? Jule was—"

"Demonstrative. I wanted to walk out until you looked at me. Deer in headlights, my friend. You didn't know?"

"I thought she had a fiancé, back home. Look, Hal, can we—you and I, maybe—get together and do something?"

"Like what?"

I sat up, parted blind slats. "We can have dinner, catch the sunset on the Parkway—"

"Sounds reasonable," she said. "I'll meet you—"

"I'll pick you up. How soon can you be ready?"

Halla doesn't waste time. We went to the Mountain House in Boone for the sloppiest, spiciest ribs I've had all year. Then, an hour or so before sunset, we headed for the Parkway. When we stopped at a crossroad, a car behind us slowed down before its driver could show up in my rearview mirror. Halla twisted her neck to look up at a cliff.

"What's up there?" I said.

"I used to eat a lot of lunches on that ledge, several years ago. That's *the* Starling Head."

"It is?" I squinted up at it. My young correspondent Shannon wrote about bonding with her stepfather on the Starling Head. Curious as any fan, I said, "Can we get up there?"

"Now? We can get a spectacular view of the sunset up there, but it's quite a hike. Are you sure you'd want to?"

"Are you any good at hiking?"

"If it's less than ten miles a day. Are you serious? Turn here." She directed me to a trail into thick woods below the bluff. Traffic was thin, but the road wasn't deserted.

"Here's the beginning of the trail, but—what's wrong?" Halla said, after the twenty-somethingeth time I checked the rearview mirror. That car was still there.

"Nothing." Not that it mattered, but it bothered me. I checked again as I swung the car off the road.

"If you leave your car here, it'll get stripped," Halla said. "Rumor has it this is trash-Bellers' turf. They're our local legend, a gang of merry moonshine vigilantes, kind of. I don't believe in them—the Resort management discounts their existence—but all the bad elements hang out here. Go up around that wall and park in the day guard's space."

I drove up the hill to the guardhouse. "You know this place?"

"I used to work here, in the lounge manager's office. I booked Roland in the lounge to play the piano, and Crystal to sing, and that's where Roland met Janelle." For a moment she brooded. "When Janelle promised to produce his album, he told me she had more to offer him than I did. I suppose he meant emotionally . . . " She sat up straight, pointing. "Park here, under the Bremco security light. It's the safest place."

The dark car drove by us, toward the Resort. I said, "Hal, I think we're being followed."

Halla's eyes opened wide. "Followed? Who? Why?"

"Police. We're suspects in a murder case, remember?"

She let out a sigh. "You had me in creeps for a minute."

"Look, let's lose them."

She considered several answers, came up with, "How?"

"The studio's near here. This is what we'll do—"

As I talked, her smile grew. "How old are you really?"

"Thirteen? Fourteen?" I stuffed my keys into my pocket.

"You don't look a day over seven and a half. Let's go."

We had maybe half an hour to spare before sundown. As if we'd never heard of time, we got out and sauntered to the Studio, ten minutes down the road. I unlocked the front door, shut it behind us, turned on an office light, led Halla through to the back of the building. We came out through the little door that leads to the Dumpster, circled to the bottom of the trail.

Halla took us up by the easy way. There's a quicker path, but it's steeper, and the light was going flat, dissolving into shadow. She led me up to a comfortable ledge, about three feet below the top rim of the bluff. "I used to sit and eat my lunch here, and dream about Roland. Later I'd eat here and cry over Roland.

It was the only place I could have any privacy. See that knobby peak over there? That's Grandfather Mountain. I think it was a volcano, millions of years ago. You can see five counties and two states from here—we're in Beller County, and we can look across Watauga County over there. Grandfather's in Avery County, and Ashe County's that way. Johnson County in Tennessee's beyond that. How far are we from the car, do you think?"

I considered. "I'd guess—twenty minutes, at least, to get back down this cliff, then—"

"Stand up and turn around. Look through the bushes."

I did. The cliff topped off at the level of my waist. Beyond a line of bushes growing on the bluff was a grassy clearing, benches, a drinking fountain. We'd climbed to a golf tee. I'm serious, someone built a golf course at the top of a rough hike through thick woods. My car sat thirty yards down a cart path.

Halla settled on our rock ledge. "It's Starling Resort's private course. Surprise." I don't ever want to lose her.

We sat side by side to watch the sun sink into an unparalleled light show. She stirred as the sky faded to purples and greys. I slid an arm around her and held on. "Wait. You have to see this." She relaxed, not snuggling exactly, but not batting me away, either. "Watch the hillsides," I said.

It happened the way it had that evening on the Parkway. As the world darkened, the lights came on all over the hills, like tiny candles in a wilderness. It was fully dark when I spoke again. "I guess you've seen that before—"

"Not like this," she murmured. "Not with someone who actually looks for it—wait—Did you hear that?"

"Hear what?" and I heard it, too. A crying cat—no, a child's low whine: "I want to go home. Please? It's dark."

Shannon. It had to be Shannon. I didn't move. I was stupid to come here. Poor kid, if she knew I'd sneaked up on her—

A man's voice muttered, "No, Baby, you don't want to go yet, it's perfect out here." The voice hoarsened. "You know what you do to me. Here, look at this."

"No. I can't see—I don't want to bond—let go of me—"

"Come on, Mimi, you never complain while we do it."

Shannon's stepfather calls her Mimi. She hates it. I heard

his breathing quicken. I might be wrong, but—

Beside me, Halla stiffened. Together, we got our feet under us, twisted around to peer between laurel bushes. A man and a little girl seemed to be wrestling less than ten feet away, on the other side of the bushes.

In the uncertain light we couldn't make out faces, only figures. He ran a hand over her hair, down her back. "Relax, Mimi—What's—You're wearing that damned leotard! I told you not to—" We heard the sound of a smack, a whimper.

Halla hit my arm. "Give me your keys."

I pulled them from my pocket. "What for?"

"Give me your keys! He's abusing that child! You get his attention, I'll take her to your car, we'll get her away."

"Here. Be careful!"

"You son of a bitch—" Halla sprang to the top of the bluff using my shoulder for leverage. Like a kamikaze linebacker she bulled through the shrubbery, straight into the man's middle. Without stopping, she hooked the little girl around the waist, hauled her toward the car.

The molester staggered a step or two, recovered balance, started after them. His mind on his prey, he didn't see me coming until he ran spang into my fist.

I thought I shattered my hand again. Geez, it hurt! I turned away, cradling it to my chest. He shuffled in the grass, got to his feet. I wheeled around in time to catch a kick in the stomach. It winded me, and I stumbled backward.

He towered above me, a menacing shadow, and another shadow sprang at him. Halla hadn't stayed tamely locked in the car. Fearless, fierce as a tigress, she grabbed an ear with one hand, hair with the other. He snarled like a cornered rat, flung her off. She landed against a tree with a thud and a cry.

I reached for his collar and yanked. He reeled away and twisted my shoulder. I found myself on my back in the grass. He loomed against the sky on the edge of the bluff, landed another kick to my ribs. As I tried to get up, he struck for my face. I pulled aside. The punch missed, but a heavy ring he wore took a chunk of skin off my cheekbone. He was beating the stuffing out of me.

Stray starlight glinted on his teeth. I was down and he was

loving it. This guy likes hurting weaklings. Cringing like a weakling, I levered myself up. "No, don't," I whined. "Leave me alone—" I moved away from Halla. "Please—let me go—"

Another step back, another pathetic whimper, and he lunged after me in the thickening dusk. I let him get close to me, then sidestepped, catching at his ankle. As he hit the ground, I aimed and kicked, and I'm not ashamed to tell you that I enjoyed it. "Happy bonding, Slimeballs."

He folded up like popcorn shrimp, rolled around, climbed to his feet and ran up the hill, his footsteps fading in the dark. I leaned against a tree and retched up everything I've eaten since puberty. Then I looked for Halla.

Halla tried to pull herself up against the tree. I eased her down. "Sh-sh. Relax. It's okay, he's gone, it's over—"

She swallowed a sob. "I think my knee's wrenched—shoulder's dislocated—Oh, shit—He wanted to get away—"

"It's dark. Let's get you and Shannon out of here."

"But I can't—" Halla gripped my arm, looking past me. Her eyes stretched open in slow horror. "Oh, my—God—"

Half a dozen young men stood around us, all sizes, all shapes, all mean. "That's him. That's the Pigshit," a deep voice said. "Can't do it with a real woman, can you, Pigshit?"

It is every city dweller's worst nightmare—a wilding gang, vicious as sharks. Like sharks they have no natural enemies, no rules. If they find you out after dark, they tear you to pieces for fun. Years ago in New York, I bought some guy drinks, he beat me up then shouldered me home, and we met up with a gang like this. He dropped me and tried to run. I passed out. When I came to, he was still alive, so I went for help. He has never forgiven me. If Hal and I were lucky, these animals would kill us before they finished with us.

I drew my wallet out of my hip pocket, tossed it to the feet of the weedy guy in front of me. When there's nothing to try, you try anything. I said to Halla, "Where's your bag?"

"At home." Halla's voice cracked. She saw what was coming as clearly as I did. In the middle of a golf course, nobody would hear us. "It's the trash-Bellers," she whispered. "I can't believe—I never thought—" She was shivering.

I wrapped an arm around her. Her face was right there.

Sometimes, when you stare into the jaws of Hell, you catch a glimpse of Heaven. If you're smart, you grab it. I laced my fingers into her curls. "Listen to me," I said. "I love you. *Don't forget this.*" I put my mouth to hers and kissed, so hard that our teeth clicked together. I went on kissing, willing her to block out the horror around us.

And Halla kissed back, leaped to meet me, sweet and rich as music. For one brief second, we closed our eyes and shared a piece of Paradise. A hand grabbed my hair, tore me away.

My arms were twisted like pretzels behind me. I heard Halla gasp, "Matt! Oh, my God, *don't*—" A butane lighter like a flame-thrower zicked to life at my face, filled my universe. I tried to get free, but the grip on my hair was tight.

Someone growled behind me. Whoever held my hair jerked it, spoke again in a thick local dialect. I couldn't put the sounds together to make sense, didn't bother to control my breath. What was the point? "I d-d-don't-d-on't—"

A deep voice, basso profundo, boomed in front of me. "What's the matter, Pigshit? You can't talk straight?"

I squinted, tried to make out the face before me. It was a ski mask. "N-n-no, it's n-no-n-ot—"

"My brother said 'Where's the kid?' We seen what you been doing, Pigshit. We see everything at Starling Resort, know what I mean? Where'd you hide the kid?"

Dear God, Shannon's only ten years old. Why can't they leave her alone? I did my best to breathe. I could not afford to stammer. Shannon couldn't afford it. "I—I t-told her to ru-run—get help—the Resort—that way—" I couldn't point. I rolled my eyes toward the Resort, away from the car.

A question in front of me, an answer from behind. Incomprehensible, but I knew exactly what they meant. The butane flame made a pass at my face. I winced, closed my eyes against the heat. It didn't help. The basso rumbled, "My brother said no little girl ran up to the Resort. Where is she?"

I snapped my eyes open. "She *didn't*? Then where—?"

The flame caught a stray hair on my eyebrow. It sizzed, stung into my forehead. I could not get away from the fire. A new voice spoke. I didn't try to understand.

The basso rumbled, "My other brother says we got us the wrong Pigshit."

"Yes—you have—" Anything. You try anything.

"Too late, Pigshit. You know what kid we mean." The flame moved in closer. My face would be charred hamburger before they finished me off. "You keeping her for yourself?"

Another voice. I caught my name, and the word "Strongbow." They always want to beat up Strongbow. The flame pulled back, the deep voice purred. "Well, looky here. We got us a hee-ro. You kill my wife, Hee-ro?"

"I d-didn't—I'm not a—he-hero. I'm an—actor—"

"Hold him still. Let's see how a hee-ro acts."

If I hadn't vomited my insides out before, I would have now. My breath came in sobs. The grip on my hair tightened, my arms were twisted into knots. The flame lowered, caught at my moustache. As the charred smell seared my nostrils, a moan of pure terror floated out of me.

"Freeze! Police!" They all froze. A dog roared.

I barely heard it. My universe snuffed out with the flame. They dropped me, melted into the night as I groveled on the ground. Grass and sweet earth mixed with the smell of burnt hair. Reality fitted together again.

Hal.

"Hal?"

Her face was a grey blur in the dark, sweat-shined. Halla was going into shock. I can't remember ever feeling this helpless. I tried to ease her. "Dear God, what did they do to you?"

"Nothing. They—I can't get up—" She reached for me.

I tried to hold her still. "Careful, dear— your shoulder—"

"No—" her voice was a thread. "One of them put it back in. See?" It moved. That meant nothing to me. I had to do something, think of something.

"Sir?"

With a tearing gasp I found myself on my feet between Halla and the voice, menacing it with a rock as big as my fist.

The dog growled. A crisp word, a clink of chain, and the dog was silent. "Easy, sir. Take it easy. The lady looks tore up.

You need me to call an ambulance—Damn. Mr. Logan?"

That took a minute to soak in. "Who are you?"

"Sheriff's office. Slocum." A flashlight popped on. I shied violently. The light held steady on a County ID long enough for me to peer at it. Then the light moved to the face of the person holding it. Shadows sprang weirdly upward over an ordinary face that matched the photo on the card.

I tried to make sense. "Surv-surv-veillance?"

"No, they lost you. We're investigating an assault out here. Looks like there's been more than one. Can you put that rock down for me?"

I lowered the rock, stepped to one side. "Yeah. Yeah, I need an ambulance. There's Hal, and a molested child in the car—at the guardhouse—" Slocum got busy with a radio.

Halla clutched my ankle. I knelt down to her. "You told the Bellers she went—" Her eyeballs shone as she glanced toward the Resort.

"I lied." It couldn't possibly matter. I stroked damp curls off her forehead.

"Oh, my God. Go away—Go on, I'm going to bawl."

Slocum added to that. "You need to move your vehicle so the ambulance can get in here, and then if you can get the young'n out of there, too. Are you all right? Your face—"

"I'm okay. But Halla's knee—she's going into shock—"

"Matt, go *away*." Halla sounded near the breaking point.

Ten yards from my car I knew it was empty. Of course I ran to it, hooked fingers under the handle. Locked. My hand came away stuck to stretchy, fragrant strings. Bubble gum. Grape. I hate goo. Embedded in the gum was my car key.

I managed to keep a grip on myself. When we were kids, Meranda and I used to unstick gum by rubbing it with dirt. I dug up a divot. It still works. I unlocked the door, searched the car. There's no place any child can hide in that car. The rest of my keys were on the floor.

My wallet lay on the front seat.

Dear God. I clutched the steering wheel, fought for control. The ambulance was pulling up the hill. I moved the car, climbed the hill to Hal and the K-9 unit.

Slocum said, "Where's the young'n?"

"She was in my car, but she's g-gone. My wallet was on the front seat—Dear God, the trash-Bellers took her—Look, Shannon's ten years old, she has brown hair—eyes—I don't know what color—You've got to—"

Slocum spoke into the radio, then to me: "You say she's Shannon? Shannon what? Can you give me her last name?"

"N-no—I d-on't know, her first name's not Shannon—she calls herself—Look, tell them to put out an APB—"

Radio in hand, Slocum planted himself squarely in front of me, made me see him. "Mr. Logan, calm down. I can't understand you when you're like this. Settle down, okay?"

I nodded, breathed, gathered limp fragments of myself, and held on, hard. "Look. You have to find those trash-Bellers; they took Sh-Sha-annon—That rodent was m-mo-mol—you know— and then—Dear God, those subhuman troglodytes took her—"

"You're sure it was trash-Bellers?"

"Yes! I mean—look, Hal said they were—and one of them called Crystal his wife, so—that's it, he's her husband! Look, you've got to put out an APB—Ken—B-B-eller—"

Still commanding my focus, Slocum tucked the radio into his armpit, made a T of his hands. "Time out, Mr. Logan. Calm down. I reported it in, okay? The Sheriff's on it right now, this minute, okay? Now, listen to me. I need you to settle down. It's probably not as bad as you think. Trash-Bellers, they don't go after little kids. Likely, they'll take her home and see she's safe, hear me?"

I nodded, half believing him.

"—and then what they'll do, they'll go hunt the guy down that was doing that to her. I tell you what, Mr. Logan, you don't even want to be around when they catch him. Get a trash-Beller mad at you, and you might as well just break your own thumbs and save yourself a heap of trouble. Okay? The young'n's probably the safest one of us, you hear me?"

I shook my head. "She's j-ust a lit-little ki-kid—"

His radio spoke, meaningless static. "Just a minute. You're doing fine, now, you hear? You take a deep breath. I'll see what they want, okay, Mr. Logan? You hear me?"

I nodded, breathed obediently as he turned away to speak

with his radio. In a moment he turned back. "Okay, the other call turned out to be a false alarm. Let's concentrate on you. These amb'lance folks can take care of your face—"

"No!" I caught myself. I had to stay sane for Shannon, for Halla. "My face is fine. I'll fol-f-ollow you to the hospital."

At the hospital I parked somewhere, strode into the emergency room. It was like coming back to a place I knew in my sleep. Scaled to country-town size, the ER here is Park East Hospital all over again. I knew how to find the main desk, where to look for the men's room.

When I came in, they were wheeling Halla to X-ray. She stopped them a moment, talked to a nurse, looking at me. The nurse reached over the counter for a phone.

I saw that Halla was checked in properly. The desk operator said, "Somebody might ought to look at your face."

"No." My jaw shoved sideways. "Leave my face alone."

"But you need to—"

I fought an urge to yell, and Bradford stood there, all six feet-something of him, wearing the rabat and collar of a chaplain. "Hey, Matt. You all right?"

My head cleared. "Tell them to leave my face alone. Where are the phones?"

"Over there. Nobody'll touch you till you say so, man."

No one I knew was at the Sheriff's office. I left a message. When I hung up, Shannon was still lost. I went out and moved the car to a conventional parking place, collected my jacket and the clipboard. Coming back in, I got a good view of the emergency area. Across from me was an unobtrusive door with an EXIT sign above it. That kind of door led to utility stairs at Park East. I was ready to bet what was left of my moustache that this one did, too. All I had to do was find out what room they'd put Halla in. Bradford was still there. I went to the men's room to assess the damage.

The cut on my cheekbone stopped bleeding some time ago. There are burns over my eyebrow, beside one nostril, above where the left side of my moustache used to be. Half of my moustache is gone. I'll have to shave it and grow a new one.

Damn. I like this moustache. It's not spectacular, but it's red, and it's thick, it has a good shape. I like it. Damn. *Damn!* It feels weird.

There wasn't much I could do in the john except soak off dried blood. I cleaned up as well as I could, promised myself a shower and change of clothes, and got out of there.

The burns are starting to hurt. The bruises throb. At least with a clean face I don't look like somebody in a bad action movie. I'm cold, sweaty, nauseated. The Sheriff's going to want answers. I'd better wait here. I'm starting to stiffen up. I've struggled into my jacket to warm up. I've just had another go at calling the Sheriff's office. No joy there. . . .

[Inspector Quin—
I wrote this out while it was fresh. I'm going to give it to the first deputy I see. I hope you spike the sonofabitch—MTL.]

.9.

TARA: LATER TONIGHT
DETECTIVE FEVER

Dear Mouse,
    Writing helps. Reality looked more habitable after I
    put all that stuff on paper. Bradford was sitting a chair
or two away from me. I took off my glasses, rubbed the heels of
my hands over my eyes. When I could see again there was a
pair of razor-creased grey pants next to me.

"Who did this to you?" Pike sat down.

"I don't know."

He fisted the arm of his seat. "Sir, you're a moron. In case
you don't get it—"

"I hope I broke his nose." I detached pages from the clipboard, passed them over. "I signed and dated it all." As Pike took
the papers I tried to steady my hand. "Shannon's stepfather—then
trash-Bellers—w-anted—Sha-Sh-annon. You have to f-find—"

Abruptly he stood. "You need help. Come on."

I stayed where I was. "Nobody's touching my face."

"For God's sake. I meant—"

"My plastic surgeon's in New York."

"He wouldn't do anything they can't do here. Sir—"

Bradford said, "If you don't take care of yourself, what
good are you to Halla?" I pushed down near-panic, nodded.

People who work in emergency medicine find amusement wherever they can. Strongbow gibbering with fright over having some
minor burns and a cut treated was amusing. The doctor on duty
politely repressed all but the upcurving crows-feet around her eyes
as she patted the paper-covered table. "Hop up, Mr. Strongbow."

I hoisted myself up, submitted to the preliminaries of temperature and blood pressure and all that. The doctor checked me for massive body damage, no problem. When she brought a wet swab into face range, I stiffened.

She held it up. "This'll sting some. Try and hold still."

"*Hold him still . . .*" I swallowed, jerked my head in a nod, clenched everything. Of course it stung. It burned like the lighter flame. That wasn't the point. I concentrated on keeping still. The paper crackled as I gripped the edge of the table, watching her gloved hands.

She snatched up gauze to blot sweat before it dripped into a burn. "Are you all right?"

I couldn't stop shivering. "It's j-just a ph-obia."

"Here, this won't hurt—triple antibiotic ointment. Your face has been injured before."

I unclenched teeth. "It's been through a windshield. And a lot of surgery." The teeth clamped together again.

She squinted at the cut. "That's not deep. We can use butterfly strips. No stitches." She was quick and gentle. Within minutes she turned away. "Okay, all done."

I slid off the table, walked to the waiting area, made a clutch at something. Bradford popped into existence at my elbow. "You'd better lie down, right here." He didn't so much help me lie down as prevent my head from hitting the floor. "Hey, can somebody give me a hand?"

"I'm all right," I mumbled.

Someone eased me out of my jacket, folded it under my head. Cussing at herself, the doctor wrapped a blood pressure cuff around my arm. I drifted backstage in time . . .

Find Shannon Hal needs Mouse's laughing . . .

("B.P. eighty over fifty. S'pose we put his feet up.")

They took Shannon's picture Hal needs me . . .

("Pulse a hundred six. Let's get some oxygen on him?")

Hal's calling Nancy smells like Crystal—Hang on.

That wasn't right. I knew that couldn't be right.

("He's coming around. Mr. Logan, you all right, here?")

"*. . . little darlin' right here I thought it was you till I got a good look . . .*"

An ammonia capsule cracked under my nose, smacking me back into the ER. I struggled to sit up.

"Mr. Logan, lie down. Did you want to stay overnight?"

In a hospital, with IVs, people waking you at all hours to give you a sleeping pill, gowns that don't cover your butt? "No. Thanks. I want to find Nance—"

"Okay, Matt, rest a few more minutes," Bradford said.

"How many more minutes?"

"Until you start enjoying yourself."

I made myself sink down again. "Right. This is fun. May I go home now?"

Another check on blood pressure and pulse, and they unstrung the oxygen. "Okay, try sitting up," the doctor said.

I gave up on seeing your mother. I forgot why I had to see her, remembered why she won't see me. "I need a shower."

"That you do, Buddy," Bradford took my elbow. "You ready? I'll run you home."

"No. I have my car—"

"Like hell you do." Pike was among those helping me to my feet. "You stick a key in that ignition and I'll have you pulled on a DWI."

I goggled at him. "I'm not drunk!"

"Yeah, but if you're not impaired, what are you?"

Right.

Bradford's car has automatic safety belts that slide into place when the car starts. As the strap came at me I threw my hands up in front of my face. Geez. I twisted to the door, straining at the shoulder belt. A wave of grief rolled over me, solid as a dump truck, knocking me flat. I gripped the armrest with both hands, willed it to pass.

Bradford got going without comment. It's a short drive to Tara—maybe ten minutes. By the time we got there, the grief had dissolved. It always does, Mousy, but these attacks are crushing while they last. Once the worst was over, I sat back in the seat. Bradford said, "It's okay to cry, man."

"I can't. Not for the last three years. Look, thanks for—"

"What happened three years ago?"

"Nothing. I spent my first two weeks in treatment weeping.

Then I woke up one day, started blubbering as usual, saw my-self in the mirror, and said something like, 'Oh, shut up, you stupid slob.' So I did. I don't want to—"

"The Bantu say if you name a thing out loud, it loses its power over you."

"I wrote it all out for Lieutenant Pike," I said.

"That's not the same as hearing yourself say it."

I stared at the windshield. "But—won't they—see us?"

He shook his head. "Not with the light off."

I took it all and dumped it in his lap—the terror of fire at my face, the loathing I felt for a man I knew only as Shannon's stepfather, the horror being lived by an anonymous little girl, the stunning discovery that when I kissed Halla, she kissed back. It took some time to run down. Then I said it again, and a third time, too, I think. It was nothing but words when I finished, except for the part about the kiss. The more I talked, the more important that kiss became. "Look, are you going back to the hospital? Can you tell Hal—Halla —"

"Tell Halla —?"

"What I said up there—still goes? And—I'm sorry."

"Why don't you tell her yourself?"

"I can't—it's late—I'm a mess—"

"I can wait. Go get cleaned up."

That was easier to say than to do. I opened my door, slammed it shut, worked my keys out of my pocket, measured the distance between the car and our room, told myself to stop being stupid—

"You want me to walk you over there?" Bradford said.

"I'm being stupid—"

"You're being smart. If you were stupid, you wouldn't be scared. I'll go with you."

So, with six feet and more of Bradford between me and the dark, I got into the room. Tony hunched in his corner, process-ing words like mad. He growled, "I don't want to hear about it. Let me create in peace, my good God." His fingers didn't skip a beat on the keyboard.

Skirting around him, I cut too close. His blunt nose quiv-ered. "What to hell happened to you?" He turned to look. "Ah, shit. How drunk is he?" he asked Bradford.

"*Damn you!*" Every shred of fear in me flared into rage. "I am not drunk!"

Bradford closed the door. "He's fine."

"He could have asked me," I snapped. "Tony, damn you, you could have asked me."

"Okay, my God's sake." Tony put aside his computer to look me over. "So you haven't been drinking?"

"Of course not! I can't believe you're asking me that."

"So what happened?"

"It's—a long story. D'you mind if I get cleaned up first?"

"Go, my good God." He sighed. "You smell like a corpse." As I collected clothes and ducked into the shower, Tony said to Bradford, "Talk to me. I'll create later."

I treated myself to a thorough shower and a complete change of clothes. It did wonders for my outlook, Mouseling. I came out feeling rather sheepish about barking at Tony. Bradford had apparently provided him with an explanation. Bradford is one powerful talker. I haven't seen Tony this mellow since Tamra Speranzo triggered the rewrite.

For Tony the point wasn't how I felt, it was whether the burns can be covered with make-up by the time we start shooting. "At least they used a lighter. Cigarette burns last for months. Your moustache—"

It was oddly bracing. My brain hadn't idled on the way home. "Look, Tony, I can get good yak-hair from Charlotte. Let me fill it in till it grows back. A week and a half, two weeks, max. Let's not shave it, all right?"

"Whatever." Tony picked up the phone. "I need a reasonable facsimile when we start production. Yeah, Dora," he rasped to the phone. "Bring Phina. Halla's crocked her knee, Matt's face and our schedule's shot to Sheol—"

Dora and Phina came in as I was ready to go out. Wide eyes stared. "My word, Matt, what happened?"

"It's a long story. Ask Tony." I shouldered past them. Outside it was just as dark as before. Bradford stood ready in case I needed him. I gathered nerve, took a broad jump across the open space to the car door. No demons clawed me down before I fell into the seat.

"Look," I said as I settled in. "Maybe I ought to have faith, but visiting hours are—"

"You got that right," Bradford said. "You ought to have faith. Chaplains get to fudge. It's easier to do things legally."

I dodged wide to the left. The shoulder strap missed my face. "Why would you think I'd—?

"Maybe I'm wrong."

So much for the utility stairway. I buckled the lap belt, used the ride to get a grip.

Bradford's handling of the dragon at the desk was a masterly blend of blarney and blackmail. I got to Halla's door legally, tapped on the jamb.

"I'm awake." Halla's voice floated on nothing. I slid around the door. I don't know what I was afraid of. I'd spent most the evening afraid of one thing or another. I guess I'd got used to it.

"Hey, Matt!" In the half-dark, Halla reached with both hands. I walked to where I needed to be. The novelty of being wrapped in each other's arms took a while to wear off.

We both asked, "Are you all right?"

We both nodded, our cheeks moving in tandem.

We laughed a little, and Halla pulled away. Her eyes filled with tears. I brushed at one with my finger. "Sure you're okay?"

"I'm a bit sore, and the painkiller makes me weepy. I've been worrying about you."

"I'm all right. I mean it, Hal, I'm fine. It looks a lot worse than it is. How's your knee?"

She frowned down at it. Even under the covers the knee looked swollen. "They say I'll need—anyway, they'll let me go, day after tomorrow, if I behave myself and don't develop complications. I'll need crutches for a week, and therapy, too. I'm sorry, Matt."

"What for? I'm the one who—"

"No, I should have—Wait." She patted air in front of my face. I obediently closed my mouth. "If you apologize to me, and I apologize to you, they cancel, right? What do we do now?"

I could think of any number of things to do, but she had a bad knee. Halla's eyes wrinkled down at the corners. "Besides that. Matt, I have to tell you—rats, here I go again." I passed her a box of tissues. "Thanks." She blotted. "You don't have to—I won't hold you to what you said up there. We were scared. It was dark. We reacted. The End."

"No." My jaw pushed sideways. "What are you talking about? I mean, yes. Look—"

She braced herself so that she wouldn't need to lean on me. "We're too old for games, Matt. I'm over Roland, but I may never get over the way we split." She set her mouth in a line. "I know you're not serious, and I can't afford to be. I—I do like you. A lot. Okay? I do. If you want to play around, maybe—but I won't live with you."

"*Live* with me?" My revulsion surprised me. "Play around? Hal, you're not getting it. Look." I sat facing her on the bed, held her shoulders to make her see me. "I've liked you ever since the day we met. Remember the morning of your interview, when you helped me get rid of Crystal Beller? I've lusted after you since—since longer than I want to admit. But now, tonight, I saw it. I love you. I've done enough things wrong in my life, Hal. I don't want to play around. I want to marry you."

"Marry me?" she said, as if she'd never heard the word. "No. You don't want to marry me. Not this century. We've known each other for what? A week? Two? This was our first date. Matt, we were scared. We thought we were going to die. We grabbed a last kiss." She let out a sigh. "And it was sweet. But it wasn't real. We're alive. It doesn't mean anything."

"It does to me." I pulled her toward me, but she twisted away. I let her go, slid off the bed. "I'm sorry, Hal. Look. I've wanted you for a long time. Before we met, I didn't know what it was I wanted. I know, now. It's you. I love you. But it has to be right. I can wait till it's right."

"Forget it, Matt. You have no idea of who I am. This isn't love, it's nothing but reaction." She worked herself down to lie against the pillows again. "You'll feel better in the morning. Let's be realistic. How's that little girl?" and she sat up again. "Oh, no. What is it?"

"She's—Hal, she's gone."

"Gone! Where? How?"

"When I went to move the car, it was empty. The key was stuck under the door handle with bubble gum. Hal, I—"

"Who took her? That man—the one who molested her? No, the bubble gum—he'd never let her take the time, and he sure wouldn't bother about it himself."

"N-no, it's worse. I think—it's trash-Bellers. They left my wallet on the seat. You remember I threw it to them?"

She shifted to a more comfortable position. "Then she's probably all right. If the legends are true, they'll take her home, and then go after the molester."

"What—You've lost me. Do these guys rob from the rich and give to the poor, too?"

A chuckle. "Well, they rob from the rich, anyway. They have a reputation for being incredibly hard to prosecute. Some-one wrote a song about them in the sixties. The town Bellers tried to have it suppressed, so it became quite a local hit at bluegrass festivals. Roland still plays it at the Resort, but it sounds better on a banjo. I wish we knew who she is."

"I think she's been writing to me, using an alias. She once mentioned she and her stepfather go up to the Starling Head. That's why I wanted to see it tonight. If it's the same little girl, she lives here in town. I don't know much more—"

"We have a description of the molester. He's about your height and weight, with a moustache and shortish hair. The Bellers thought he was you till they got the lighter close."

I repressed a shudder, put my mind to work. "And she's ten years old, with brown hair—She says straight out that Shannon's not her real name—"

"Ten? Are you sure? She's pretty small for a ten-year-old. She's strong, though. Before she realized I was on her side, she almost got away."

"She says in her letters that she takes gymnastics."

Halla nodded. "That explains her strength. A lot of little girls that age do gymnastics."

"Yeah. My kid does, too—I c-couldn't see anything else—"

Halla reached out and took my hand. Her touch is strong and gentle. "Matt, go home. You're finished. Go away and let me get some rest. I'll be fine."

"I'll see you in the morning."

"Tomorrow morning—no. Or, not too early, okay? Noon?"

"I'll wait till you're awake. Good night. I love you. Get used to it." I lifted her chin. "If I kiss you, will you kiss back?"

"Um . . . " Her face is wonderful. Some undiscovered nerve pathway must connect it directly to her brain. She thought about refusing, then decided not to, and lifted her face for a short peck. Even that was good enough.

It was deliriously good enough. I slipped out, headed for the parking lot. Mousekin, I felt like facing a thousand dragons. My keys were in my pocket. I could probably drive home now, and there was Bradford, standing by my car, his pipe glowing.

I stopped. "What are you, following me?"

His Cheshire grin floated in the dark. "More like looking out for you. I was asked to."

"Asked to? By whom? Pike? No, Hal. Right?"

"Do you not need looking out for? You think there's not at least one cop waiting for you to drive your vehicle out of this parking lot?"

Oh, well. It'd be interesting to see if his safety belt could slide into place without spooking me.

◇◇◇

Phina and Dora were still here, Mouse. I presume Tony filled them in. Dora was being tactful, and Phina was being brave. The Sheriff won't let any of us leave the county, so Dakota's still around. Phina actually had to tell him, in words of one syllable, to find somewhere else to sleep. 'Kota gives conceited cretins a bad name.

Dora was saying around the pen in her teeth, "Or replace McKee, keep our schedule—"

I pushed the door shut. "No."

Phina rolled eyeballs. "I thought he was gone."

"We're brainstorming, looking at options—" Tony said.

"Well, that isn't one." I came in. "Tony, look—"

"We can't afford delay. Shooting around Sarah'd cost—"

"Hal is Sarah. You all saw her auditions."

"How long till she can use her knee again?" Dora said.

"Only a week or so." I sat down on my bed. "Look, it's

personal, sure. I need this show. With the cast we have—"

"It's not the cast, it's Halla McKee," Phina sneered.

"Have you got any complaints about her work?" I countered. "Or her attitude? Or—"

"All right, already!" Tony gathered papers. "What do you propose we do with this schedule—subject to nobody important getting arrested for murder, of course?"

In the dead silence we looked at each other. Dora ended it. "I hate this. Can we at least pretend to believe none of us did it? I myself doubt we did. Anyone could have done it."

Anyone could have done it. They were off. Wilkie Collins calls it detective fever. They all had theories about the murderer, and they all wanted to expound. Too worn out to think, I threw myself backward on the bed, bent my arm over my eyes, tried to let the talk swirl around me.

Phina said, "I bet it was Crystal's husband. The spouse is always the first suspect in real murders. He never went in to worship the Star, because I was recording all the time. Even when I didn't have him in sight, the sound of his tools—"

Tony cut her off. "You just gave him an iron-cast alibi."

Dora said, "He could have faked the sounds, and sneaked over to Matt's dressing room. Maybe she told him to meet her. That's it—" She stubbed the end of the pen on the table. "He set up the sound of tools, and met her in the dressing room—"

Tony sighed. "*And* he knew Phina's camera was acting up and she'd be working, *and* he knew when she'd point the camera away from him—make a real plot, my God's sake."

Phina said, "Okay-okay, as a theory it needs work. *But!* What if his cousin Ron—the honor of the family and stuff?"

Silence. They couldn't buy it. "Who has a better idea?"

Dora said, "Wait. Wait. We can narrow the time frame. I saw Crystal run to the ladies' room, about ten minutes after that fight with Matt. Did anyone see her go back?"

I sat upright. "Ah, for crying out loud! How many times do I have to say it? I didn't fight with Crystal in my—"

"But we heard you, didn't we, Tony? So did Yvan, and Halla, too. You're the only actor on the set who doesn't have a Southern accent. We all heard you in there—"

"No, you heard somebody else."

Dora and Phina traded a look. "Who, for instance?"

"I don't know—look. It's no surprise that Crystal broke into my room. It's a habit she has—"

"Had. She's dead now."

"Okay, had. Cat burglars should take lessons from her. Inviting a guy into my room is exactly the sort of thing she'd do. But I wasn't the guy."

Phina said, "She was good at getting into places. Maybe she got into the wrong place at the wrong time and saw something she shouldn't have?"

Tony growled, "You writing my next script?"

"It was the wrong place, at any time," I said. "I didn't—" Silent stares. "I didn't do it." I sounded overdone even to me.

Tony said, "No, remember? We agreed, none of us did it. But Gabby was out on the floor exploring—"

I couldn't let that go by. "Gabby? Come on, how desperate are we? Gabby's only six years old."

"No, but how about Gabby's mother? She admits she hit Crystal," Dora said.

"No, hitting's not killing," Phina said. "Okay-okay! I got it! Gabby's agent! Listen—Crystal knew about something she did—misappropriated money or something—and she blackmailed her, so she lured her into Matt's room and, boom."

"That's it!" Dora crowed. "I can't stand people who buy hundred-dollar scarves, and know how to tie them. She'll be a pain over Gabby's contract, too, I bet. I vote for her. Gabby's agent—what's her name—" She pushed her braids back out of her way. "Where's my clipboard?"

"Harper," I said. "Janelle Harper. Mrs. Roland Harper."

"Harper? I never heard of any Roland Harper."

"Halla's son's father. He plays piano in the lounge at Starling Resort, and put out an album a few years ago. Janelle produced it, and he married her."

"Sounds like a soap opera. And Crystal sang there four nights a week—Oh, I got it!" Dora waved her pen in the air between two fingers. "Listen—Crystal sang there—so, what if she sucked him in, and they had an affair, and Halla found out and—"

"Halla and Roland split years ago, Dora. He married Janelle. Why would Halla—"

"No, no, how about if *Janelle* found out about it—yeah, Crystal told Janelle about her and him on the set that day, and—boom. Yeah. That's my theory. How's that?"

Phina's mind was on another track. "No—you know what, I know if Halla did it, it'll ruin Matt's day, but Halla has admitted she didn't like Crystal."

Tony sputtered. "Who did? I don't care who throttled Crystal, I'll pay the defense lawyer. She blackmailed me; she blackmailed Matt and trashed him. She drove you nuts, Dora, on that shower scene. We know what she was like with any straight male. If she and Halla went after the same man—"

"Hal doesn't 'go after' men, and she didn't have time to kill Crystal," I said.

Dora ignored me. "She and Crystal were always up for the same parts, and they both used to work at Starling Resort. Halla worked in the manager's office, 'cause Crystal beat her out for a job singing in the lounge. I have their résumés on file. They've been rivals for years."

"Halla got this job. Crystal didn't. Halla has no motive."

"None that we know of, but they were rivals. We don't know where Halla was at the time, you have to admit that."

"We don't know where any of us was at the time. We all have to admit that."

"Okay-okay. You know what, I'll be the suspect," Phina offered. "We were all outside the Canteen, she and 'Kota—"

Dora swept on. "No, no, none of us. I got it. How about that adorable lawyer—Matt's ex-wife's husband? There ought to be a name for that relationship. Maybe he cheated on his wife at the Resort, and Crystal blackmailed him, and the prenuptial agreement says he doesn't get a dime if a divorce—"

"In my dreams," I said. "Crystal was alive when he and Nance left. I saw her vertical and behaving herself right before they went. He doesn't need money. He's a superlawyer."

Dora took the pen out of her mouth. "Behaving herself? Are you sure it was Crystal?"

Phina snorted over a laugh, then held up her hand. "I got it!

Okay-okay. I bet we could make a case for him being the killer. Say he was seeing *Crystal* on the side, and she—"

"No," I said. "Wyndham never met Crystal—"

"He must have. He's staying at Starling Resort, and he's *male*; she was working there, and she was *Crystal*," Dora said. "When they talked in The Studio, the day of the murder, they looked like they'd met before. Remember, Tony? In the morning, before we got started?"

"Yeah, I remember—they talked for two seconds," Tony said. "This is real life. The guy's a newlywed, his wife's pretty, he's not about to fall in love with a lounge singer."

Phina slapped papers together. "Anyhow, the police must have asked the Wyndhams what they did after they left the studio. He wasn't cheating. That's a fantasy." Phina's face was pale and ravaged. If this were my screenplay, Mousy, I'd kill Dakota off in the first half-hour.

"It is not fantasy. I deduced it," Dora said with dignity. "Listen, if one of them did it, we're cleared. He's cute and everything. I liked him. He's a lot like Matt. But—"

"He is not anything like me!"

"Sure he is. People always remarry the same type, over and over. He's likable, like you. I liked him."

Tony said, "He's great. We all liked him, who didn't?"

"I don't," I said, "but that doesn't make him a murderer. Nancy'd say it makes him socially acceptable."

Phina tightened already tense lips. "Okay-okay. Let's get real. I think it's obvious the motive was blackmail, no matter who strangled her. So, who can we eliminate?"

"You give Crystal's husband an alibi," Dora said.

"Tamra only hit her." Tony added. "The murderer wouldn't hit, or couldn't, for whatever reason."

I put in my bit. "Halla didn't have time."

"As far as we know," Phina said. "Okay-okay, so maybe she didn't. I say let's decide 'Kota's it and get some of this work done."

"Nuh-uh." Dora tapped her pen. "No, 'Kota's one person we know who actually had a good reason to want Crystal alive."

"Yes," Phina stated flatly. "It was Dakota, because—because Crystal threatened to tell me what they did, and he was afraid of me. And I did slug him."

"Okay, it's Dakota," Dora decreed. "Okay, Tony? Matt?"

A glance at Phina, and Tony nodded. "It's 'Kota. Matt?"

"I guess so. Tony, what about your rewrite? Are we wasting time doing this now?"

We took Dakota as our working hypothetical murderer, buried our heads in shooting schedules. Sure, it's screwy. Show people don't always think the way the reasonable world thinks. A pretty girl has been murdered, we're all suspects, and all we want to think about is how to keep on making our movie.

The schedule Tony originally set up was flexible, because you can't be sure of the weather in the mountains, but tinkering was a headache. The question was whether Halla's knee would be up to shooting exteriors at the horse ranch next month. We cobbled something together, called it a night. Once Phina and Dora were gone, Tony curled up over his rewrite again. His gaze was intense, but it wasn't the baleful glare it had been.

I can smell burning genius as well as anybody. I took the clipboard out of his way and wrote this out. I think at last I'll get to sleep, Mousekin. You, too.

It's late, sweetheart. Daddy misses you. Think of poor little Shannon as you go to sleep tonight, honey. At least you have three parents, and all of them, including your old Dad, love you.

..10.

TARA:
TOO EARLY

Dear Mouse,
     So much for trying to sleep. Whenever I dozed off, some horror from last night came crashing through, and I'd sit bolt upright, wondering what hit me. I got a couple of hours' sleep in the morning, before Tony's alarm went off.

I sat up carefully. "When do you want me where?"

"Take the weekend off. Frolic in the forest. Dally in the daisies. Romp among the roses. I'm rewriting, damn you."

"Damn me? What did I do?"

"Shut up. At least we haven't started production yet."

I shut up with a private grin, and set my mind to getting up. My back and shoulders groan with every move. I have a huge bruise on my ribs where I took a kick. I might as well get used to it. I'll probably feel worse tomorrow.

Getting up was not as easy as I planned. You can't spend a chilly spring evening standing around a golf course with your arms tied in a knot behind you, and expect to get away with it the next day. Not at my age. I've felt this way before, mornings after Strongbow got another working-over. The only thing that's missing is the hangover.

I knew I had something to be grateful for.

I took myself through the morning routine very, very gently. My shower was long and steaming hot. As I creaked through getting dressed, Tony muttered at his screen, "You going to stay in all day? Agonized groans distract me."

"I wouldn't dream of distracting you. I do it all for you,

Uncle Anton." My mind raced ahead to the hospital, and it made me cocky. "Shall I pick up the mail before I head out?"

Tony stopped punching the keyboard for a second, deliberately turned to stare at me. "Last night, some bozo beat the snot out of you, and then a band of merry men damn near burned your face off. You're a mega-star—"

"Mega-has-been."

"Yeah, right. How many millions have you made off *Strongbow*? It's still rolling in."

"How many millions have forgotten my name? I'm lucky you gave me this chance—"

"Man, you ought to be screaming your head off to the papers right now. But no-o-o, it's, 'Shall I pick up your mail, Uncle Anton?' It's probably too early for the mail anyway. You're a star, my good God. Make like one, will you?"

"Geez. I thought you wanted an actor, not a media event. I'll be back in a few minutes."

In the front office, Ma'am shook her head. "I thought y'all were going to sleep in late. Haven't gotten the mail yet. Something came for you last night, though, after you went back out with that preacher." She handed me a tightly folded page torn out of a school notebook.

I all but snatched it out of her fingers. "Where did it come from? Who brought it? Did you see her?"

"Not her. I didn't have to see him, I know a trash-Beller when I smell one. He snuck out before I could get my gun."

"Trash-Beller? A trash-Beller brought this?"

"I tell you what's the truth, Mr. Logan, you better take that thing straight to the Sheriff, and don't have nothing to do with it afterward, you hear?"

I nodded. "Exactly what I plan to do, Ma'am. Thanks."

Maybe I shouldn't have handled it—I've done plenty of shows about fingerprints—but the minute I was in the room, I wanted to read Shannon's letter. Feeling Tony's look, I said, "It isn't the mail, it's a fan letter. Local. You want to see it?"

"No. Shut up." He went back to his keyboard. I opened the paper carefully.

"Dear Mr. Matt Logan,

"Thank-you for helping me. That lady said it was you. Some men took me home. I am sorry to go away, but my Mother gets mad if I stay out after dark. Please do not try & find me & do not tell any one, please. He said, I will go to reform school, if anyone finds out what I do to him, & my Mother can not do without me. One time, I tryed to tell her, but she says, I am lying. I thought up how to make him to stop, in your car. We learned about STDs in Health. I will put a cut on my lip & make it dirty. Then I will tell him that I have another sore just like it, you know where. He will be too scared to try again. Please, please, do not tell.

"Thank-you very much.

"I love you.

"Shannon."

That settled it, Mousy. I had a stop to make before going to see Hal. I gathered everything I'd received from Shannon, and headed out. The walk loosened me up, lifted my mood. If we can identify Shannon, stop what's happening to her . . .

At the Sheriff's office, Quin had her head buried in paperwork, while a high school kid tried to file more of it away. I hesitated. "Sorry, I'm afraid it's important."

She shut folders with an all-the-time-in-the-world smile. "Hey, Matt. No, you're fine. Come on in, sit down. I hear you had a rough night, last night. Does Golde know you're here?"

I'd enjoy her Southern charm more, but like Lady Macbeth's madness, it has method in it. She has a murder to solve, the Press won't be patient, and I'm a promising suspect. I handed her Shannon's letters. "This isn't about Crystal. I thought you should see these. They're from the little girl who was molested on the Starling Head last night. Is it your job, or—do you want them?"

She wanted them. Each letter got pulled out and examined, last one first. Finally, her mouth set in a grim line, Quin picked up her phone, and her fingers crawled over the number pad. As she waited for the other end to pick up, she glanced at me.

"Appreciate you bringing in the envelopes. You sure made her easier to find. The postmark's local. Yes—" she said to the phone. She dealt thoroughly with Shannon's case. When she hung up, she swivelled to face me. "You heard? They've been having trouble over her. That statement you wrote last night was the only evidence that she exists."

"Ah, for crying out loud, you thought I made this up? Hal's in hospital because of—"

"No, a child wrote these, and she has been victimized. Even I can tell that. And she's not a trained victim."

"A trained victim? What's a trained victim?"

Quin clamped her mouth into a thin line. "I hate these cases. I hate 'em. I wouldn't work in Child Protective for anything. Give me a nice, clean chain-saw serial killer, long as you keep the kids out of it." She glanced up, saw the high-schooler staring. She gave the kid a second look, and went on. "Some kids get beat up from the day they're born, to where, by the time they can talk, anybody can do anything to them and they won't tell. Shannon's not like that. She tried, she said No, she told people, she tried to fight him. Trained victims don't try, they don't let people try for them. I hate that. Doctors call it Stockholm Syndrome, and battered child syndrome. I call it pitiful."

The kid turned back to the file cabinet, red-faced. Quin sat up in her chair. "We'll find her. There's only four elementary schools in Beller County. We'll find her. Did you happen to write more of your journal?"

"Did you happen to arrest Ken Beller?"

"I knew you'd ask me that. Three of his brothers give him an alibi, and his cousin's the public defender. We couldn't hold him. I'm sorry, Matt."

"But I can identify him—"

"By sight? According to your statement, they were wearing masks, and that lighter blinded you."

I shuddered. "No. Not by sight. But his voice—"

"You know what Beller Hutter could do to you in court? I'm sorry, Matt. One thing, Ken's left the county. He's just over the Watauga County line, but he's gone."

"Sure, for how long? Sorry—I'm a little jumpy."

"I'd be more than jumpy, if I'd met trash-Bellers of a dark night. You take care, you hear?"

◇◇◇

I headed across the parking lot to the hospital. I had to wait
while some doctor finished with Halla, before I could go into
her room. She lay flat and still, staring at the ceiling. When I
came in, she flopped a hand out toward me. "Matt . . . ?"

I rejected the notion of attempting a kiss. This wasn't right.
Her hand had no strength in its grip. Her eyes were all wrong.
"Hal, what's going on?"

A single knock at the door: "Ms. McKee?" and a gurney
wheeled in, with scrub-clad people attached to it.

Surgery. Halla was doped up for surgery. She hadn't told
me she needed surgery. "What're you doing?" I said stupidly.

"I told you to wait till noon," she murmured.

"But—you didn't tell me. Why didn't you tell me?"

She squinted at me. "Why should I? I don't need your con-
sent. Go away till I come out—"

"No, I love you—Didn't you think I'd want to know?"

"Since when am I obligated to . . . to . . . " She was drifting
away, under the sedative.

Someone took my arm. "We have to ask you to leave."

I shook the hand off, ignoring the twang of pain it caused.
"Leave me alone—Hal—Listen—!"

"Sir, stand back. I don't want to call Security."

I stuffed my fists into my jacket pockets, backed off. There
was nothing I could do—or would want to. Halla needed surgery, which everyone knows is full of risks, and no one told me;
I couldn't do anything, and I was sick with rage.

Once she was gone, wheeled into the "Authorized Personnel Only" elevator, I had nowhere to go, nothing to do.

The waiting area is a charming place, almost entirely built
of windows, overlooking a small park. Anyone down there could
look up and see me. I recoiled all the way back to the elevator.
Its doors happened to open and I backed onto it, let it carry me
to the ground floor.

Chapels are usually on ground floors. Chapels rarely have
clear windows. I found it easily. If I sat against the wall, no one
could see me unless they were looking for me. I'd be safe in the
chapel.

Maybe I dozed off. I hadn't had much sleep. I got back to the world with my head on folded arms over the seat in front of me. Bradford sat beside me. "You okay, Matt?"

I started up. "I have to go to Hal—" What did she call it when your muscles shriek with pain at the very thought of movement? Sore. That's it. I was sore.

"Let me call to see if she's allowed visitors," he said. "No sense moving till you have to."

"Yeah. Thanks. I mean—thanks."

Halla was ready for visitors. Taking the elevator wouldn't hurt as much as taking the stairs, but taking the stairs would loosen me up. I'm an actor. I can't afford a body that doesn't work. I took the stairs, stopped at the desk. It's a good thing, because access to Halla was restricted.

"Are you family?" the desk dragon said suspiciously.

"I'm her fiancé."

"Man. The once and future lovers." The dragon went to Halla's room to ask, came back. "She's still a bit groggy, but you can go in."

Halla gave me a miserable glare. "You are *not* my fiancé."

"I know, I only said that so I could get in. Thanks for playing along." She turned her head to the window. "Hal, I shouldn't have blown up that way. I was scared for you—"

That roused her. "I make my own decisions—I will not give up the right to make my own decisions. Even if I ever marry, which I hope I never do, I will not give up the right—"

"I don't expect you to. I won't give up the right to kvetch if I don't like the decisions you make, either. Is that clear?"

She did her best. It wasn't enough. The glare disintegrated, her eyes pointed down at the corners. "Damn it, no fair. I want to have a tantrum and you make me laugh. Sit down. I can't stand the pain vibes you're emitting. How's your face?" She reached to touch it, pulled her hand back.

"Not as bad as it looks. What about your knee?"

"I can't believe you lied to them—the trash-Bellers. They burned your face, but you—"

"What was I supposed to do, hand Shannon over to those animals? Come on, Hal, think."

"But—I was afraid they'd kill you. I kept thinking about it all night. Does it hurt now?"

"My back feels worse. I mean it, Hal. I was more scared than hurt. How about your knee?"

"Well as can be expected, I'm told. Roland was here."

"Right. You have the look. Flogged. Deflated. I hate to see you look like that."

"He said I have to forfeit my week with Danny. I can't pick him up. We have to pick him up ourselves, or we don't get him. Roland's making the most of it."

"Hang on. You once said his stepmother picked him up from school."

"She's Roland's wife. Spouses count as—oh, no. No. I won't go there, Matt." She frowned at the ceiling. "It's not you. I can't deny I like you, but I—Ow, rats!" She winced.

I sat, folded her hand into both of mine. "You okay?"

"Yeah," she sighed. "There's that, too." She let me keep her hand. "But I don't want to hear 'We wear the chains we forge in life' when I make bum decisions."

"Sounds as though you're looking for a decent human being. A friend."

"You hold my hand like this, and kiss me the way you did last night, and want to be friends?"

"Why not? My parents are friends, always have been. You and I were born to be friends, Hal. Look at the way we worked together that day Crystal tried to blackmail me—"

She snuggled her cheek on our laced-together hands. "You know how I look after I've been talking with Roland." Suddenly she gave a sharp sigh, cuddled down, and slept.

I stayed with her the rest of the day while she drifted in and out of sleep, with regularly spaced doses of painkiller to keep her going, and people stopping by regularly for tests and vital signs. It was exactly what we needed, both of us. When visiting hours ended, they ejected me.

I did a lot of writing while Halla slept. I ought to toss it down the first john I come to.

No, Mouse, I'd better not. There's the bit about Shannon, and the one about Inspector Quin here. I'd better keep it.

At least by now I can drive my car. After a day of sitting in one place, I couldn't have managed the walk. I keep savoring the memory of Halla's cheek cuddled on my hand. If I could find Shannon, and see you once again, Mouseling, I wouldn't have much more to wish for.

.11.

TARA: MORE THAN A BIT SORE: MAY DAY

Dear Mouse,

If Halla wasn't scheduled to go home from hospital today, I'm not sure I'd bother with getting up this morning. The second day after you've been knocked about is worst. Your body creaks and your mind hates the world. Moving is the most painful thing I can do. Being with people is the hardest thing I can do. They're also the two best things I can do.

I could use a meeting, but it's only six o'clock in the morning. The first meeting isn't till noon, and writing isn't helping this time.

I have it. Bradford said he holds an early morning prayer service in the hospital chapel. I'll eat, go in to straighten out my head there, then report to Hal. I can finish this later.

◇◇◇

Later: Nancy's suite, Starling Resort—For Inspector Quin. As I came off the elevator, I heard a familiar sound track. Two friends of Halla's were with her, and had put one of my worst efforts on screen. By the sound of it, the movie was funnier than the producer ever meant it to be. Laughter and one-liners tumbled out the open door into the corridor. As I walked from the elevator to Halla's room, the three women cheered like kids at a Saturday matinee.

"Bodies always scream when they fall out of closets," Halla said. The body screamed and fell out of the closet.

"The teeth! Get the teeth!" the short, dimpled one rooted. "I bet that would be worse than going to the dentist."

The tall one shuddered at the bit with the teeth. "How do you suppose they got Matt Logan to star in this turkey?"

"He's not the star." Halla's voice was a low chuckle. "That cloak is the star. I want it. They couldn't have made the movie without that cloak."

"I know! They said, 'Hey, Matt, grow a beard, put on a Prussian uniform, and act in our movie, and we'll let you wear this neato cloak.'"

I knocked on the open door. "Actually, what they said was, 'Hey, Logan, put this cloak on, and we'll give you a job in our movie.' The beard saved on make-up."

Six dismayed eyes stared. I watched a black tentacle slither out of the well, wrap around my neck and pull me in. My scream echoed down, down, down. Halla took a breath to speak. I held up a hand for silence. A distant splash. I lowered my hand. "There, you can talk now. I'm dead."

The dimpled one broke first, sputtered, gasped, and fell into musical giggles. The tall one has a face like a Botticelli Madonna in a cheerful mood. She turned her back. Halla tried to look contrite, but it was no use. Her mouth tightened down, her eyes deepened, her face caved in to dimples. "Nuh-uh, we've seen this one before. You walk again."

"Yeah, my agent renegotiated."

Her friends traded glances, stood up. "We'd better—"

"What, and miss the rest of this?" On the screen my horridity was paused, quivering and unfocused. "Come on, it's a classic," I pleaded. They didn't really want to go. They zapped the monitor, and the film went on.

I found a spot and settled in. The last time I spent a morning in unremitting silliness, I was too drunk to remember much of it—only that it was with my Mouse. I lost a lot, drinking. I had no idea how I've missed laughing like that.

The cheerful Botticelli is Rose, and the dimpled one is Kayla. They finished packing things into a bag by the time the doctor arrived to let Halla go. Tactfully, they vanished long enough to give me a word with her. "Am I redundant?" I said. "I wanted to drive you home."

Halla worked her knee brace over the edge of the bed. "I

have to do some thinking, Matt. A lot of thinking. I've never been—wanted. I always did the wanting."

"You don't hang around with people of taste, obviously." I linked hands behind her straight, strong back. We flowed together as if we belonged that way. "I want you, Hal. Get used to it. Has anyone ever told you that you're beautiful?"

"Whenever they're after something. I never believe it."

"Why not? I do." I traced the line from her cheekbone to her jaw with the back of my finger. "Of course, I am after something. I want a wife, and nobody else will do."

"Matt, go away. Marriage is out. Learn to live with it."

"I'll bite. Why? You kissed me as though you like it. Do you?"

"I guess—Yes—I thought about it all night. Heaven knows why, but—I can't get away from it. But it didn't really count, can't you see that?"

"No, I can't. Why did you kiss me back, if it didn't count?"

"I thought it was my last kiss, you know that. Matt, please. I can't live in your world. Whenever you change your socks, your publicist calls the tabloids. Nobody around you can move without someone splashing it in front of a lot of lonely, crazy people. I won't live that way. Publicity's one thing—"

"Wait, Hal—in the first place, until this murder happened, no reporter's looked at me in almost three years."

"Crystal Beller's murder boosted your career—"

"No!" I cried, revolted. "Is that the way you think it works? It doesn't. What do you think—"

"Wait. Let me show you something." She clutched my jacket for support, and leaned down to one of the bags her friends had packed. After a fumble or two, she drew out Friday's edition of the *Probe*, tossed it flat on the bed. "There." The headline wailed:

"**PRE-TEEN SOBS: 'MY MOM DIDN'T DO IT!'**"

The pre-teen in question was Dannal.

Shadows deepened around her eyes. "I won't lie to you, Matt. I like you, a lot. But I will not expose my child to this."

There was not much more to say. I kissed her softly, she kissed sweetly back, and I left her alone in that hospital room, waiting for her friends to take her back to her empty apartment. So much for my new love life.

◇◇◇

In our bathroom at Tara lives a tub equipped with hot running water. Very hot running water. That was where I needed to be—in the midst of large quantities of very hot water. I've overdone everything. I was tired of aching, and I had to think.

I debated stopping at the office for messages. Probably a good idea. I left the car running and ducked in. Ma'am was ready for me. "You got to hear this. I don't know what to tell you." She activated a message machine.

Nancy's voice wandered out, all question marks and dashes. "This is for Matt Logan? It's Nancy? Wyndham? The police were here last night—about that girl?—who was killed? I can't cope—Can we talk? Suite 416?—I can't go on—I don't know—what to do?" *Click.*

"When did this come in?" I snapped.

"Maybe an hour ago, while I was checking stuff."

"Can you make a copy of the tape? May I have it?"

"I did." She handed it past the 'Sharon Beller, Proprietor' sign. "Sheriff'll likely to want to hear this thing."

"They'll hear all about it if I have to drag Nancy in by the hair. Thanks, Ma'am."

The steering wheel of my car was still warm from my grip of a minute ago. I should have got a speeding ticket on the way to Starling Resort. Never mind. The Sheriff has me under surveillance. Maybe my tail would be around if I needed him.

Everybody knows that the character with some vital bit of information ends up dead before the police hear about it. Real murder may be different, but I didn't want to risk it.

At Starling Resort, the security is elegant and careful. A handsome bit of beefcake with the face of Prince Charming intercepted me and asked civilly what I thought I was doing.

"I'm Matt Logan. Mrs. Wyndham asked me here."

"I'll check, sir." He consulted a designer phone, keeping a discreet eye on me. I tried to look harmless and well-bred. That's not easy with a damaged face and little over half a moustache. "I'm sorry, Mrs. Wyndham doesn't answer."

"Has she gone out?"

"Not since I've been here."

"She couldn't have got past you?"

"I doubt it, sir—Sir, what are you doing?"

"I'm getting into this elevator."

"I can't let you—" People were coming in, needing atten-tion. "I'll call the Sheriff—"

"Do that. Ask for Inspector Quin." I forced closing doors apart. "We may need an ambulance, too."

As the elevator rose I paced tight circles. This was point-less. Life isn't a screenplay. Of course it was okay. Nancy was probably having a nap or something. She'd scratch my eyes out for coming up like this.

I dived between doors and made for the Wyndhams' suite. It must have been my lurid imagination that made the silence sound so stifling. I knocked, and the door opened at my touch.

"Nancc?" I listened. I knew she was there. "Nancy?"

She wasn't in the outer room. I hadn't really expected her to be. The bedroom door was open about half an inch. She was there. I was certain she was there. I stepped toward it. "Nancy!" Nothing. Leaving caution behind, I barged in. She lay on the bed, horribly still and livid.

I strode across the room to her. "Nancy!" I clapped my hands above her face. "Mrs. Wyndham!"

No response.

"Anastasia Russo!" I clapped again, barely missing her nose. My big hands made a sound like a rifle shot in that silence. Nothing. I put my ear to her half-open mouth, watched her chest. She wasn't breathing. Damn.

I tilted her head back, blew two breaths in. I probed her neck for the artery, praying I'd feel a pulse. My prayer was answered.

The answer was No.

Damn!

I called for help, but nobody had followed me up here.

Nancy must have spent an hour on her make-up. Her hair was morning perfect, slightly ruffled where it had slid around on the pillow. She wore a fancy, easy-access nightgown, twisted loosely around her bent legs. Two pill bottles stood on the dresser next to an ice bucket, champagne bottle, a flute glass, and dam-ask napkin. One vial was tipped over, one half-full.

Oh, Nance.

I hauled her down to the floor and felt for a pulse again, to be sure. If there was a right time for Nancy to commit suicide, this wasn't it.

No pulse. I fought off the sense of futility, opened her gown, measured, pumped, and counted. You count out loud so anybody passing by might get curious and stop to help. Fifteen compressions, then two breaths.

Fifteen and two—fifteen, two—*Come on, Nance.*

In the middle of the fourth cycle she gagged, turned away, cried, clutched at her chest. I straightened, took a breath for myself. "Lie still, Nance. You may have a ruptured cartilage or two. Lie still." I picked up one of the bottles, held it at arm's length, tried to read the label. My arms aren't long enough, and my glasses were in the car. I had to find help.

She stared with unfocused eyes. "Why . . . why . . . ?"

"Mouse needs her mother. Stay with me, Nance. Where's the telephone?"

"My husban' . . . hates phones in . . . bedr'ms . . ."

"Nancy, wake up!" I clapped hands above her face again. She opened her eyes. I leaned down close to her. "Nance, listen. If you go back to sleep, I'll push on your chest some more. Understand? Stay awake!"

For a brief second she saw me. Her hand, delicate as a bird's claw, held my wrist like a vise. "Matt—whore!" She made a face, tried again. "I know why—she's a whore?"

A knock at the door, and it burst open. Heavy footsteps muffled in the carpet. "In here!" I shouted. "I need help!"

Nancy's grip on my wrist loosened. She plucked at the lace on her gown, strained her chin into her neck to frown at it. "My husban' hates . . . ?" I tugged the gown together over her chest, dragged the spread off the bed to cover her.

Security appeared at the bedroom door, Prince Charming with attitude. "Sheriff's on the way up, Buddy. You better—"

"Good. Now get an ambulance. She's overdosed."

"On their way. You better have a good—Holy shit." He came in far enough to see the bottles and glass on the dresser. It activated the right impulses. He brought his radio to his face.

I said, "Look, I've done CPR. She's breathing on her own, but she's in and out of consciousness. Tell Rescue—"

"What's your name?"

"I'm her ex-husband. Look, you have to—"

"The ambulance is coming. Are you all right?" He hunkered down beside me. Now that he decided we were on the same team, Security sounded genuinely concerned.

"Thank you, I'm fine. It's Mrs. Wyndham that's—"

The radio spoke. "Rescue is coming up in the elevator. Mr. Wyndham just came in with Miss Wyndham. They're coming up, too. We couldn't stop them."

Miss Wyndham, my Aunt Fanny. Mouse is Miss Logan. Never mind. It was good of the front desk to warn us.

Medics surged in with oxygen, drug kit, stretcher. They called reassurances and instructions to Nancy as they hooked her up to machines and IV bags. Security faded off. I got out of the way, answered questions, tried to make myself invisible. If Wyndham saw me—

He pushed in. "Oh, my God, what are you doing?" His face looked puffy; his voice was hollow, as if he had a heavy cold. He moved uncertainly; his feet seemed to have trouble finding the ground. This was hitting him hard. He came to Nancy, knelt carefully beside the stretcher. The medics gave him a moment with her.

"Nancy. Baby. Don't try to talk, okay? Nancy, can you hear me? It's Nigel, Baby. Just rest. Don't say anything."

"Mommy?" Mouse crowded in behind him. "*Mommy*!"

I didn't say anything. I'll swear I didn't make a sound, but her head spun around to me. Wyndham caught the movement, stood up and put himself between us before I saw what I was looking at. "Come away, Baby. You can't see this. Oh, my God, this can't be happening to me—"

They packed Nancy up and wheeled her out. All the medics went with her, as Inspector Quin and a deputy arrived with someone from Starling Resort Management. Wyndham hid Mouse somewhere, came back and tapped a finger on my shoulder. "You're in contempt of court, you know."

"Sorry, Nancy called me. She said she wanted to talk."

"She's not talking now. I'd really like you to leave." He stopped and stared as the deputy began ferreting into the bathroom with evidence-gathering technologies. Attempting suicide must be a very serious offense in this county.

Wyndham crossed the sitting room to plead with Quin for some privacy and respect. I headed for the door.

On my way out, Quin called to me. "Matt, would you mind sticking around a while? You might could help us out."

"I—He—I was asked to leave—"

"This is an investigation, Matt; you're a witness. You want to have a seat there?" She waved at the sofa, which curls around half the room to form a coliseum.

"May I use the phone?"

Quin smiled. "Why, sure, soon as Kelly's done with it. Tell Golde 'Hey' for me, will you?"

Kelly released the phone and I made the call. Golde Silver was out of the office, so I left a message, saying I decided to talk with Quin. I could call her later.

Wyndham had sequestered Mouse in the kitchen-bar behind the couch, screened by a wall of trailing plants. I found a seat in one corner of the arena so that I could see part of her head without looking as if I was trying to. Wyndham's no dummy. He stepped around the vines, imposed his back across my line of sight, spoke to her. I could see a bit of her hair move as she nodded. He spoke to the Manager, who led Mouse out with an arm around her shoulders.

Quin established herself at the desk in the front room, graciously offered Wyndham a seat facing her. He sat, nervously aligning the pen set with the edge of the desktop, picking up Quin's micro recorder to put a worn notebook beneath it, to shield the glossy wood from scratches. I doubt that he gave her much help. Most of his answers came with headshakes, shrugs, and apologetic smiles. Kelly, working in the bedroom, took up more of his attention than Quin's questions. In time she dismissed him so he could get to the hospital and be with his wife. He left reluctantly; Kelly all but pushed him out the door.

My session was more thorough. Paying no attention to her recorder lying on the notebook, Quin took me through my story

from the time I got here until the medics arrived. None of it
was particularly difficult. I gave it to her in as many forms as she
wanted. Soon she went after another angle. "How'd you happen to
be so handy, Matt?"

"Nancy called me at Tara to talk about the murder."

"What'd she sound like when you talked to her?"

"Oh. Sorry. I didn't talk with her, actually. She left a message." I dug into my pocket, handed over the cassette.

She received it like a treasure, put it next to the recorder
without skipping a beat. "If I had any gold stars, I'd give you
one. Not many'd think of bringing that along. Now, you heard
the message, and you high-tailed it over here—I been told you
violated the speed limit on the way, but that's not my job—why
couldn't you just call her back?"

"No, I didn't want anything to happen to her—"

"Happen to her? Like getting herself poisoned? Why?"

"Look, in movies it's what always happens. I didn't want
to risk—"

"Who'd poison her? Kelly says your fingerprints are all
over that pill vial."

"But—hang on—didn't she do this to herself?"

"We're trying to find that out. How did your prints get on
her pill vial?"

"I picked it up to read the label."

She pointed at an amber vial on the desk. "Do you care to
show me?"

"I was on the floor beside Nancy—" I hesitated. "This isn't
the same one."

"No, we don't want to smear your prints on the real one."

"Oh. Sorry, I wasn't thinking." I mimed what I'd done,
using the pill bottle.

Quin nodded, left it where I'd placed it. "Kelly?" she called.

In the bedroom, Kelly looked over his shoulder at her.

"D'you care to see if these prints are the same pattern as on
her pill vial?" Quin aimed a grin at me. "He just got that pretty
fluorescent powder. If I hadn't brought him here, he'd have
dusted Lieutenant Pike's golf clubs for prints. Couldn't let him
do that."

Kelly got busy with the vial. In a moment or two, he nodded. "That's it, Inspector, except for her prints. We got us an empty bottle of champagne in the bedroom. Real fancy. And a glass—they got a weird pattern of prints. You'd think the bottle'd be eat up with them, but—you might ought to look at them."

Quin nodded. It didn't sound right, but they probably—

No. It wasn't right. I said, "Hang on. The glass and bottle of champagne should be eaten up with her prints? What do you mean by 'eaten up'?"

Kelly put up with the foreigner who didn't speak the language. "I mean eat up. Them prints ought to be stuck all over the glass and bottle and all, but the only ones on the bottle's high up, and there's nothing but partials on the glass."

"On the stem of the flute or the bowl?"

He looked to Quin, shrugged. "See for yourself." He pointed through the bedroom door at the flower-painted bottle and tall, slim flute. Dabs of orange powder covered the neck of the bottle; smudges spotted the stem of the flute.

I shook my head. "There's nothing wrong with those fingerprints. Not if they're Nancy's."

"Are you serious, Matt?" Quin said. "Those are Mrs. Wyndham's prints, right, Kelly?"

"Sure looks like them."

"Right. And Nancy would handle a flute glass exactly that way," I said. "That bottle's right, too."

Quin said, "You want to tell us about it?"

"Look. Nancy worships champagne—the sparkle, the glamour, all of it. She says she fell in love with me because I can cork a bottle of champagne with a cavalry saber."

Quin laughed. "Wouldn't a corkscrew be easier to find?"

"Yeah," Kelly kicked in.

"Only nineteen people in the world are officially able to do that," I protested. They traded amused glances. "Sure, it's an atrocious way to treat champagne. But it impressed Nancy."

"And the prints on the glass—?" Quin said.

"Champagne has a mystique, a ritual. It goes flat if it gets warm, so you want to keep it as cold as possible. You hold a flute like that one by its stem so the heat from your hands won't kill the fizz. The bottle you handle by its neck. When you pour, you wrap it in a napkin, to insulate it. So if Nancy poured her champagne out of this bottle, there wouldn't be any finger-prints below its shoulder. The napkin kept it clean."

"She went through all that trouble for a suicide?"

"Her last champagne? Absolutely. It's like a last kiss. She'd linger over every detail."

"But isn't this a real expensive kind? Why would she take a substance with it if she's such a connoisseur?"

"Nancy's no connoisseur. You could put garlic juice in cham-pagne and she wouldn't care. I don't think she'd notice. She has no sense of smell. She likes the champagne aura."

Quin nodded thoughtfully. "Nice, Matt. That's real nice."

"Sorry?"

"It sounds so creative. But what if we look at it at a differ-ent angle: you set your ex-wife up with a bottle of poisoned champagne. She calls your motel, says she knows something we don't know, and do you care to come talk about it, and the motel manager hears the message. See, you didn't count on that. So you come tearing over, you wipe the bottle and glass, put her fingerprints in all the right places, create this fine story about riding in to save her, and anyone with half a heart would buy it. Trouble is, some people don't have a heart. You knew she had something, yours are the only non-resident prints in here, and trying to revive the body is the kind of thing you do."

"I didn't—" No use. "I didn'ts" never impress murder in-vestigators. "Look, she is still alive, isn't she?"

"Last I heard. You still in love with her, Matt?"

"No. I have a sorry feeling that I never really was."

"Then, why did you—?" The questions kept on coming, re-peating themselves for several millennia. I tied myself in knots, trying to keep track of the charges and speculations. In the middle of it, Kelly stuck his head around the bedroom door. "Inspector, you won't like this."

Quin switched off the recorder to give him her full atten-tion. "What've you got?"

"The wine in the bottle tests clean. Stuff was in her glass."

"Are you sure?"

"Dying's sure, but this is likely. We'll take these in for tests, but you can smell the difference even without the reagent strips. I hate it for you, Inspector."

Quin nodded. "Sure you do. Thanks." She reached over and switched the recorder on again. "We're still recording this, you're aware of that, aren't you, Matt?"

I nodded. The recorder didn't hear it. "Right," I said.

"You want to give us this in writing?"

"Look, am I under arrest?"

"Not yet. Don't leave the county. You don't have to give us a write-up, you're aware of that, aren't you?"

It took a minute, but I couldn't see that this would do me more harm than I've done myself. "When do you want it?"

She stood, waved at the desk. "Now's not too late." She threw in a charming smile. "We sure appreciate your help, Matt."

◇◇◇

So I went down to the car for my clipboard and glasses. As I stepped out into the spring sunshine, Wyndham came in, looking drained. Mouse wasn't with him. I angled away, but he changed course and came toward me.

I said, "Look, Quin had questions, and now she wants—"

"Yes, I got interrogated, too. All this crime scene investigation—why can't they leave us in peace?"

"Yeah. I'm sorry about—How's Nance doing?"

He couldn't seem to focus on anything for long. "Nance? Oh. Nancy. They pumped her stomach. You'd think they'd allow her some privacy, but the policewoman kept sitting—"

"But Nancy is alive?"

"Barely. I hear you tried to save her—I'm grateful—"

"Forget it. Look, I have to write—"

He put a hand on my arm. I disengaged it. He said, "No, you don't forget a thing like that. Let me buy you a drink."

"No, thanks. I'm supposed to—"

He passed a hand over his face. "No, I mean it. There are a few things I need to know. Nancy's been confused—this murder—I don't see why they go through all our lives like this. You'd think suicide was a crime. Hey, a drink doesn't count if somebody buys it for you, isn't that the rule? One drink. Please."

I don't like being pressured to drink, but his new wife was in critical condition after attempting suicide. He deserved any information I could give him. "I'd rather have coffee, if you don't mind." Quin could wait.

Starling Resort has a huge atrium, with a microcosmic jungle in the middle of boutiques, shoppes and a cutesy café. This was the wrong time of day for coffee. What they brought was at least half an hour old, one of those flavored coffees the shoppes bill as "gourmet" and charge three times their worth for. All the sugar in the bowl couldn't save that dreck. I did some fierce acting.

Wyndham ordered a ginger ale. It came with fruit on a skewer and a paper umbrella to make it look dangerous. "What happened to your face?"

My face wasn't the point. "What do you want to know?"

He finished the ginger ale in one pull, stripped the skewer. "Did the police say anything about why Nancy did this to me?"

"Quin wasn't confiding in me—Hang on, it couldn't—No, the fingerprints proved that Nancy handled the glass—"

A cube of pineapple stopped halfway to his mouth. "Fingerprints? What fingerprints?"

I explained about the fingerprints on the glass and champagne bottle. "But Inspector Quin didn't say—"

"What didn't she say? Please, I—I'm a bit lost, here. It's my wife we're talking about, and they think it's my fault. What did that detective ask you?"

"Oh, sorry. I was thinking—There's been a murder, you know. Maybe they have to make sure that Crystal's killer didn't try to kill Nance." I frowned at the molasses-and-asphalt mess in my cup, and reeled off the gist of my interview with Quin. "Don't ask me what Quin thinks," I ended. "I stopped trying to read the police mind long ago."

He nodded thoughtfully, running the end of his skewer in and out of the drink straw. I pushed my cup aside, and shoved my chair back. He looked up. "Wait. Let me ask you one more thing. What did Nancy say to you—before the police came?"

I wanted to be gone. "Look. Nancy wasn't making any sense." I concentrated, staring into the little jungle. "She asked why, and then she said that you hate phones in bedrooms—"

"Correct. No business in the bedroom. What else?" The last of the fruit disappeared.

"When I told her to stay awake, she said she knew why Crystal was a whore, then drifted into the ozone layer. She said you hate something. She wasn't coherent. Look—I'm sorry."

"What else? What did she say I hated?"

"Nothing," I said. "She didn't finish the line. I told you every word. I'm sorry if it's—"

"No, it's good, you've eased my mind, trust me. Here—" He snagged our waiter in passing, offered to sign the tab.

The waiter sighed. "Sir, we're not connected with the hotel. If you read the sign—"

Wyndham slipped a credit card on the tray. "I am grateful for your effort to save her."

"I didn't do it for you, or for her," I said. "I told Quin—"

"Speaking of Michaella—"

"I'd rather not."

"Excuse me, sir—" The waiter bent discreetly over Wyndham. "The sensor won't take your card. It could be damaged. Do you have, like, another card? We accept—"

"I don't have the other ones on me. Are you sure?"

"Here." I stood, handed over a bill. I don't like fuss.

Neither did the waiter. "Thank you, sir," and he left.

I said, "Look, I'm sorry if I wasn't any help, but—"

"No, I'm grateful—" His attention drifted. I gathered myself together, waved the waiter's change away. Wyndham came back to me without warning. "I want to apologize for the way she acted the other day. You know, when you said you'd call your lawyer. Beane's a good man. Call him. See what he says."

My jaw moved sideways. "If Mickie tells me, live in person, she wants me to sign her away, I might consider doing it."

"That's what I mean. No reason why you can't see her."

I gave it thought, and had to remind myself to breathe. "Alone. I see my kid alone."

"Hey, I'm grateful, not gullible. Don't push it."

"I didn't mean—look. We could use the fountain there. You can sit at that table and keep an eye on us. But I meet with her alone. No interruptions."

"And then you'll sign?" Wyndham said.

"That depends. If I decide she'll be happier—"

"She will, trust me. Call your lawyer. You can use my phone." He drew it out like a gunfighter.

"I have my own phone, thanks. I'll call tomorrow."

"No, get it over with now, what do you say?"

"But—Nance—"

"Trust me, she wanted this as much as I do. Come on, do it for Nancy. Call your lawyer, see what he says. He gives you the go-ahead, you can see Michaella the minute Nancy's out of the hospital, one way or the other."

My throat squeezed on my windpipe. I could do it. I could talk with my Mouse, tell her how I've missed her, tell her that whatever happens—it's what I've always wanted. I made myself breathe. "I'll c-I'll call."

He couldn't do enough for me. He bullied someone into letting me use an office where I could have privacy and time. I figured there was an even chance that Brewster was out somewhere, but my lawyer was right there, right up with me. When I explained, he said, "It took you long enough."

"Sorry?"

"How long have you been trying to get visitation with that kid? She's growing up, away from you. Wyndham's crazy about her, from all I hear. Listen, Matt, this'll sound harsh—"

"You've never pulled punches before."

"You have some sweet memories of you and her together," Brewster said. "But how often were you sober all those years?"

He had me. Drunks are good at telling themselves fairy tales. "I—I never thought of that."

"She may not be as glad to see you as you are to see her. Have you ever made amends with her?"

"I've never been allowed to. That's one thing I—"

"Listen, Matt—"

"I know. Look, I'm not going to say you've made me happy or anything, but thank you. I might have made a—a clumsy blunder. Thanks, Brewster."

I stayed in the office a few minutes to rearrange my head after I switched the phone off. It's not easy to convince yourself that your dearest dream has never been anythig more than a self-made fantasy.

Wyndham was there when I came out. I set my jaw, nodded. "If I hear it from her—but I have to see her first."

He aimed a pat at my shoulder. "You're doing the right thing. We'll call you—"

I moved out of reach. "No. In person, or no deal."

"I know. Trust me, I'll take care of it. I can't make plans now, but give me a few hours. I'll call you tomorrow."

So I got back to Nancy's suite late.

Quin and Kelly were wrapping up the flute glass as I came in. "Where have you been?" she said. She gave me a second look and her face changed. "Matt? What happened?"

"Nothing. I ran into Wyndham. We talked. F-amily stuff." Abruptly I strode to the desk, sat down with the clipboard.

Even when I'm writing for Quin, my mind slips off into "Dear Mouse" mode. I read somewhere that you can grieve over a lost hope as deeply as you can over a lost child.

.12.

TARA:
SOME RESOLUTIONS

Quin had me sign what I wrote, and then she ejected me. "Get some rest, Matt. You look like someone run over you with a manure spreader." Charming.

I swung into my rental car, started up. Driving took all my concentration, until I fitted the car into a parking place. The steps were a challenge. If I focused on each next one, I could keep climbing. At the top I leaned into the door frame, pushed a button. What was wrong—Oh. This wasn't Tara.

Inside, Halla called, "Just a minute!" A fumble at the door and she stared at me, hanging between her crutches, her face blank with surprise. "Matt! How'd you know—Come in—"

I stepped into chaos. The place smelled like cinnamon, fresh bread, and cat fur. Fluffy, cream-colored kittens with faces like pansies scattered across the room. A mature version with a face like a brown velvet fist adorned the back of the couch, flipping its tail to let its young practice killing.

"I hope you're not allergic to cats," Halla said, limping into the kitchen area. "Find some place to sit. Don't be shy about ousting somebody; humans outrank cats here. Let me get the rolls out—" One of her crutches clattered to the floor. "Rats! I keep forgetting I can't do that."

I strode across the linoleum, got a hold on Halla and the hot pan. I was quick: it burned my hand only slightly before I slid it to the nearest surface. The cinnamon rolls it contained were spicy, hot and gooey. "Were you expecting someone?"

She leaned into me, turning her face to my shoulder for a moment. I put both arms around her. Nothing in the world is as

comfortable as holding Halla's body against mine. I shifted sideways, hoping she wouldn't notice how much I like it. I needed
to hold on to her. Apparently she needed me, too. She clung
close. "I bake rolls when I'm low," she said, after a moment.
"They'll go to my neighbor. You want one?"

"No, thanks. I—I didn't mean to come up here."

"Oh. Well—" She shrugged one shoulder, pulled away.

"No, I don't mean—Hal, why do I act like a jerk when I'm
with you? I guess I came like a hunted animal, run to earth—"

"No, it's good. Usually I like being alone, but today—Can
we sit down? I get tired—" Her face looked haggard.

"How about the couch? Here—" I scooped a kitten out of
the way with one hand, settled Halla against an oversized cushion with the other. The kitten jumped indignantly off my hand,
clawed up and reported to its mother for a snack.

I sat beside Halla, and she huddled against me like a puppy
seeking warmth. I sneaked an arm around her. "What's going
on? You seemed fine, this morning. If I remember correctly,
you ran me off." I gathered her closer.

She stiffened, made a move away.

I held onto her. "No, tell me about it. You'll feel better;
women always do in screenplays."

She sat up and glared at me, her mouth tightening and one
dimple deepening. I love it when she tries not to laugh. I shrugged.
"Come on, what can it hurt?" I pulled her close, settled her head
on my shoulder.

In a moment or two, she loosened up, let herself drape against
me. It all came out: how the helpless terror haunted her, how
she'd tried to stay awake in hospital until the sleep medication
came around because narcotics deaden dreams, how she dreaded
the night before her, alone with her horrors, denying herself the
sleep aid, now that she was home. "I locked my door, and I
want to push my dresser in front of it, but I can't keep it out,
what they did to you. I didn't even yell, I was too scared. It's all
I can think about. But I won't take a pill, I can't have another
addiction, I have Danny—"

"You shouldn't be alone. You need someone with you—"

"I can't—I don't know anyone who would—"

"Sh-sh, Hal—Sh, dearest—Let me hold you—" Pulling her close, I laid us both backward, let her cry into my shirt. Soon enough, the storm eased. She turned in my arms, her responsive body molding to mine. No use asking what started it. I kissed her hair, her cheek, a wet eye. Her face turned, our lips slipped into place, we kissed.

It lingered long, deep and heady, like skinny-dipping in red wine. Her touch was firm, her back supple and smooth. She moved with me easily as dancing. Dreams I never knew I had clamored to come true. Fastenings loosened at a touch; we explored each other slowly, savoring. As a delicious curve slid under my hand, a kitten pounced.

We struggled to sitting positions with a single laugh between us. Halla eased her brace onto the coffee table. "Oops. Ow! I'm sorry, I forgot the cats. I'll—Ow, damn it!"

"Are you okay? Here, let me—"

"I'm fine, a bit sore. Rose says I push myself too hard."

"You do." I lifted the kitten to its mother. It delved into the big cat's side, purring. "Do these things have a father?"

"And a solid gold pedigree. They pay my rent. They're Himalayans, worth about a month each, here." She slipped a hand up my arm and across my chest. "Do you want to—"

I fetched a deep breath, put her hand away from me. "Hal, no. Not now."

"Not?" She frowned, her eyes puzzled and hurt.

I sat up, buckled my belt. "I'm sorry. I shouldn't—"

She propped herself up. "What, 'sorry'? I started it."

"We both started it. It doesn't matter. I—Let's not."

Panting a bit, she thought of several comebacks. "Why?"

"Because—" Carefully I placed her hand on her knee brace and left it. "Hal, look at me. You know I want you—"

How could she miss it?

"—but I want to do this right. I've done too many things wrong in my life, Hal. I love you. I want you—a lot. But I don't want to have you until after we're married. I want to do it right, with you."

The sun sank low. A stray beam from the late sun gilded the blind slats with fire. "Well. I've never been treated this way before," she whispered.

"I won't apologize for stopping, Hal."

"I guess—I'm not used to being treated like a lady."

"You are a lady. I wouldn't treat you any other way. Look. Maybe—I'd better go."

"No! No, I don't want to be alone." She tugged the edges of her shirt together. "But—I suppose if you want to go, I can't stop you." She was losing a fight to keep her voice clear. "What's left, after all? You won't make love without marriage, and I won't marry you."

"No, look—Hal, please—this publicity will all die down within a week after they solve the murder—I'm not famous enough for them to waste ink on. Don't say never, please? There are ways to protect the kids. Hal, don't shut me out."

"It's not you. You had nothing to do with it. But I'd give Dannal up to Roland before I'd let—that tabloid thing—happen again."

"Hal—Geez, Hal—I'm sorry—"

She may not have heard me. "And it looks as though I'll have to. You should have heard Roland on the phone, an hour ago. Janelle's out of town, but when she gets back, they'll go straight to the best lawyer in the county."

"No. Hal, no, you shall not lose your child. I won't let that happen to you—"

"Neither will I." She turned to face me squarely. "Given a choice between you and Danny, I'm sorry, but I choose Danny."

"As I would choose my—Mouse—but, Hal, it doesn't have to come to that. We can—"

"Oh, sure, if we live on a guarded estate and keep pit bulls. I won't live that way. I'm sorry—you'd better go."

I stood up, moved to the window. "Look, you can't stay here alone. Isn't there someone you can call?"

There was Kayla. Halla wasn't ready to talk, so I made the call. No problem. Kayla likes the cats as well as Halla, it seems. I rang off. "She'll be here in an hour, she says. Look, have you eaten anything since you came home?"

She shrugged one shoulder. "I—No—I can't remember."

"Right. I can make an omelet with an attitude. It'll be something to do while we wait for Kayla. Would you like that?" She didn't object, so I poked around her kitchen. With occasional directions from Halla about the location and use of implements, the omelet came out fine. She ate nearly half of it, with some surreptitious help from the cats.

As I took the utensils and started cleaning up, she asked from the couch, "Matt? What brought you up to my place with a face like the end of the world, this afternoon?"

"Nothing." I started hot water running into the sink. As it splashed, I called, "Do you like coffee?"

Halla cried, "No—Matt, damn it!"

"You don't want coffee?"

She pounded the cushion beside her. "You want us to be a pair, you get me to spill my guts into your lap, but when you have trouble, all I see is your back? How fair is that?"

"Hal, you don't want—I can't ask you—"

"Yes, you can, it's only fair. Leave the dishes."

"I—You're not in any shape to—"

"I'm better, now. Please, Matt, I have to do something. Talk to me. You came up here for a reason." Suddenly her eyes turned down at the corners. "Or are you too macho?"

I leaned my hips on the sink. "Oh, you're very good—"

"Do you want to tell me?"

Father's stroke happened just two hours after they got word of the wreck. Mother's never shown that she blamed me by so much as a word or look. Maybe I'd feel better about it if she did. Meranda showed up while I was in intensive care, and Nancy acted loyal in public, but once I landed in detox, I considered myself on my own. Nobody has to tell me that most of what's happened to me in the last three years has been my own fault. I never thought anyone else could be on my side.

I lifted a kitten out of a chair, sat and let it roam on my knee. It tied itself into a knot, lapsed into a coma. Telling Halla about this afternoon didn't take long. When I finished, we sat silent for a while in her dimming apartment. She stirred first. "So Mouse isn't your ex-wife?"

"No, that was pure luck. If the *Probe* hadn't made that mistake—Geez. Anyway, Nance kept tabloids away from her. She never saw the story. Hal, I'll do whatever it takes to keep you from losing Dannal." I stared into the gathering dark. "I know what it's like to lose a child."

"Tell me."

I began awkwardly, with the easy part, what I know only from other people's descriptions. I have no conscious memory of that day. "I had to drive her to school one day. I'd chased a hangover with tequila, and I smashed into a tree. They found her covered with blood. The seat belt was buckled under her. The blood was all mine; she wasn't even bruised. I went face-first through the windshield, crushed my hand. Life isn't usually that kind."

Now that I'd started, talking was easy. "My first week in treatment, I was served with the restraining order. I—I've only had a couple of glimpses of her since. You have no idea how I envy you with Dannal."

"You still miss her."

"Every second. I keep on trying to get the court order changed. I always lose. I've never been allowed to say good-bye, or I'm sorry, or—at least I'll—get to see her this way."

"How much do you remember about her?"

"All of it—I hope. Nance and I—we lost our first baby. Mouse happened almost the minute Nance was able to let me touch her again. When they came home from hospital, Nance was too exhausted and depressed to get up when the baby woke at night, so I did it. I'd clean her up, fix a bottle for her and a drink for me, and we'd sit in the rocking chair and have a party. One night—it must have been well after midnight—I played variations on the alphabet song. Mouse sang the whole thing, three times. She was two and a bit. I can't say the neighbors were as impressed as I was."

Halla said, "Was she the little darlin' Crystal taunted you with, that day in your—?"

"No! What is this thing everybody has about—Look. Crystal and I exchanged a couple of acid lines that morning, but that was all—I mean all—the contact we had that day."

She stared, wide-eyed. "But I heard you. I was trying to open my door—"

"And you banged it twice, and then went down the hall?"

"Yes, how do you know—Good heavens."

"You remember now? I was across the floor by the kitchen set, talking with—"

"That's right, I wondered if any of the rest of us would get a chance to meet him. I can't believe I've been so dim! I have to call the Sheriff's office, right now."

I fetched the phone. "I'd appreciate it."

She stabbed buttons, made competent noises, answered repetitive questions. At last she switched the phone off, her mouth set and grim. "They didn't believe me."

"Did they record it?"

"Yes, but—"

"Then they have it. Thanks for doing it."

"But if it wasn't you, it must have been the murderer."

"Not necessarily. We thought it was the murderer who hit Crystal, but that was only Tamra. Let's not jump to conclusions." A car door slammed in the parking lot downstairs. "I think Kayla's here. Get some rest, Hal."

◇◇◇

As I slogged into the room, Tony and Dora grabbed me for a meeting. I had just enough energy left to pay attention to the rough schedule they'd patched together to accommodate Halla's knee injury and Tony's rewrite, as far as it's gone. It made sense, which means that Dora did most of it. I congratulated her, agreed to show up when they wanted me, saw them off to dinner, and found the phone. I wasn't looking forward to this call, so I'd better get it over with. "Hello, Mother, it's Matt."

"Of course it is, dear; no other man living addresses me as Mother. Are you drunk?" My family always ask.

"No. How's—how's Father doing?"

"Wonderfully. I think his right hand's gaining strength." Optimists see the glass as half full. My mother parties down if the inside is still wet. "Do you need money?"

"Not in the last twenty years. You always ask."

"The mother-mystique. It gets your mind off your father. Why did you call?" Mother hates to waste time on the phone.

"I'm—look, if I si-igned M-M—I m-mean, if-if you—"

"Breathe, Matts."

I did. "Yeah. Sorry. I mean, if W-Wyndham ad-adopted Mickie, would your grandparents' rights be—you know—"

"No, they're not related to anything you do. Are you considering releasing her, lamb?"

I nodded, which didn't go through the phone line. She was silent, giving me time. "B-Brewster says—they tell me he—Wyndham loves her. I—was drinking most of her life—"

"I think it would be best for both of you, Matts. Your father disagrees, frankly, but I like Nigel. He's like a slim Santa Claus without the beard. This must be painful for you."

"I'm okay. Thanks. I have w-work. Work distracts me."

"Oh—work." She dismissed work. I should know better than to lie to my mother. "Do you know anyone there? Someone you can talk to, alone?"

"I prefer to keep my life private, Mother; don't worry. Well, there's this—I mean, she's—"

"Darling, you've found somebody. Who is it? The shrew in your movie?"

"Mother—"

"The mother-mystique again. You've brought her name up every time you've called. What's she like?"

"Well—a lot like you, actually. You know—"

"That's no good, lamb, you don't talk to your mother. Thank Heaven. I hope she's younger than I am?"

"My age, or thereabout. You're incomparable, Mother. Look, give my love to Father—"

"No—tell me about her. Is she pretty?"

"No. She's . . . How much time do you have?"

It was the longest talk I've had with my mother in years.

Letting Mouse go is rather like reconstructive surgery. I'm told I'll be better off, I know it's going to hurt a lot, and so I don't let myself think about it. When I wake up at night, I run lines in my head, to block it out of my mind. I'm a working man; I can't afford to brood.

.13.

PARKWAY:
FIRST DAY OF PRODUCTION

[*Inspector Quin: I should have let you know about this earlier, but it's been a long day. Here it is.*]

This morning, early, I got a phone call. It wasn't anybody I wanted to hear from. "Hi, how're you doing?" Wyndham asked, as if he wanted to know.

My diaphragm heaved. "Nance—Is she out of hospital?"

His cheery voice came down several notches, emphasizing its hollowness. "No. I don't know how much longer she can hold on. I wish they'd let her go peacefully."

"I'm sorry. I—I didn't realize—What can I do for you?"

"I got a question. They didn't search you before they let you leave our suite yesterday, did they?"

"Search me? No. Why?"

"Did you happen to see my pistol while you were there?"

"Geez. No, weren't you wearing it?"

"I don't carry it unless I need to. You know," he added.

I swallowed resentment. "Have you reported it missing?"

"I decided to come to you first. What did you do with it?"

"I never saw it."

"I don't want to make a big deal out of this. We have to consider Nancy and Michaella. Had you gotten rid of it by the time we talked?"

"I told you, I didn't see your—"

"I don't want to go to the police over this."

I gritted teeth. "Look. I'm sorry for you, and all that—"

"Why are you being so evasive? It doesn't do any good. If my gun doesn't turn up in the next couple of hours, I *will* report it to the proper authorities, and I *will* get a new one. Got that? I just want to feel secure." He rang off. It was getting late. I didn't have time to call Golde Silver about it, so I had to go to work in that frame of mind. Fortunately, I'm playing a jerk.

The studio is still in the grip of clue-hunters, so the schedule's had another overhaul. With the weather set for a dry spell, Tony took us to the horse ranch to shoot exteriors.

We had to get complicated permission slips or something from the Sheriff, because the horse ranch is in Watauga County. The site's probably crawling with unobtrusive deputies from the two counties, but most of us have forgotten to care. Today we started production.

That meant I had to get up on a horse.

I know that there are lots of people who love horses. You may be one of them. Me, I don't like horses. Sure, I like to look at them. I like to watch other people ride them. But they're big. They have blunt instruments on the ends of their legs, where most animals have feet. They don't like me.

The scene itself is a snap. Badger has been bragging to Andrea about being a great cowboy. One morning, Sarah takes him out and puts him on the Dun. Badger falls off, looks up to see Andrea watching him. A stunt guy takes the fall. All I have to do is hit the ground and look stupid. A snap. Julien enjoys it.

At seven this morning, with a yak-hair moustache and an extra layer of make-up to hide the healing burns, I took a deep breath of crisp air and approached the horse. Tony and Dora, squinting against the slanting sun, waited. Phina and her camera crew waited. The whole team of electronics experts waited. Halla, in old-fashioned jodhpurs, with freshly brightened hair, waited, her braced leg dragging behind her out of camera range. I took a deep breath, stepped up to the mounting block. The horse turned its head and looked at me.

I must not hesitate. I've been having lessons, so I knew I could do this. I grabbed the back of the saddle with one hand, a fistful of mane with the other, put a foot in the stirrup—

"No!" Halla said, automatically.

Out of the corner of my eye I saw Tony twirl his hand. Phina kept things rolling. I prefer to be warned when I'm supposed to improvise, but this was no big problem.

Halla narrowed Sarah's eyes. "What are you doing?"

Badger slapped a tan, unresponsive neck. "Getting up on this nag, if you don't mind, Little Lady."

Sarah nodded. "Good. Do it again, just that way."

"Okey-dokey—" I repeated what I'd started to do. Halfway to the saddle I saw what was wrong, swung back to the mounting block, feeling like a fool. "See? I was checking something out," Badger said.

"Put your *left* foot into the stirrup, *if* you want to face forward," Sarah sneered.

I did. As soon as I sat in the saddle, Tony yelled "Cut! Print that—print it! My divinities!"

The crew stirred, exchanged grins, shook themselves into working rhythm. Tony raved. We were all kinds of immortals. "*Can* you do it again? Make Uncle Anton divinely happy?"

We worked with the horse all morning. Badger got up, and Sarah showed him how to handle the reins, and then the horse took a step or two out of the frame. After that first look, the horse was completely unaware of my existence, as far as I could tell. Badger clucked at it to make it go, but I doubt that the horse took the slightest notice.

Lunch came sooner than I thought it would. I caught up with Halla as she arranged her crutches under her arms. We asked, "Are you okay?" We both nodded.

Halla stopped by the wrangler who was undressing the horse. As he hefted the saddle to the top of the fence, she said, "Tim, hey. If this were a chestnut, I'd call him Babe."

"You'd call him right," Tim said. "Like his new paint job?"

The horse butted its head against Halla's shoulder. Apparently that's the equine idea of a caress. Halla melted. "Hey, Baby, do buckskins have more fun?" The horse lowered its head and nudged its face under her arm. She played out a blatant love scene right there in front of me with this horse, scratching between its ears and rubbing its face.

As we came away, I said, "I'm jealous."

"Babe was bottle-fed; he's like a puppy. I teach riding here, sometimes. Do you want me to skritch your ears?"

"Not my ears, and not until we're married."

She dimpled, and then stopped to face me. "Matt, don't. I won't marry you. Please—"

"Sorry, I couldn't let that go by. I'll wait, but you shall marry me, you know, sooner or later."

"'*Shall*?' So correct. Where did you go to school?"

"Different places around the known world. Father worked for the State Department. *Will you, nill you, I will marry you.*" I looked around. The crew had gone in to lunch. "Look. I have to finish falling off the horse, and Julien and I have the hayloft scene this afternoon, but—" We headed for the ranch house and lunch, as I struggled for words. "I—I need a favor."

"It's yours, short of marriage. What is it?"

"It's—Look. I've had some riding lessons, but—well, you saw me. I have to look competent for the rest of this production. Can you give me lessons after work, or something? If it's too much—but I'll take you to dinner, drive you home—"

"Sure." She aimed a grin sideways at me. "Why was that so hard to ask?"

"I feel like an idiot. Are you sure you're not too tired?"

"Are you sure you're okay?" She turned to look at me straight on. "How's your back?"

"Loosening up. I've felt worse."

I spent several hours after lunch working, first falling in the dirt, then rolling in the hay. After I cleaned up, Halla and I met like conspirators in the indoor ring. The horse stood dressed and ready, with its wrangler in attendance. I stopped. "Hasn't this one been working all day?"

"All's he did was let you get on and off," Tim said. "If you don't ride him, I will. Work his kinks loose."

Halla showed me around the horse, and then had me sit on top of it, my arms folded, and my legs dangling down, the stirrups crossed on the saddle in front of me. The beast walked around the ring, as she called orders—"Keep your heels down— Move with him—Head up—Move with him—Sit up—Heels down—" The first time I fell off, I thought it was my last. The horse turned, lowered its head to blow on me. I froze, watching huge, hard hooves, each one potentially packing half a ton of horse. Any one of them could crush whatever part of me the beast decided to trample first.

Halla hobbled toward me through the deep mulch. "Matt! Are you all right?"

"So far. I—Hal, what—what do I do?"

She stopped, her mouth tightening downward. "Keep your heels down next time." She added with a straight face, "Right now, take the reins and mount up."

"But will the horse let me?"

"He's waiting for you. Don't waste his time. Pat him and tell him it's not his fault. He won't hurt you, Matt. Come on."

Gingerly, I obeyed. The horse graciously accepted my apology. Under its smooth hair, muscles lived warm and very strong. A huge, powerful beast was letting me do these things to it, without showing the slightest resentment. That's what's so astonishing about these animals—not their size or grace or strength, but their incredible tolerance for idiots like me.

Halla is very wise. She allowed us a good, long—what did she call it—skritch—before she called us to order again. By the time the lesson was finished, so was I. Forty-five minutes of riding around a ring on top of a walking horse is a lot trickier than you'd think. I was drained.

Was that the end of it? No-no-no. Halla insisted that I undress the horse and clean it up. I covered my nerves with some white-knuckled acting. That beast still had hooves and powerful, square teeth. Under Halla's supervision, I rubbed the horse down and put it away in its stall, checking to see that it had water and feed.

Halla went with the wrangler to help clean the saddle and stuff. I stayed a moment beside the stall, watching the horse crunch well-deserved hay. The whole stable was a quiet symphony of feeding animals, salty, sweet smells of beast and fodder. I could hear Halla and the wrangler talking in the tack room. A few light bulbs strung along the rafters multiplied rather than dispelled the shadows.

I can't tell when the talking faded off. I'm not sure I didn't do some fading myself. I was startled wide awake by a rustle in the dark. I can't be sure how it happened. I stepped away from the stall door and it rattled sharply. As I spun back, the door opened, and a rough hand shoved me between the shoulder blades. I stumbled into the stall. The latch clicked into place.

The beast loomed through the half-dark, gazing at me with a few bits of hay hanging out of its mouth. Horses are strict vegetarians, I've heard. I backed up against the wall farthest from the creature, praying that it would not resent my intrusion.

A deep, bass voice came apparently out of the horse. "Well, looky here. Our hee-ro."

Dear God, that voice. Ken Beller was right there in the stable—somewhere. "P-please." I breathed, urgently. "Look, whatever you do, d-don't hurt the horse. Please don't—"

"You lied to me, Hee-ro. We found the kid in your car."

I straightened; my hands knotted into fists. Don't ask what I thought I was capable of. I've always considered myself a wimp. "What did you do to her?"

"Let her out and seen her home, what'd you think?"

"Hang on, you know where she lives? Who is she?"

"Quit playing hero, Hee-ro. She don't want nothing to do with you. We found the gentleman and we showed him more'n he ever wanted to know about the birds and the bees, know what I mean? He won't likely touch nobody that way for a spell. You let her alone, you hear me?"

"But if you know—"

"I know everything. Her, him, you, your gal, your ex; hell, I know who killed Crystal."

"Who? Look, it's murder. Anyone who kills once can kill again. You're in danger—"

"I know what I'm doing, Hee-ro. You don't. How's that mustash of yours?"

"You're a vandal. That moustache was a work of art. Look, at least tell the police—"

"Shit. Quit aggravating the horse." The stall door rattled and swung open. It took me a moment or two to get myself together and through it. I latched the gate carefully, thinking hard. I decided not to mention this to Halla. No sense in scaring us both silly. I took her to dinner, drove her home, got a hug at her door for it, took a detour up on the Parkway to write this. Driving's when I do my best thinking, outside the shower.

Some misfit has stolen Wyndham's damned gun, a murderer is running around loose, and they're probably the same person. Ken Beller says he knows who it is. I hope this helps you. I'll bring it around and hand it in to whoever's at the Sheriff's office now, then go back to Tara—MTL.

.14.

TARA: ALMOST LATE:
THE ARRESTING DOG

Dear Mouse,
    You'll like this. A County car was parked across the entrance to the lot when I got in to Tara this evening. I parked beside the office, walked around the building. Tony, Dora, and Phina sat outside, arguing their way through a drift of papers. A couple of deputies moved in and out of our rooms, apparently at whim.

I came to a halt. "What's going on?"

"Search warrant," Tony said, without looking up. "Listen, Dora has an idea about Halla. Right in our faces, if we knew where to look. It's why I keep her around. Get a chair."

It was better than brooding, Mouse. Work insulates me from my life. That's not a bad thing, some nights. I dragged a white plastic chair from somewhere, sat among them. "What are they searching for?"

Phina tossed a crumpled paper accurately into the wastebasket they'd brought outside with their work. "Evidence. Clues. Who knows?"

"What's this about Hal?"

Dora handed me a rough draft of some kind. I strung on my glasses. If I concentrated on shooting schedules, I could forget other things for a while. Dora said, "The weather's supposed to be dry till Saturday. See, if we shoot from scene sb-256 on, and get as many ranch scenes done as we can this week, we'll be that far ahead. Halla can use Sarah's crutches. Her knee sprain can stand in for the broken thighbone, and you'll get the riding behind you."

Phina grinned. "The Demon Dun horse came in from Illinois. He's all ready to go."

I sat up straight. "No way. I won't get on that animal—"

They passed around a smirk before Tony said, "Take it easy. You only have to ride the quiet plug. Guess who doubles for you, riding—Dakota. He turns out to be an expert on a horse. We had to find another murderer. We voted on that guy Wyndham, okay with you?"

"Sure, why not?"

"Good. Next week is supposed to be dry, after Tuesday. We can crash Badger's car then. Dora, I want a junk car, not too fancy. I rewrote Badger losing his car. It doesn't get repossessed; he totals it. I want a good visual."

Phina sneered. "Everyone crashes cars," she said. "I want something more. We already have fire, when the ranch gets torched, so I want something—how about a flash flood? Badger's car gets swept down the canyon in a muddy—"

"And we fit a whole new set into the budget—where?"

"We'll do Scene asb-181 through to Sarah's fall after we do the horse show," Dora said before Phina could answer him. "Halla should be ready to ride then. How's that?"

"You see? She's a genius," Tony said. "We can crash the car after the—" He stiffened, squinting. "My good God, do you see that animal move!"

Phina straightened, the sneer dissolving from her face. The Beller County K-9 unit, Slocum and dog, had arrived to back up the search warrant. The dog looked like a shaggy Rin-Tin-Tin, with Siamese-cat markings—light tan body, and dark face, paws, and tail. It's a beautiful animal, huge and well muscled, moves like a helium balloon. Watching it was pure pleasure. You don't see dogs like that in Central Park, Mousy.

Phina dived into the room she now shares with Dora. We could hear her negotiating with one of the searchers for the use of a couple of her cameras.

Slocum set the dog to snuffling all over our rooms, even the bathrooms. Tony pushed a wry smile to one cheek. "Searching for drugs," he said.

"Drugs?" I said. "Why drugs?"

The way he looked at me said I had a lot to learn about some things. "Wake up, infant. All the movin' pitcher folk do drugs, everybody knows that. Like, River Phoenix? Robert Downey, Junior? Lawmen do this, every location I shoot on. My good God, that dog must have taken ballet lessons." Phina and Dora were as unbothered as Tony. A question I'd never had the nerve to ask even myself evaporated and blew away.

The dog found nothing incriminating and kvetched about it, whining, begging to keep on searching somewhere else. Slocum showed it the wastebasket we were using. Nothing. The dog whined for more. Phina came out of her room with a compact camera. She's a sucker for great movement, and every move that dog made sang. She approached Slocum.

Phina's usually an abrasive personality, but when she wants something, she can look like a waif painting by Keene. Her huge, black eyes glow, her face gets sweet and wistful. I'd swear her hair shines and her cheekbones pop out to cast shadows. Slocum fell hard, started calling her "Cutie." Tony, Dora and I silently promised each other never to let Phina forget that someone called her *Cutie.*

Slocum put the dog through its paces, while Phina knelt in the middle of the parking lot with the hand-held camera. She sat down and shot some more. By the time she thought she had enough, she was lying prone in the gravel.

Slocum grinned, showing haphazard dental work. "Want to see Tabu here arrest a guy?" He winked. "You're going to like this, Cutie. Which one of them's the slickest?"

"Matt's slick," Dora said, before I could react.

"Sounds to me like she's lying," Slocum commented. Country doesn't mean clueless, Mouse. "You snooze, you lose, Young'n." Your old Dad's well over forty, Mousekin. Slocum may be past thirty, but I doubt it. I like this guy.

He unsnapped the leash from the dog's harness, had me stand in the middle of the parking lot. "I want you to run to that vehicle for me. When you get there, freeze and put your hands up. Don't move, now."

I have never yet refused a stunt. On the other hand, the stunts I'm asked to do normally don't involve a dog that would kill me on command. I did a quick calculation in my head about who'd be responsible for my death, decided it was Slocum, so he probably knew what he was doing, and I was reasonably safe as long as I followed directions.

I was about to push off and run when Tony called a halt. I hoped he had second thoughts about getting me mauled. He rummaged in his car and came up with Badger's hat and jacket. "Badger's car gets impounded," he said. "It'll be great. Get dressed. Come on."

"What, I have to change my pants, too?" Badger wears tight jeans. I like loose khakis.

Tony squinted at my hips. "No, it'll be a long shot. Ask and you shall receive. Phina, my fairy, are you happy? We can save thousands on this scene."

Slocum chuckled at me. "Friend of your'n?"

"Used to be." I shrugged into the jacket, donned the hat.

Two deputies stood by their car, spitting discreetly. Phina waved them out of the picture. Nothing scares her away from a good shot. Slocum seconded Phina, so the deputies moved.

All dressed up for the kill, I checked that dog and handler were set, pushed gravel, sprinted for the car. It's hard to explain. I had no hope of outrunning that dog, but I ran, hard. Within touching distance of the car I skidded, halted, froze. Then I remembered, threw my hands up above my head.

The dog rattled gravel. I looked over my shoulder.

"*Freeze!*" the dog snarled. I whipped my head around to the front, decided to stay that way till time ended, or Slocum called off his dog, whichever came first. The dog added something unprintable.

"Oh, Yesss!" Phina breathed.

Slocum came up, said something to release the dog. I stayed where I was, thank you. "You're fine, you can relax now. You get that, Cutie?"

I ventured another look behind me. The dog sat next to Slocum's leg as the deputy talked with Phina and Tony, a few yards off. I lowered my hands; the dog never acknowledged my existence. I guessed I was safe for the moment. Adrenaline drained out of me, fizzing all the way.

One of the deputies shifted his tobacco wad. "Old Tabu's a pretty good dog," he remarked, to be neighborly.

"You didn't see Tabu from where I was standing."

They grinned. The other one spat, shook his head. "Nope. You were fine. Tabu's a good dog."

Did you think that was the end of it? No-no-no-no-no. Phina got serious, set up lights, took measurements. Tony wanted close-ups. Slocum cleared it with the dispatcher, and signed Dora's form so he could play the arresting officer. Tabu hoped I'd try something funny so it could tear my throat out. We worked in the parking lot till well after dark. For the last shot, Slocum had Tabu leap over Phina as she lay flat on her back with the camera chugging. It'll be a terrific shot. The whole scene scared the bejazus out of me.

It must have been close to ten when Phina and Tony decided they had what they wanted. Slocum took off the dog's harness and spoke. The dog danced around its handler, begging, cajoling. Slocum pulled a floppy stuffed thing out of the patrol car and offered a tug-o'-war. The dog transformed into a pup, windmilling its tail, growling gleefully, pulling and shaking the toy, bounding after it like a springbok whenever Slocum got it away and threw it. At last, with a laugh and a tussle of the dog's ears, Slocum opened the rear door of his patrol car and spoke. Tabu sprang up and landed in a cage that took up most of the back seat.

"You keep police dogs in cages?" I said.

"Crates," Slocum said. "It keeps him restrained, like a seat belt. You wouldn't believe the number of people that lets a dog or a kid ride loose in a vehicle. Then they wonder why they take a fender-bender, the kid hits the dash and crushes his face in. Riding a kid loose in the car's a criminal offense in North Carolina. It ought to be against the law to ride a dog loose, too. You can get jail time for riding a kid without a seat restraint, but people still do it. Hard to believe, ain't it."

A surge of physical nausea sloshed around my stomach. You were riding loose when I smashed my car, Mousy. What ever made me think I had the slightest claim on you all these years? "At least they don't always get hurt," I muttered.

Slocum was inexorable. "Don't you bet your kid's life on it. You maybe once in a blue moon see a kid killed when he's riding restrained. A kid that wasn't hurt wasn't riding loose. I can practically guarantee it." He gave the dog a last rub or two under its chin and closed the crate.

For the first time ever, I faced cold, bare facts. I could have killed you, Mouse. By every physical law known to science, you ought to be dead. When the time comes, I'd better sign the adoption release with a decent good grace, and leave you to be reared by the people who deserve you.

We played the sequence on the monitor, and that's when I saw what they'd been doing with me. Tabu chased me down, almost had me, when I stopped with my hands in the air. The dog slammed on the brakes in mid-leap, landed sitting, and drooled. That first time, when I peered over my shoulder, I barely missed being its supper.

I'm not sure how Tony plans to work that scene into *Demon Dun*'s opening, but it'll be there, probably behind the credits. After the scare I've had, he'd better use those shots and get an Oscar for them.

Dora waved a phone in the air. "Matt, it's for you. You have a visitor at the office."

"Why didn't the clerk send them around to our room?"

Dora handed the phone over. "The regular guy's out sick. This is the owner. Harry Houdini might get past Sherlock Holmes, the Marine Corps, and the IRS, but he wouldn't get past Sharon Beller."

Deputies crowded into our room, wanting to see every take we'd got of the dog chase and Badger's arrest. I put the phone to my ear, leaned against the car, turned my back. "This is Matt." On-screen, Tabu snarled at me. The deputies cheered. I plugged my other ear.

Ma'am said, "Mr. Logan, I got a lady here, says you want to see her. I think it's another damn reporter. She said I better call you first, but I can kick her out. Want me to?"

"Er—no." You don't kick journalists out unless you plan to retire to Greenland tomorrow. "Did she give a name?"

"She thought I ought to know it. Let me kick her out."

"No, I'll come around. I think I know who it is." I rang off, and a metallic shudder shook my spine. Damn. Only one "reporter" I know expects instant, universal recognition. Your Aunt Meranda's mean, Mouse. In Rome once, she hung all my underwear out on the—never mind. I strode around to the office, wrenched the door open. "What are you doing here?"

Meranda turned, one eyebrow arched, her fine jawline slightly off-center. "The local defenders of the law called me in for a grill session after your murder mystery here, so—What the hell happened to your face?"

"Why can't you leave me alone?"

"You don't think I'd leave here without seeing you?"

"Since when do you care what I don't think?"

"That's your problem: you don't think. You react. You moralize, stuff only a rag like the *Probe* could print. 'Reality keeps me sober?' I'm embarrassed to be related to you."

"Hang about. Did you say—?"

"I said I'm embarrassed—"

"I heard you. 'Reality keeps me sober.' That bit didn't get into the article." I can't believe I didn't put it together till now. "*You* bought my journal from Crystal Beller?"

Ma'am leaned powerful arms on the counter. "Why would a reporter want to do you like that?"

"I am not a reporter, I'm—Can't we do this somewhere else?" Meranda demanded.

"Because she's too old to drape my underwear out in public, Ma'am. She's my sister."

"Nobody trashes my brother. That's my job. You don't—ever—talk to me that way. How dared you hang up on me?"

Ma'am pronounced, "You got no call to turn around and sell his diary to the papers."

"Sell it, hell, I practically had to pay them to print that drivel. I'm surprised he managed a complete sentence."

For maybe the first time in her career, Meranda von Kozak failed to steamroll her victim. "Do you have any idea of the damage you could have caused?"

"Cut the melodrama, Brat. If Michaella saw the thing at all, at least she'd know you love her. That's more than Nancy ever told her. You ought to thank me for letting her know."

"The first—the only time I tried to see her, Nancy pulled her out of her school. She'd gone to that school since she was three; she loved it there. Maybe you've forgotten how much you liked starting out in a new school every time Father was reassigned."

"Nancy's a twit. She didn't have to disrupt the kid's life."

"Maybe not, but she did it. If I make a wrong move, my— M-Mickie pays. You knew that. You knew it."

"I did not. I wondered why you'd been behaving so nicely all this time. So blackmail's the way to your heart?"

I swung my back into her face. "Ma'am, you're right. It's another damned reporter. Kick her out."

The skull under Ma'am's lacy dress glared. Meranda actually skipped a beat. "What—Wait a minute—Very well, Brat— Matts—I'm sorry. I shouldn't have done it."

"Look, get out, g-go back to the White House. I'm sick of you and your k-k-ind. Geez, c-an't you leave the ki-kids alone, they can't c-con-trol—" I stopped to breathe.

"Kids-zz?" Your Aunt Meranda holds one of the most passionately coveted jobs in the world, mainly because she never misses anything, ever. "You said kids, plural. Whose kid-zz? You've stopped talking about Mickie."

"Forget it. Go home and expose the Vice President." I reached for the door.

Meranda planted her back against it. "What kids-zz? What are you talking about?"

I may have mentioned pit bulls in connection with my sister, Mousy. The only really smart move was to give it up. "I don't suppose you actually read the *Probe*?"

"My favorite literature, next to *War and Peace* and the *Congressional Record*. Wait a minute, I'm getting something—'*My Mom Didn't Do It*'? Is this about the Mom?"

"Hal," I told the post card rack.

"Hal? And what's a Hal when he's at home?"

"Not he."

Headlights swept across the front window. Ma'am, until now a fascinated audience, straightened up. "Y'all want to go

Dear Mouse . . . 179

somewheres else? I got paying customers." Meranda caught my arm, hustled me outside.

"Hang on." I closed the door behind me. "Hang about. How did you know 'Reality keeps me sober'? Crystal kept that sheet."

"She did? Then you must have written it twice. Your writing's full of those little moralities. What about this Hal?"

"Leave her alone."

"Look, I admit it: I was wrong, I shouldn't have done it. I wouldn't admit that for the President. Enjoy it. What's Hal, and why does her cub matter?"

We walked in no particular direction, across the road and up the hill. Ma'am watches TV, but she hadn't recognized Meranda von Kozak in faded jeans, without the lip gloss and designer ensemble. Meranda's tall like Mother, so our steps matched comfortably.

I said, "Halla works on *Demon Dun*—"

"Eyes? Hair? I'll check a Barbie doll for the rest."

"Not if you want to know Hal. She's—"

"Pretty?"

"No. Good. Strong. Kind. Smart. Funny. . . . " I went three more paces before I noticed Meranda wasn't with me.

She'd stopped, hands planted dramatically on hips. "My God, don't tell me my little brother's growing up at last? No, don't get mad again. This Hal—Halla?—objects to having her kid in a tabloid's headlines. I can't say I blame her, but it'll be yesterday's news tomorrow. Why not tell her to get over it?"

"She can't afford to. Dannal's father and stepmother object, too. I gather they can pay for better lawyers than Halla can. They have joint custody now, but—Damn. *Damn!*"

Meranda stood still, said nothing. It's one of her most insidious tactics. In the dark, I couldn't see her face, but I knew it was being open, sympathetic, vulnerable. It's a look they teach you in journalist school. Nobody does it better than your Aunt Meranda. The woman's a bloodsucker. Resistance is futile, as the queen pointed out. "I'm—rel-releasing her for adoption."

"So Mother told me. What the hell are you thinking?"

"Mickie's better off without me. I'm no good for her."

"Sure, who told you that? Look, Matts, don't underesti-

mate Mickie. Strong women run in our family. Logans breed
strength, Logans marry strength. Stop wallowing in that damned
self-pity of yours and fight."

"I've fought for three years. It doesn't do her any good, and
I'm tired of losing."

"My God, you're such a wimp. So, who planted the story
in the *Probe*, the kid's father?"

"Roland? What are you talking about?" I realized with a
shock that my sister was being tactful, changing the subject.
"I—No. No, Roland threatens to take Halla to court over it."

"Somebody in charge of the kid had to authorize that story.
Tabloids don't print just anything, you know."

"Sure, models of discretion, those rags."

"Look. Why did the *Probe* say 'Mouse' was Nancy?"

I stopped to frown at her. "The reporter got it wrong—"

"Get a clue. I did some editing, or they wouldn't have
touched your journal, no matter how juicy it was. Which it
wasn't, I hasten to add. Some guardian released the story about
Whatsername's—Halla's kid; otherwise, it wouldn't have seen
the light of day."

"This explains why you were billed as a dethroned princess—unnamed. So what does the *Probe* hold sacred?"

"Their bottom line. Irate parents tend to win lawsuits."

I shook my head. "I don't get it. Hal's dumping me to keep
Dannal's name out of the tabloids. Roland's only waiting for
his wife to get in from Florida before he sues for custody. Who
else could authorize a story about Dannal?"

"I suggest you find out before they print a sequel."

"Find out? How?"

"Cheat. Use your brain. It's your quest, for God's sake. Do
I have to tell you everything?"

I can't say we got cozy, but for the first time in years I came
through a talk with my sister, and neither of us wanted to throw
mudballs at the other.

.15.

SHERIFF'S OFFICE: GUNS AND HORSES FOR INSPECTOR QUIN

This morning, Tony was dressing by the light of the pre-dawn news broadcast on TV when I came out of the bathroom wearing only a towel. Phina knocked once on the door and barged in. She glanced at me, barely hesitated. "Oops, sorry, Matt. Tony, I got it. I can make the jumping stunt work. Listen—I hang out under the hurdle, Dakota rides the horse over it—"

Tony held up a hand: "Sssh, what was that? Listen!" A portrait, probably from an overexposed snapshot, filled the screen: scruffy face, cocky smirk, bad teeth, baseball cap.

"Okay-okay, but Tony—"

"Sssh!"

She ssshed. The voice-over was saying, "So far, no arrest has been made, but the Beller County Sheriff has confirmed that a relative of the victim was questioned and released earlier this morning. We have also learned that in the course of the questioning, actor Matt Logan was accused of the shooting. You may remember Matt Logan's dressing room is where the body of the victim's estranged wife, starlet Crystal Beller, was found earlier this week, strangled by a tie that was a part of Logan's costume. This is the second murder in less than two weeks for the once sleepy town of Beller Mountain . . . "

"Ken Beller," Tony said. "Son of a bitch who burned Matt's face. What do you think of that?"

I secured the towel, gaping like a stranded fish. "How?"

"Shot, on the golf course. It looked like suicide—gunpowder residue on his hands and everything—only they can't find the weapon."

I groped around the nightstand for my phone. Golde Silver's machinery directed me to wait while it rang through to her bedroom. I don't know when she sleeps. She came directly to the point. "Where were you last night between sunset and nine-thirty?"

"On the Parkway at sunset, just driving. I can't prove it. I didn't see anyone but a fox and a few deer. Geez. Was it Wyndham's gun?"

"They haven't found the weapon. Listen, this is important. Can you be sure whoever talked to you in the stable the other night was Ken Beller?"

"It was the same voice I heard up on the Starling Head. I hear it in my nightmares."

"God, what a witness. Where'll you be today?"

"Working, if they don't arrest me."

She didn't chuckle audibly. "Meggy hasn't even decided it was murder, yet. Hate to disappoint you. Don't leave the—what do you call it—the soundstage?"

"The horse ranch? I won't, but—how can she believe Ken Beller would commit suicide?"

"I don't think she believes anything right now. They appreciated your writing, the other night. Why not call me?"

"I tried, but all I got was your machine—"

"I have call forwarding, if you'd've just waited a minute. Never mind," she said before I could reply. "Thanks for calling." She rang off, too busy to annoy me.

Phina barely acknowledged the interruption. Not much distracts her when it comes to getting the right shot. She pitched her idea as I put the phone back. "Tony, listen, we get an intern to toss dirt at the lens, so Matt can—okay-okay—Matt, you're off the phone? How brave are you?"

"Craven coward. Don't even think about it. Does anyone mind if I get dressed?"

"No, listen—you won't get hurt. We put that pit of mulch all around the outdoor jump to cushion falls. It's about two miles deep. Be a sport."

"Why did we hire Dakota?" I demanded.

Phina reddened, looked to Tony.

I mentally kicked myself. "I mean, what's Dakota's job?"

"Oh." She shrugged. "Doubling you, but Matt—"

"Bingo." I said. "Let him do his job. It'll work, Phina."

It didn't work. Phina tried everything, but there was no way to film the Demon Dun horse leaping over the camera, without making it obvious that I wasn't on top. We wasted half the day on it, while a dozen extras in horse show costumes stood around getting paid, and deputies from two counties hung around, surveilling or protecting or whatever.

Standing in the stirrups, butt in the air, fingers gripping the horse's mane, I cantered my sweet-tempered plodder up to the jump—Halla's taught me to enjoy cantering—while Phina filmed from the far side of the hurdle. An intern tossed a clod of mud at the camera to hide the edit, and then Dakota rode the Demon Dun over the jump, like a demigod on Pegasus.

Badger's no demigod, and the Babe's no Demon Dun. The camera didn't buy it. With lunchtime approaching, Phina stood up, her face set like concrete. Her shoulders looked as if they wanted to heave the over-observant camera into the mulch pit.

I dismounted, handed Badger's riding crop to a props person, fingered the buckle of my helmet. Dakota rode the Demon Dun up close to Phina, leering, rubbing her nose in it.

I abandoned cowardice. "Phina, hang on, what if you lower the jump to about that high, and I ride the Babe over it? I think I can stay on long enough for you to get the shot." I reached for the crop again. "Tony, do you want me to try it?"

Phina's face lit up as brightly as it did when she first saw Slocum's dog. "Would you?"

"It's a special technique," Dakota objected. "This isn't for amateurs. You can't do it."

Tony ignored him. "What does Halla say?"

"She's in physical therapy this morning," Dora said. "Her make-up call's for noon. D'you want to wait for her?"

I took in a deep breath, maybe one of my last. "It's almost

noon now. Can we try?" Dakota got down from the Dun, handed its reins to a wrangler, headed for Wardrobe.

"No, 'Kota, stick around," Phina ordered. "We might want to use you again." He came back with a martyred sigh.

I'd made up my mind to suicide, so I decided to enjoy the ride. The Babe canters like a rocking horse. I rode all the way around the ring before steering for the jump. As it came at us, I assumed the position, grabbed two fistfuls of mane, pressed my legs into the horse's flanks, and went soaring over the hurdle.

Alone.

The horse declined, thank you. Forefeet planted before the jump, it skidded to a stop and ducked. I tumbled over its ears into the deep, soft mulch. The horse mouthed its bit, shook its head, and stepped daintily over the jump to look down at me.

Only Dakota laughed out loud, but everyone else on the site wanted to. I handed out the Famous Grin, collected the reins. "Let's try it again."

We tried again. The horse refused again. "Push him," Dakota called. "You got to push him harder!"

I pushed as hard as my legs could squeeze. This time I was ready. I only shifted to one side when the horse refused.

"Come on!" Dakota called. "What do you think that thing in your hand is for, anyway?"

I looked at the crop I'd been carrying. The horse turned its head and nosed the toe of my boot. I straightened in the saddle, and the crop fell to the ground. "Oops," I said. I sat back, lowered my hands. My leg pressed, my fingers tightened on the reins. The Babe took a single, amazingly precise step diagonally backward. The crop snapped under half a ton of hoof.

"Geez. Sorry," I lied. I scratched deep into the roots of the mane. I doubt that I could get a horse to do that again in a thousand years.

"What are you doing?" Halla, on time for her noon make-up call, surveyed us, frowning. "You're not trying to jump the Babe?"

A deep silence all around. Tony broke it. "What's the problem? You know something we don't know?"

"Apparently I do. Babe doesn't jump."

Tony glared at the wranglers sitting on the top rail of the

fence. "Babe doesn't jump," he rasped. "You have a mouth, I have ears. You couldn't say it?"

The wrangler gawked. "I'm sorry, Mr. Pornada, I didn't know. I'm one of Dunny's wranglers. From Illinois."

Another wrangler hastened to add, "We don't know nothing about this one. Tim's his wrangler. He's in the can."

Halla said, "If Babe can't step over it or walk around it, it'll hold him till Doomsday. We could keep him in a playpen."

Tony spoke for us all. "Shit."

Phina tucked what she felt firmly behind her face. No director of photography should have to look like that. I said, "Hang about!" It got their attention. "The other horse jumps, right?"

"Like a bird," Halla said.

"You can't ride him," Dakota said. "You couldn't hold him. He'd run you all the way to Graceland before he stops."

I looked to Halla. "This is important, Hal. Is there any way I can stay on the Dun horse until it gets over the jump?"

"You'd just be a passenger. He's a sweet horse, but . . . "

I turned to Tony. "Let me try. Come on, I've been falling off all morning. It hasn't killed me yet." I appealed to the Demon Dun's wranglers. "Would it bother the horse?"

Halla said, "Dakota could take him over the jump, and he'll get used to what we want. Then you get up on him—"

"And stay there," Phina kicked in.

With a new shot of energy, we temporarily forgot about lunch to make it happen. Once I was on the horse, Halla moved to its shoulder for some last words with me. "Dunny's a lot of horse, Matt, but he knows his job. Just sit there and let him do it. If you want him to do something, just think about it—and don't think too hard. Keep your legs down; grab mane, not reins. Try to move with him, the way you do on Babe, okay?"

The Dun was exactly what Halla said—a lot of horse. Moving with it was easy. I felt its power through the saddle. Riding it gave me a hint at why Halla and Dakota get so passionate about horses. The Dun did for me what it had done for Dakota, and I rode a horse all the way over a jump for the first time in my life.

The landing was rough. I ended up in the mulch again. Phina pulled a fist of air into her side. "Yesss! Got it!"

I sprang up, dusting off my seat. "No, I know what I did wrong. Let me do it again."

"Matt, are you crazy?" Tony said. "You don't have to— Did you hit your head?"

"No, I want to do it right—I wasn't ready for the down side of the jump. Hal, what do I do, lean back?" I reached for the Demon Dun's reins. "Come on, one more time?"

The wrangler handed me the reins. "Man, you got guts."

Guts had nothing to do with it. Exhilaration swept me along like a fresh river. "Look, I can do it. Let me try."

They let me try, and I did it. It felt like climbing Mount Everest, winning the lottery, leaping a tall building at a single bound. I gave a whoop and the horse gave a leap or two, but I was too jazzed to get scared and fall off. I grabbed mane, collected the reins. The horse started listening to me again. I called, "Did I make it mad or something?"

"He ain't mad," the wrangler said. "He's just picking at you. Dunny knows a amateur when he carries one."

"Yeah, amateur, that's me. One more time, Tony?"

Again I rode Pegasus over a two-foot jump, and Belerophon never had more fun. On the other side, Demon Dun did some more "picking," and shook me off. It came back, lowered its nose and blew on me, to show no hard feelings. I collected the reins, gave the face a rub, rolled over to get up.

"Ow!" Something hard and mean dug into my shoulder. I pushed away mulch. A smallish, shiny thing emerged. It had a hole in one end. Geez. *Geez*! I took off my velvet helmet to cover it. "Get the horse away," I snapped at the wrangler.

They came from all sides:

"Good God—Matt, are you okay?" Halla said.

"Got it! It's beautiful!" Phina said.

"Matt, don't move. Where do you hurt?" Doc said.

"What are you doing?" Tony said.

"What have you got?" said a voice I didn't know. A folder flipped open above me to show a Beller County ID.

I removed the helmet. "I think you're looking for this."

It was time for lunch break. Deputies from all over swarmed onto the area. Phina stayed out there to guard her cameras and film. I don't know what's going to happen to the footage, but Phina's sure to fight for it like a crazed bobcat.

They let me clean up before I came in here to answer endless questions about how I found Wyndham's Vickers in the mulch where I'd been riding expensive horses for five hours this morning. They let me call Golde Silver, of course, but I don't think it made much difference. With my lawyer's blessing, I stayed to lunch on somebody's mom's fried chicken, cucumber salad, rhubarb pie, and syrup-sweetened iced tea, while I wrote this out.

We got the shot, anyway. The sulfur smoke gets added in post-production. Things could be worse.

.16.

MONDAY BEFORE MOTHER'S DAY:
HOMEWORK TIME

D ear Mouse,
I emerged from the Sheriff's office after answering
maybe an hour of questions and writing a statement,
and got back to the site in time to knock out a solid chunk of
Badger's scenes with Sarah, Gideon and Andrea. The horse
show scenes have to wait until deputies from two counties finish with the hurdle set. Tony cussed under his breath in his
native language—not Hungarian. Romanian? I'm still trying to
place it. He grabbed Dora for another schedule overhaul. It's a
pain for the extras, too. A lot of them have to take time off real
jobs to do this.

There was no riding lesson today; I had to drive Halla to
the school to pick up Dannal. I was looking forward to it.
Dannal's a decent kid, Mousy. He lives his own life between
split parents, making the best of what he has. Inevitably, I suppose, I wonder how much you and he have in common.

The air this evening was sharp and fragrant. The sun takes
longer to set these days. With the crew gone, the dust was set-
tling on the mulch pit. The sweet plug that I ride had been turned
loose in the corral for some reason, and I strolled over to lean
on the fence and look at it, while Halla got cleaned up.

The Babe dropped whatever it was doing and came over to
greet me. I should have known. I stepped back. It pressed its
chest against the rails and stretched its neck to reach me, giving
off a tremulous growl. Nobody was around to tell me not to

touch the horse. The horse told me touching it would be fine. I reached toward it, and it reached toward my hand, pushing its face against my fingers. I gave in, skritching and stroking. It's amazing how pleasurable it can be to give pleasure to someone who likes it. "You should give Halla some pointers." I told it. It nodded, pressed for more rubs.

"Terhune calls horses the dullest creatures, pound for pound, in the animal kingdom. Do we have a meeting of the minds?"

I didn't bother to turn. "I thought you went back to Washington. What is it now?"

"You know who planted the story about Halla's kid?" Meranda said.

"No. Thanks for the wild-goose chase. Journalists don't reveal their sources to judges, much less to—"

"Have you ever heard of a J.J. van Dyck?"

"J.J. van Dyck?" I thought, shook my head. "No. Never heard the name."

A crutch knocked against the doorway, and my day improved significantly. Meranda said, "I take it that's Halla."

"Yeah." I made the introduction in form: "Halla McKee works with me here. Hal, this is my sister."

Halla offered a hand and a smile, searching for a resemblance between us. "I'm sorry, I can't say I've heard much about you," she said, and gave a shy laugh. "I'm sure you're tired of being told you look like Meranda von Kozak, but she's one of my heroes."

Meranda raised an exquisitely plucked eyebrow into the shadow of her disreputable hat. "No, actually, I can't say I hear that terribly often."

Halla had a second, sharp look. "Good heavens. I'm sorry— am I chewing shoe leather? Matt never mentioned a sister."

"I'm glad to hear it. That story about your son—"

I sneaked an arm around Halla's waist. "Meranda's an execrable sister, not worth mentioning. Pretty good journalist, but—" The light in Halla's face had gone out. I brought her closer. "Hal, do you know a J.J. van Dyck?"

She all but snorted, pulled away from me. "Why? Did she offer to represent you?"

"Represent me?"

"You could go farther and do worse. She did well enough for Roland before they married."

"J.J. van Dyck is Dannal's stepmother?"

"Hello," Meranda said softly.

"She uses her maiden name professionally. Why?"

Meranda broke the news. "She arranged the *Probe* article about your son."

The reaction was exactly what journalists live for. Halla froze, wide-eyed. Cataclysmic things happened behind her face. After a moment, she said, very quietly, "Are you sure?"

"I'm a—what's that cuss-word you use, Brat?—journalist, that's it. I know how to dig up these details."

It took Halla no more than an instant to suppress the chaos in her head. Stiffly, she offered another smile. "It was nice—" she swallowed— "I'm glad I met you." She turned to me: "Let's not keep Danny waiting."

As we drove to the school, Halla was light years away, buckled into the seat beside me. Her face set and still, she watched mountains pass without sound or sign that anyone occupied her body. It was worse at the school. She went in while I waited in the car. After several minutes, she came crutching out again, with deep grooves between her brows. "They say he took the bus. We'll have to meet him at the apartment. Matt, I don't like this."

Neither did I. I remember enough about the last days of your mother's and my marriage to wish I were anywhere else. There is no right side in a domestic quarrel, Mousekin. Grimly, I drove us back to Halla's apartment. The only side I could legitimately take was hers.

As we swept into the parking lot, she sat up. "Good God, that's Roland's car. I knew something was up. I knew it!"

"Take it easy, Hal. Don't jump to conclusions," I said. It had no effect, of course.

I parked behind Roland's car, blocking it in. Halla was out and limping toward the stairs before I turned my engine off. At the top, Dannal, carrying a backpack, emerged, shepherded by Roland. Halla met them halfway, her crutches braced against the stair rails, barring the way. The fight was on.

I should have turned away, but Dannal's face was white, flat, stony with misery. It could have been any child caught in parental crossfire.

Mousy, it could have been you.

I don't remember getting out of the car, or climbing the steps. I have a vague feeling I did it three or four at a time.

I caught her by the shoulders, forced her to face me. "Halla, stop it," I barked, into her eyes. "You can't win this way. I mean it, Hal. This is not the way to win."

She tried to twist away from me. I held on. "Let me take care of it. Listen to me! This won't win for you, Hal."

She struggled, and I gave her a tiny shake. "Look at Dannal. You can't let him see you like this. Look at him!"

Her eyes wavered, and she looked at her child. Tears welled up, spilled over. She wrenched away from me. It took her too long to crutch up the stairs and slam the door.

I turned to Roland. "Harper, right?" I said heartily. "Roland Harper?" I held out a glad hand. "I've been hoping to run into you again. Look, do you have an agent?"

He took the hand, raised it in a warrior's clasp. "Hey, brother, thanks for getting her under control. Yeah, I have an agent in Nashville. Why?"

"There's a guy in New York looking for your type right now. He specializes in singers." This is perfectly true; Nick Orange started handling Elvis impersonators last year. I slapped pockets. "You have a piece of paper?"

Roland did, and I wrote Orange's name and fax and phone numbers on it. "Fax him a picture and résumé," I said as I wrote, "and can you spare a copy of your album?"

"I still have a bunch of them in my attic," he said eagerly.

This was too easy. "Look, he's not going to waste your time." I added postal and electronic addresses. "I worked with him for a year, then he told me up front he couldn't help me anymore." True again: I came to his office drunk one day, and Orange had me escorted out. "I'd get that album off to him as soon as possible, if I were you. Tell him I sent you." I handed Roland the paper.

Roland accepted it like an award, read it reverently. "I can't believe this. Matt Logan's agent. Thanks, man."

I stopped him as he reached for Dannal. "Look, I know all about court orders," I said. I threw in the Famous Grin. "You don't want to fool with them. Are you violating one now?"

He launched into some of what had been said between him and Halla. I held up a hand. When he paused, I said, "Look, I get around. There's some inside information about that *Probe* article that I'm not at liberty to talk about. I know someone who can, though—she's an agent. Do you know a J.J. van Dyck? She has a local number, actually—"

"Man, you're kidding! Know her! I'm married to her!"

I laid on another coat of honey. "Married—that magnificent woman is J.J. van Dyck? You are one lucky guy. Look, ask her about that article. Then—well, you'll know what to do, I guarantee it. And call Nick Orange soon."

He was all thanks and celebration. I moved my car, and he left Halla's place.

Dannal stood passively where he'd stopped when the fight between his parents began. His backpack trailed beside him. I looked down at him. "Are you all right?"

He nodded, mute.

"Good. Let's go back to your mother. Shall I carry that?"

"No, I can take it. Thanks," he remembered to say.

Halla stood in a chaos of peanut butter, kittens, strawberry jelly, and bread. As I opened the door, she exploded. "Look at this! The cats are out, my kitchen's a mess—"

I caught her again. This time, her attention was easier to grab. I said, "Hal, it's okay. I'll see to the mess—"

"The way you 'saw to' *that*? Thanks! Roland took my—"

I turned her to face the door, and Dannal.

She stared motionless for a full second, then began to shake. I turned her to me, put my arms around her and held on. "Take it easy, Hal. Easy does it. Don't let him see you like this. You have to calm down. Can you take a steamy bath, or read a steamy novel, or something?"

She nodded into my jacket. I could feel her strength as she pulled herself into tight control. Soon enough, she raised her head, wiped her face, turned to Dannal. "Danny, I'm sorry you saw that," she said. "Did the peanut butter fight back?" She dipped a finger in a patch of jelly. "Someone's been bleeding."

A little, relieved smile loosened his face a bit. "Yeah, I think the bread won."

"Help Mr. Logan clean up the mess while I have a bath, will you, darling? Do as he says, and if you finish before I get out, start your homework. No piano until it's done, okay? Put the cats in the other room. It's their supper time." She said to me, "I'm presuming a lot—"

"Go on, Hal. We'll be fine."

Dannal let his backpack fall and gathered up the mother cat. It tribbled in his arms. Five kittens dropped everything to follow their mother into another room, their tails stiff and conical. Halla reached to his head as he passed, kissed his hair, then slipped into her room.

I shed my jacket, rolled up sleeves. Dannal and I got to work on the mess. Peanut butter was smeared in all kinds of unlikely places, usually accompanied by jelly. I soaked a sponge. "Look, your parents both love you—"

Dannal slapped at a puddle of jelly with the dishcloth. "Ah, don't hand me that crap!"

"Crap?"

"*Dannal*!" His mother emerged from her room.

I dropped the sponge, herded her back. "Hal, it's okay."

"But he can't—"

"Please, Hal. Let me." I kissed her forehead and turned her around. "You're not *compos mentis* right now." She leaned back against me, and I let my arms wind around her. For a moment, I wondered what it would be like to be married, and have the right to lock Dannal out of our bedroom for an hour.

Time. She needs time. I called myself to order, steered her into her room. "Go on, Hal. We'll survive."

As I turned to the kitchen, Dannal pushed a truculent shoulder to his ear. "Sorry."

Actually, I didn't feel too *compos* at this, myself, Mousekin. Dannal scrubbed at the counter, his face deep red. I tried again: "Look, I—I need to know. Why is it crap?"

"I said, Sorry," he muttered sullenly.

"No, I know, but—look, I'm not offended. I don't want to harass you. I said the wrong thing, but I don't know why it was wrong. I need to know. It's important."

He eyed me suspiciously. "Why?"

"I—I have a daughter about your age. I rarely see her, and I don't want to—er—hand her any crap. I thought—"

Dannal left the jelly puddle to instruct me. "It's like, *duh*. Like, what's the point? I mean, you know your parents love you, so what? It doesn't give them the right to keep on jabbering, trying to win. All they care about is winning."

"But what if a child doesn't know?"

He rolled his eyes up. "Either you know they love you, or you know they don't. It's still *duh*. It's no excuse."

"But if she really doesn't know? She hasn't seen me—"

"You might think she doesn't know, but if she thinks she knows, it's still the same thing. Saying you love her is *duh*."

"I see. Thanks. I—We'd better—"

"Yeah." He returned to the mess on the counter. I tackled the refrigerator. A large blob of peanut butter had splatted on the floor behind it, half-hidden behind the back corner. As I bent down to get at it, I heard a sound like static on a bad audio system. I investigated. "Two questions."

Dannal ran fresh water over the dishrag. "What?"

"One: is this one of your cats?" I picked the kitten up. It forsook the peanut butter and turned its energy to the job of chewing my thumb, purring like marbles in a blender.

Dannal dropped the rag to rescue me from the Fanged Fuzzball. "Corrigan! Dummy, you don't belong out here."

"How can you tell its name? They all look alike to me."

"Nobody purrs like Corrigan. He always gets lost, no sense of direction. What's the other question?"

"How—I'm just curious, of course, but—how did you manage to drop peanut butter behind the refrigerator?"

"Oh. It fell off the knife when I jumped up to get the bread off the top."

"Couldn't you get the bread first, and then the peanut butter? Just curiosity."

"Oh, yeah. I didn't think of that. Come on, Corrigan."

The kitten went in to dinner, but when the mess was cleaned up, Dannal let the cats out again. "You're not allergic, are you?" he thought to ask. "They help me with my homework."

"Isn't that cheating?"

"Yeah. Don't tell anybody."

As he hauled his backpack to the table, I remembered the peanut butter mess. "Look, do you need a snack? I noticed—"

"Oh, right. That's what I was doing when Pa came." He made a move to get up.

"No, hang on, I'll get it. Any special instructions?"

"No, however you want to do it, it's fine."

It wasn't, of course. I had to slice a piece exactly one centimeter thick off the homemade loaf, mix the jelly and the peanut butter together, and I was absolutely forbidden to put a piece of bread on top. Dannal added, "Can I have some milk?"

I settled him with snack and homework, and myself with the clipboard, and here we are.

Dannal has just slapped a book shut. "Done." He tossed his pencil away. It skidded across the table to the floor. Two kittens attacked and killed it, then wrestled each other for the bragging rights. "Do you want to see my piano?"

.17.

EDELWEISS MOTEL:
LONG AFTER BEETHOVEN BOOGIE

Dear Mouse,
Dannal's piano shares his room with the cats. It's not unpleasant; in any case, who noticed? His piano is a six-foot Steinway grand, with a good, wide bench. I sat on the left, bass side. Dannal sat beside me. I spread my hands over the keys, flexed my fingers.

"You can play it," he said proudly.

"Thanks." I ran some scales to warm up, and played a bit from Saint Saëns's "Pianist" because it's silly and I like it. The piano's in great condition and beautifully tuned. You don't come across an instrument like that very often when you're traveling, Mouse. I thoroughly enjoyed it.

"Nice, huh?" Dannal's as perceptive as his mother.

"It's great."

"It used to be Pa's. He gave it to me when Janelle got him his Bösendorfer."

"Bösendorfer. Wow."

"Yeah. A nine-foot concert grand. It was his wedding present. Can you help me with this?" He shuffled through sheet music, spread a book open on the stand.

"Sondheim." I dug out my glasses. Sondheim composes sophisticated stuff.

He pointed. "It keeps going bonkers in there, somewhere. I can't figure out what's wrong. Watch this."

He played perhaps two notes when his mother's voice

called from inside the bathroom. "Is all your homework done?"

"Yes!" we both called back.

"Okay, have fun."

Dannal is good. Technically he's excellent, and artistically he had one or two surprising insights. Sure, Sondheim says a lot that he missed, Mouse, but what Sondheim has to say usually isn't anything a ten-year-old has any business knowing.

Halfway down the second page, it became intricate mud. Dannal took his hands from the keyboard. "See that?" He shook his fingers in frustration. "I can't figure out what's going wrong."

I worked out a few of the chords, scowling over Sondheim's fiendish accidentals. "Okay, look. This D is flat here, right? Then—" I played some— "it flats again here, so you have a double flat. Have you got that?"

He nodded. "Yeah, that's no problem. But watch, where the D goes natural again, down here?" He played down through the natural. Sure enough, turgid mud.

I tried it myself. Either the music had been printed wrong, or— "No, hang on. That D's double flatted, but this is a single natural. Have you tried popping it up only half a tone? Sondheim's pretty careful about things like that."

"But my Pa says—okay, let me try it—"

It worked. From the other room, Halla called, "That's Sondheim. I know that!"

Dannal's eyes met mine. The corners of my mouth were up; his tightened down, a look I am coming to know. He held up a palm. We slapped five. Not my style, but there it was.

"You'd better take it through once or twice, to set it," I said. "That thing's a witch."

"Yeah, Sondheim's unreal." He played through the rough spot twice. He had it.

"Are you going to get into trouble for playing this kind of thing? It's rather advanced."

Dannal snorted. "Everybody wants me to play this—" He started banging out Beethoven's *Für Elise*. Every ten-year-old piano student has it. I've always loved it.

"Hey, hang on—hang about. Don't abuse *Elise*."

Dannal stopped the noise. "All I have to do is play the notes right, and everybody thinks I'm a genius," he scoffed.

"Hang on, look. Don't answer, just think. Is there anyone you know who's really—er—cool? If they smiled at you, it would make your day?"

His ten-year-old face was a blank. He shrugged.

"Right. Give me a minute." I concentrated, remembering the good times I had with your mother, before my drinking got out of control. Nothing. There's nothing there any more.

I thought of the day Halla swung that wallop at me—no, that was too happy.

I thought of you. That would hurt too much and ruin it. But—I had it. I pictured you smiling at me, forgiving me. That was it. I held it in my mind and played, *Für Michaella*.

It's a short piece. When I finished, Dannal was frowning. "I thought it was only an exercise."

"It can be anything. Think of Corrigan. Play Corrigan."

"Okay . . . " Doubtfully, he sat up, his hands hovering. Then this side of his mouth tightened down and he began.

At the end, a laugh echoed from the bath. "You said they all look alike to you."

Dannal and I swapped a grin. "That was Dannal."

"Oh."

I got another idea. "Do me a favor? Play it again. I'd like to try something."

He obliged, and I played a bass variation I'd composed years ago. It was working, and then Dannal hit a clinker. I glanced at him. His eyes pointed downward. I kept playing. It happened again. He was throwing in a second here and there, and then an odd fourth or two. Another few bars, and *Elise* was syncopating.

I couldn't let him get away with that. I abandoned my variation and rolled into a boogie bass. That was it, war was declared. I can't tell where we went with it. It got 'way out of hand. It was loud, it was obnoxious, it was undiluted jam. It took us three tries before we got together enough to finish it off. Then a high five: "Yesss!"

Dannal's mother stood robed and toweled at the door of his

room, her eyes deep and soft. If anyone smiled at me that way, Mouse, I'd take the heart right out of my body and lay it at her feet. She turned the smile on me, and it became rueful. "You did that on purpose."

"No more Mr. Logan."

"How am I supposed to teach him respect? My neighbors will probably sue."

Dannal slid off his side of the bench. "Do you want coffee? Say you do even if you don't," he added, "because Ma lets me get hot chocolate if I make the coffee. I do pretty good coffee; Ma likes it."

Halla stopped him. "I'm sorry, Danny, not tonight."

"Ah, Ma!"

"No, dear. Mr. Log—I mean, Matt—has to go. It's nearly seven," she told me. "When Danny's home, I'm not to have men here unless they're related—"

"By marriage or by blood," I finished for her. "I know. I won't even say the next line. But—" I moved in close to her, tucked a curl under the towel. "Someday."

"Matt, no. I'll always be grateful for—"

I put a finger to her lips. "Someday. Soon." I took leave of Dannal, collected my jacket, and made my exit.

I started the car, activated the phone. Tony didn't sound civilized. "Where to hell have you been? We don't have your mobile number."

"Nobody has it. I won't be bothered when I'm driving."

"Yeah, well, it's a pain in the—have you seen the news?"

"No, I'm just leaving Hal's place. I got sidetracked—"

"Of course you did, my God's sake," he growled. "Doesn't she have a bad knee?"

"It's not—geez. I'm on my way back. I'll be there in—"

"Not if you know what's good for you," he said. "Turn around and drive out the other way. The networks all decided you're the murderer, and it's a battle zone here. The owner's holding the media off, but we can't even show our faces outside the gate. Get lost. But show up tomorrow morning," he added. "We had to hire security guards for the site."

"Wonderful." I switched on the headlights. "I'll be at—"

"Don't tell me, I don't want to know. You better hang up before they tap into your signal. See you tomorrow."

I backed out of the cramped parking lot and drove to the Parkway. In my mirror, I could see a pair of headlights following me onto the entrance ramp. I went to the Beller Gap overlook. It faces west, with a counterpart that faces east. In the sunset's afterglow I parked and got out. The other car cut off its headlights, pulled into the eastern overlook. For five minutes, nothing happened. I got in and started up again. The headlights placed themselves back in my mirror.

As I turned onto the roadway, the phone purred. Damn. I pulled off the road, flipped the switch. "This is Matt."

"Are you drunk?" Your Aunt Meranda.

"No. Geez. How did you get this number?"

"How do I get anything? Mother's worried. Are you all right? I know someone with a helicopter who can—"

"I'm okay. Nobody's tailing me but police, so far. Did you tell the media I killed Crystal?"

"No, they made that up all by themselves. Is it true?"

"No."

"Right. That's all Mother needs to know. I don't want to be heard talking with you." She cut the connection. It's been a long time since I've felt so adrift. I switched the phone off, started the car again.

I drove as far as the county line, got off the Parkway, headed back. At the first tourist trap I came to, I found a motel tucked into a side road behind the franchises. The people running the desk were too interested in the news broadcast to look under my baseball cap. Soon enough, I was holed up in an anonymous room with a vibrating bed and a couple of hundred channels on a TV perched on a rack out of reach. The control was attached with a chain to the nightstand. It's been years since I had both the time and the equipment to myself, to do some serious channel surfing. Remember how your mother used to hate it when I did that? I stretched out on the bed with the control and zapped.

I'd cycled two laps around the channels when the images began to look weirdly similar. I stopped zapping at random. A recent headshot of mine smiled thoughtfully from one corner of the screen as a beautifully groomed anchor reviewed the Beller case. I zapped.

"—deliberately dressed to resemble Julien Darcy. It's unclear as yet whether Crystal Beller was actually the intended victim—"

I zapped—

Julien appeared, her eyes large with unshed tears. She pleaded into the camera: "—come clean. Matt, please, we all love you so much. You need to stop running. Please, please, turn yourself in. If you tell the truth, and throw yourself on the mercy of the court—"

Geez. Zap—

Baseball. Zap—

"—dressing room was locked. Logan never accounted for the mysterious time gap—"

—zap—*Xena: Warrior Princess.* Zap—

"—the death of Ken Beller was murder or suicide. Matt Logan's name was mentioned in connection with—"

—zap—

"—I know *my* first instinct would be to pick up the gun as soon as I saw it. Logan's mysterious behavior on the set—"

—zap—

"—no fingerprints, only mysterious smudges, possibly made when Logan put the gun in Kenneth Beller's hand—"

—zap—Psychic infomercial. Zap—

"—give himself up. Darcy saw the victim's murdered wife, Crystal Beller, running into the ladies' room just minutes before Logan's mysterious—"

—zap—

"—mysterious disappearance. Logan was last seen at two this afternoon, wearing—"

—zap—"Moms Who Adopt Alien Clones." Zap—

"—Matt Logan was spotted entering a Myrtle Beach bar, but escaped moments later—"

—zap-

"—Logan was seen entering the Ashe County Library—"

—zap—

"—have just learned that the suspected murderer, actor Matt Logan, is the ex-husband of petite swimsuit model Anastasia

Russo. Russo was released from Beller County Hospital today after her mysterious illness cleared up, possibly because Logan was not allowed to visit her in the hospital."

Damn. Damn it. *Damn*!

I zapped the TV off, started pacing. Some things you can't escape, Mouseling. It had to happen. I tried to order myself not to think about it, without much success. Within days, I am going to see you again, probably for the last time.

I spent some time reminding myself of Dannal's advice: "Saying 'I love you' is *duh*." I tried to recall the glimpse I'd got of you at Starling Resort. You're ten years old now, with long hair. Wyndham says you have perfect teeth. I wasted energy wishing for a way to stabilize, until I calmed down enough to remember my clipboard, out in the car.

I sneaked out to get it. A shadowed figure in a room across from mine slipped into his doorway. Right. Surveillance. I came back in to call Golde Silver.

"Where have you been?" she demanded. "Is that deputy still following you?"

"There's been a guy around for the last couple of days."

"Are you still in the county?"

"I—yes—Look, I saw the news. They're saying a warrant for my arrest—"

"Now listen. *Don't leave the county*. He's your guardian angel. Long as he sees you, you're in the clear, you hear me?"

"But—Look, is there a warrant out for my arrest?"

"You didn't watch the right news reports. No warrants yet. When they arrest you, you'll be the first to know. I better be the second. Tell me this: why didn't you pick up that gun?"

"I'm not that stupid. Why?"

"Good for you. The clown who hid it is very upset. He expected you to pick it up."

"I was supposed to find it? Who hid it? Why me?"

"Ron Beller found his cousin's body. He doesn't believe Ken'd commit suicide any more than we do. I guess he watches crime shows; it's not the usual Beller style. He took and hid the gun where you were working. He figured you'd pick up the gun and get your fingerprints all over it. You pick up the murder weapon in six movies."

"I don't pick the weapons up, the characters I play pick the weapons up. Geez. Actors are not their characters. Did Ken Beller commit suicide because of Crystal?"

"Meggy's not saying, so they're not sure. Stay in the county. I'm proud you called me and not them. Nighty-night, now."

Sure. I paced some more, then ordered myself to sit down and write this out. It's after midnight, and I'm done. Maybe I can get some sleep.

Good night, Mouseling. Sleep well. Your Dad loves you.

.18.

Tara: Field Day for the Press (Not for Mouse)

Coming in to work wasn't any fun at all. It's been years since the Press got up that early in the morning to cover me. As I drove slowly through the crowd to the gate, they shouted provocative questions and catcalls:

"Hey, Matt, how does it feel to be a murderer?"

"Do you think you'll get away with it, Killer?"

"Who's your next victim going to be?"

Two uniformed security guards kept the crowd thirty yards from the gate. Several more, dressed as wranglers, were being efficient about catching creative attempts to get into the site. It was a zoo. Exactly what I needed the day we shoot the apple tree love scene, and little Gideon's birthday party.

Once past the gate and rid of the Press, I drove straight to my dressing trailer. I have not felt so out of charity with journalists, as a species, since the week after I got out of treatment. In the twenty feet or so between the car and the trailer door, I came across Julien.

She gasped, rocked back. "Oh! Matt! You're back!"

"I saw your plea," I said. "Thanks for caring, but—" I pointed to a car so ordinary and dirty that it was practically invisible—"see that guy over there?"

"What guy? I don't see—oh. You mean him?"

The man was almost as hard to see as his car. "Yes. Him. What do you suppose he does for a living?"

"I don't know what you mean—"

"He works for the Sheriff. And do you know what he does for the Sheriff?"

"Matt, you're being so mysterious!"

"He follows people. Specifically, me. I haven't been more than fifty yards away from him for the last eight hours or so. If the Sheriff wanted me turned in, he could have ordered that guy to do it any time in the last several days. Your plea was touching, but redundant."

"The network representative said—"

"They used you, Julien. I thought you had more—never mind. They wanted a story; you gave them a humdinger."

"But—Oh, Matt, I'm sorry, I really didn't know. Oh, Matt, forgive me! Please, I never thought they'd lie to me!"

I considered the privacy of my make-up table, and then the love scene under the apple tree, made up a smile for her. "There's nothing to forgive, Jule. They used you. You're the one who deserves an apology. See you in a bit, okay?"

She offered a tentative smile and a hug. Our working relationship sealed for the moment, I ducked into my trailer, wishing for Halla. She had a physical therapy session this morning, and wouldn't be there until after noon, for the birthday scenes.

The energy it took to concentrate got my mind off the real world. Tony ordered prints of three of the first four takes, and Julien and I only got better. The apple tree scene was in the can by eleven-thirty.

When Halla arrived at lunchtime, I'd forgotten there was a real world. In the birthday party scenes, I focused on Gabby, who knew little and cared less about the murder. His concern was watching nonexistent globs of ice cream and cake fly through the air, as little Gideon deliberately trashes his birthday party.

The afternoon marched by, and Halla and I met in the indoor ring after work. Halla was ordered to improve my form on a horse that jumps, so that they could put me in cross-country silks and get a few more mulch-pit shots. As soon as we knew nobody was looking, we all but fell into each other's arms: "Are you okay?" We both nodded.

I pulled back to see her eyes. "What about Dannal? Hal, I'm really sorry I—"

She chuckled deep in her throat. "He talked about you all morning, and I expect to hear more tonight. You made a hit."

"I don't think it'll be easy—what will his friends say about— have you seen the news?"

"We both have. Matt, don't worry about Dannal. His parents are split. He can keep things private; he has to, or Roland and I would drive him crazy. Let's get started."

The riding lesson had to be cut short, so that a hired chauffeur could drive her home. I left my car on the site and went back to Tara with Tony. I wore the baseball cap, and I drove, so nobody saw me. Press coverage can be a bore.

The gate and low wall around Tara were originally meant for decoration, but they did define a boundary. Ma'am placed cousins around it to keep reporters off the premises, so we had some freedom inside the perimeter. It's been a hellish day, and we still have to look at our daily footage.

<> <> <>

The dailies look good, some of the best we have so far. As Phina reset the machinery, Tony heaved a blissful sigh. "I don't know what you two did, and I don't want to, but you and Julie were clicking, there. Think you can do it again?"

Phina straightened up from whatever she was doing to the machinery. "Hey, Matt, watch this. You didn't see this last night."

It was the jumping footage. Phina had fooled with it so that the shots of me coming at the jump alternated with Dakota riding the Demon Dun horse over it. "See, I knew it wouldn't work," Phina said.

She was right. In a shot that tight, nobody sane could mistake Dakota on the Demon Dun for me on Babe. I said, "Dakota doesn't move the way I do. We don't look enough alike. What if we pad my costume, and I'll try to move more like Dakota—"

"I know what's wrong," Phina said. "You make 'Kota look cheap. Watch this—" She shifted equipment and zapped. I rode silently across the screen three times on the Demon Dun, ended up sprawled in the mulch pit twice.

Phina made the most of the falls. "Good out-takes," she said. "What'll you give me to forget I got them?"

"What'll it cost me to get them onto *Funniest Bloopers*? I know good publicity when I see it."

"Hold it—wait, go back." Tony waved his hand at the monitor. "Let's see that jump—the one where he made it."

Phina ran the second jump again.

"That's it," Tony said. "Right there—no, take it back— Look at his face—right there. That's beautiful. It looks like you know you're going to do it. Gorgeous!" Tony sat back. "That, my angels, is why I am in this business. Matt, can you do it again in cross-country silks?"

"Do I have a choice?"

"What you have is a phone call, Matt." Dora reached the phone across Tony's head.

"Tell them you're busy," he said.

I took the phone. "Thanks. This is Matt."

"Hi, how are you doing?" It was Wyndham. "I got somebody here who wants to talk to you."

A shuffling at the other end: "Daddy?"

"M-Mouse?" My voice was so hoarse it was no more than a whisper. I took the phone outside, plugged the other ear, huddled into the white plastic column. A couple of flashes gave notice of telephoto lenses behind the trees.

"Hi, Dad."

"Mouse. I've missed you. I've—missed you a lot."

"Missed you, too, Dad."

"Look—You know your stepfather wants to adopt you?"

"Uh-huh."

"Is that what you want, honey?"

"Sure."

"Oh. . . . Look, Mouse, I want to see you—but whatever happens, I want you to know—I'll always love you—" No. Geez. It was exactly what Dannal told me not to say. I tried again: "Look, I want—want you to know—"

"Stop it!" The sharp cry stabbed through the connection into my ear. "Don't love me! Don't see me, and don't love me, and get out of my life!"

I kicked myself, too late. "Mousy—I d-didn't mean—" I don't know what I didn't mean. "I'm sorry, honey—"

There was a sound like a hiccup. "Please, Daddy? I don't want you to see me."

"But you got off the plane and tried to find me—"

"No, I didn't. It was a mistake—I got off the plane by mistake. Leave me alone!"

"Okay—Mou—Mickie. I guess—that's all. I wish—"

"I don't care what you wish—just stay away. Please!"

"I—Okay. Look, let—let me t-talk to your stepf-ather."

Another shuffle. "So." His voice was not unsympathetic. "They released Nancy from the hospital yesterday."

"I know. I—I saw the news."

"Yeah. I hate all this media frenzy. I don't think Nancy's in any shape to leave, but—So, what would you say to a meeting in the atrium, ten o'clock tomorrow morning? I bet you'd like to get it over with. This has to be hard on you. And, of course, the sooner we do it, the less interested the media will be in— well, in all of us. What do you say?"

"Sure. What-whatever you like." It didn't matter. Nothing mattered. "Ten o'clock, at Starling Resort. I'll b-I'll be there."

"We'll look for you," he assured me. I rang off.

.19.

TARA: TOO LATE

Dear Mouse,
I have to accept this. I have to accept this. I have to accept this. I have to accept this. I have to accept this. I have to accept this. I have to accept this.

It is so hard to accept this.

You have a life to live, Mousekin. You've been living it without me for over three years now. Even when we were together, how much of me was with you, and how much of me was in orbit? I have to accept it.

Everybody says this is best for you. You do. Your mother does. I do. It has to be done. I have to accept it.

I'd sell my body to the Martians for some tears, Mousy.

The hours crawl by in fifteen-minute steps. It's nine minutes and six seconds until two-fifteen, AM. I'm to meet Hal at nine, we'll have breakfast at Starling Resort, to be sure we're on time to meet you in the atrium. I want Halla to be your stepmother some day, Mousekin. You may never meet her. I wish you could, though; she's a good person.

Six minutes and two seconds before two-fifteen. Words drag out from under my pen, like time from under the clock hands, or the thoughts from under my brain, too slowly for any use. Writing's no good.

I sit by the window and watch the moon move behind forty-foot pines, telling myself I have to accept this. I have to accept this. I have to accept this. I have to accept this. I have to accept this. I have to accept this. . . .

.20.

BELLER COUNTY HOSPITAL:
POST-APOCALYPSE

Dear Mouse—No.
Dear Michaella—No.
Dear Shannon—never mind. I'll just write it.
Sure, it hurts, more than I ever guessed it would. I can live with it; I've lived with worse. I did what I had to do. That's all about it. After that—

I'll start with this morning—three minutes before five-forty-five. Tony's alarm went off. It's three minutes fast. Tony growled, rolled to his feet. "You get any sleep?"

I shrugged.

"Anything I can do for you?"

I shook my head. "Thanks."

"I don't want to sound like Simon Legree, but are you going to need tomorrow off? This murder's doing tap dances all over our shooting schedule."

Moving felt strange, as though my joints had forgotten how. I made myself turn to face him. "No. Work's good. Where do you want me, when? I'll be—finished—by ten."

He puffed out his cheeks, flicked me away. "You're not on the call sheet today, remember? I got an idea about Andrea and Charlie. I'll use little Gideon, too. Then this afternoon I want to check out the studio, see if the deputies left me any sets. The interiors—" Tony was off into his own favorite world.

I got dressed as carefully as I would for an audition. Halla likes the brown shirt, so I put that on, with my *Thundercars* jeans, the dark twill jacket she rubbed her cheek against the other day, a silk to match the shirt in the breast pocket. If Halla weren't with me, I might have blown the whole thing.

She handled me like fragile china. I functioned within physical reality, but it was no use trying to concentrate on anything important. The atrium was almost empty. I seated Halla facing the atrium and sat with my back to the world.

Halla talked occasionally about nothing, needing no answers. She ordered a substantial breakfast. The only kind of coffee they had was the "gourmet" stuff, but that was okay. I probably wouldn't touch it.

Halla was lifting a forkful of hash browns when her gaze shifted from me to something behind me and she stiffened, her eyes wide. My head reared up. Halla said something I didn't listen to. They had arrived, my Mouse, with her mother and stepfather. Nance looked pale and shaky. Wyndham had everything under control. Mouse lagged behind. I stood, moved to the fountain.

Wyndham, all smiles, tried to draw her forward. She resisted, shook her head, shrank back. He caught her wrist to drag her out from behind Nancy. Mouse set her heels and pulled away, ducking behind her mother.

I didn't see her face, but I hardly needed to. "Don't," I said. "It's okay. Let me have the papers. I'll s-I'll s-sign."

He reached for Mouse. "A deal's a deal. Trust me—"

"Cut it out!" I moved to block him. "Leave her alone. Where's the re-rel-the p-paper?"

Wyndham conjured a sheaf from an inner pocket, showed me where the signature should go. He had all kinds of fine words about what a fine thing I was doing. I spread the release on the fountain parapet. A drop of water plopped on the words "Birth Parent." No use hesitating or wishing. I scrawled a signature, my pen tearing at the paper. Done.

I straightened and looked directly at Inspector Quin, pushing through saloon-style doors. Pike and Slocum backed her up. Right. Getting arrested for murder would make my day. "Look, are we finished?" I said. "She doesn't need to see this." Wyndham had another copy for me to sign, and another, for my records. And that, finally, was that.

I handed him the third copy. He pushed it back. I folded it mechanically, tried to get a look at my Mouse. She turned her face away, hid behind Nancy. Wyndham held the papers up like a trophy. No point in hanging around. I moved away from the happy family, and the police group surrounded me.

Wyndham's voice rang across the atrium. "Got it, Mimi!"

"Mimi?" I spun around.

She gasped, her head jerked up. An angry sore festered on my Mouse's lip.

"*Shannon*?"

Too late, she clapped a hand to her mouth.

I charged through deputy, Pike and Quin. With everything I had behind it, I slammed my fist into the fungal growth between his nose and upper lip. Blood spurted, soaked my sleeve. If I broke my hand, who cared? I may have taken out a tooth.

Security wrestled me from behind. I filled my lungs and bellowed. "Shannon, tell someone—*Now*, Shan! Tell Quin!" and I was on my face in mulch. With professional gusto, Security had a knee at the bruise on my ribs, tightened my arms to my shoulder blades. I couldn't see what happened to my Mouse.

An overshined shoe appeared by my face. "Let him up," Slocum said. "You got the wrong one." Security released me, helped me up, brushed me off.

Mouse stood by the fountain, poking at trash in the water. Quin took her shoulders, looked into her eyes.

Pike pulled Wyndham to his feet, his big-city voice cutting across the country drawls around him. "Nigel Wyndham, you are under arrest for the murder of Crystal Dawn Beller. You have the right to remain silent . . . "

I blinked, sucked in a deep breath. I hadn't had any sleep; things weren't registering clearly. Wyndham was under arrest?

Things happened so fast.

"Like hell I am!" Whipping away from Pike, Wyndham shoved Quin into the fountain. He grabbed my little girl, reached under his jacket with his other hand. "Get back!"

"Ah, shit—Take it easy, Mr. Wyndham. You can't —"

People swept away like blown leaves. I stood like a stump. Wyndham brandished his new pistol, hauling my child beside him. Deputies materialized at the exits. Wyndham hustled her toward one, waved the gun. The deputy got back.

I have no experience with real guns. Sure, I've popped off with whatever toy a design department can come up with, and the bang dubbed in during post-production. I knew getting shot with one was supposed to hurt; I've acted that, too. But real guns never came into my life. I am not a hero. Three long steps took me into his way. "Let her go."

He leveled the gun at me. "Get back!"

I stood still. "You think I'd rather live than stop you? You're an idiot. Let her go."

He nestled the gun under her ear. "You want to see her die? Get out of my way!"

Then I knew real fear. "No, you can't—you c-ouldn't—"

"I killed one whore, I can kill another. Get back!"

I tried not to hear that. "D-do-d-on'-don't—"

A wail from my little girl cut us off. "No!" She held on to his arm as it crossed her throat, rubbed it with a woman's caress. Tears overflowed, ran down her face. "No, Nijey, I never did anything to you, you said you loved me, you said you could never hurt me—"

I froze, appalled, staring. Through the floods, her eyes nailed me, signaled, insisted. I couldn't read it exactly, but she seemed interested in a piece of the floor three feet to my left, and six feet in front of her.

I made myself breathe, played abject submission, ducking my head, patting air down at my sides, moving a foot backward. "Okay. Okay, man, don't hurt her. Please don't—" Like a kid cheating at mother-may-I, I crossed one leg behind the other, stretched it sideways. A weight shift put me there.

Her drenched eyes approved. Like a little piston, her knee rose and fell, driving her heel into his instep. Surprise loosened his grip. She slipped free in the one direction he never expected—straight down. For an instant she coiled at his feet, then rocketed in a perfect forward dive to my arms. I grabbed her, spun, tossed. Halla, crutches braced, stood behind me, ready to catch her. Halla only had to spot her. My Mouse knew exactly what she was doing.

With my little girl safe, I whirled back to the gun. I think I had some idea that it would be better for a stray bullet to hit me than anyone else. I launched into what I'd like to have known as a flying tackle. As my feet pushed off the floor, everything went into slow motion. I watched Wyndham turn his gun around, peer into the barrel, squeeze the trigger.

We crashed to the floor together, and rolled. Something between my neck and collarbone came apart with a loud pop. Flying tackles are not advisable at my age. That arm still moved, so I hadn't broken anything. I scrambled out from under Wyndham to see what I could do for him.

There was nothing. I struggled out of my jacket, threw it over what used to be his face. Then, holding the weak arm to my side, I put my head to my knees, fought off black nausea.

Shouts, orders, screams filled the atrium around me. The floor beneath me vibrated with running footsteps. And two little, light hands tugged at my armpits. "Dad? Daddy?"

I took a deep breath and a huge risk, rose to my knees, and looked up into eyes that were my own. I can't remember the last time I saw my Mouse that close, sober. I said, "Are you all right?" First things first.

She nodded, wound her arms around my neck and hugged, as a child hugs, chokingly. I put an arm around her, held her close and safe, and bowed my head to her shoulder.

Deep inside, something thawed, broke apart, set me free.

She said into my ear, "Daddy, you're getting me wet."

"What?" I lifted my head. Two soggy stains spread over the shoulder of her dress. Tears. Geez. I caught my shirt cuff in my fingers and used it to try to wipe the stains away.

She sighed patiently, leaned sideways. With a woman's nerve she plucked the silk from my jacket and dried my face with it. It was ineffably sweet. When she got to my nose, she commanded, "Blow."

"No," I rebelled. I took the silk to finish the job myself. She looked at what lay at her feet. "I killed him."

"No. Mouse, no, he killed himself."

"I planned it that way. I made him do it."

"Nobody's that powerful, Mousy, not even you."

"But I wanted him dead." Her chin tightened.

"So did I, but he beat us to it."

She began to cry in earnest. "I hate him."

I gathered her in. "Not as much as he hates himself. He did it, not you. We're both going to have to live with that."

The rest of the world regained existence. Someone stood above us. I said, "You belong with your mother, Mousy." I set my little girl away, stood, raised her chin to make her look at me. "Don't ever think I've forgotten you, because I never will."

She nodded. I turned her to her mother.

Nancy narrowed her eyes. "Murderer!" she snarled. She screamed, "Murderers!" and raised a hand at our child. Mouse recoiled against me.

I caught Nancy's wrist. Her eyes blazed, but nothing was behind them that I could say anything to. I let her wrist go, put my back between her and Mouse. Someone nursed her away.

My weak arm draped heavily around my Mouse as the crowd surged around us. I scrubbed my eyes on the sleeve of the good arm as Quin came up, wringing wet. She reached for my child. "We need to get you to the hospital, Baby."

Mickie shrank back against me. I hugged her, and she turned, clung to me with sudden, silent strength. "Look," I said. "Let me drive her? She's not ready to go to strangers. P-please—" My voice caught, choking.

A gentle hand, warm and strong, slid across my back, pulled me together. "Matt, dear, are you okay?"

"I can't stop blubbering, Hal—"

"You're not used to it yet." Her hand moved to my shoulder. "Do you want me to—" She startled, yanked her hand away. For a second she glared at it, then at me. She snapped at Quin, "Call an ambulance—Matt, listen. We're going to walk to that bench, and you can lie down on it, okay?"

I frowned at her. Halla isn't one to order people around.

"Oh, Matt, please! I think that second shot hit you."

Mickie lifted her head with a gasp, her grip loosening.

"Second shot?" I repeated stupidly.

"Daddy, walk!" Mickie grabbed my shirt in two tight fists, compelling me toward the bench. "Come on!"

"That damned gun went off again when it hit the floor," Halla said. "One more step, dearest. You can do it—"

Now that I knew what happened to me, that shoulder began to hurt, a lot. "Hal—my Mouse—?"

"I'm fine, Daddy," Mickie insisted. "I won't leave you again, I promise—ever. Now, come *on*."

Of course medics carted us both off to hospital. They knocked me out, patched me up, settled me into a private room to finish sleeping off the anaesthetic. At least I'd stopped weeping. I did my best with the Famous Grin and thank-yous, and they left me to rest.

◇◇◇

I must have drifted through caverns of sleep for several hours after they settled me there. Sometimes I woke enough to know something was urgently wrong; sometimes I slept too deeply to know anything at all. Once or twice a needle stung, delivering a painkiller or taking a blood sample. In the afternoon, I turned over, opened my eyes. "Where's Mouse?"

Stupid. Mouse was gone. Of course she was gone. Nancy must have calmed down and taken Mouse home by now.

Why do people enter hospital rooms that way: one knock and they're in before you can say Go away or Come in. I levered myself up on my good elbow before I knew I could. "Hal, what about Mouse—my little girl—?"

Bradford came in, pulled the chair around and sat reversed, folding his arms across the back. "Hey, man, how you feeling? Doctor says you'll be all right, given rest and all that."

"Bradford." I let myself down onto the pillows, wondering if I'd regret the sudden movement. So far, the painkillers were holding strong. "I need to know what's happened to my daughter. Can you find out—her name's Michaella Russo Logan—"

"I'm 'way ahead of you, man. Your sister's been with her. Listen, you got a lobby-load of people out there. I'm screening them for you—no press, no strangers. Lieutenant Pike is here to debrief you. He might be willing to give you some answers. Halla's waiting to see you, and your sister needs to tell you about the little girl. Who do you want to see first?"

"Meranda. If-if she knows ab-about Mouse—Mickie—Michaella. Would you ask Meranda to—"

"You got it." Bradford stood, spun the chair to its proper position, and left. Another moment, and Meranda sailed in.

She closed the door, stood inside it. She said, "Michaella's fine, Matts. Don't worry about her. She's safe now."

"Safe. With her mother?" I hadn't realized how bitter that could taste in my mouth.

"No, Nancy's under arrest, as an accessory. Mickie's a ward of the court. She's upstairs asleep now. If you're not up to answering questions, I'll boot out the forces of the law—"

"Upstairs? Here—in hospital? Why is she—dear God, that damned gun—"

"Matts, stop it. She wasn't hurt—not today. She's—You need to know, and it's rather hard. Listen to me, and don't go off into a fit. Are you ready to hear this? It's nasty."

"Hear what?" I forced myself into some semblance of composure. "What is it?"

Meranda stood where I could see her without twisting my neck. "Her injuries are internal, Matts. Some of them are—as much as six weeks old. She was fine till Nancy married Nigel. There's no doubt about what's been happening. Nobody had any idea—except that the kid apparently tried to tell Nancy."

It took me a minute to absorb that. More than a minute, because Meranda was in the chair when I put the room into focus again. I said carefully, "Have you ever wanted to kill somebody who's already dead?"

"Occasionally. Mickie's a fighter, Matts. She'll be okay, given the right treatment. The chaplain tells me they treat abuse cases very aggressively here. She'll get what she needs."

"Whatever it takes." I had a hard time squeezing my voice past the constriction in my throat. "I know I can't see her or anything, but—whatever she needs—anything—"

"I know. It's all taken care of. Look, shall I get you another hit of painkiller?"

"I'm fine. Leave me alone. Nancy will calm down; she'll get M-Michaella back. I can't stop her; I s-igned—*Damn* it!"

"Don't worry about that. She got hold of the—" Abruptly,

my sister looked away, rose, circled the bed to the window and stared out, her back to the room. The emotion swelled over me like a tidal bore. I turned my back, heaved deep breaths, swallowed, shook my head, hard.

It took me a few minutes to get rational again. "Sorry."

Meranda stayed where she was. "Are you all right?"

"Yeah. I'm an idiot. It's just—I'm no good for her. I didn't even know I was looking at her, that night on the Starling Head. How could I not know my little girl? I saw what he did, and I didn't even—"

"Matts. You're not Superman." Meranda faced me again, braced her hips against the windowsill. "Forget the adoption papers. The kid got hold of them when you sucker-punched Nigel—nice one, by the way—she tore the papers up and threw them into the fountain. I suggest you destroy your copy at your earliest opportunity."

"No. That won't make any difference. Nancy'd never let her go—Hang about. How do you know so much—?"

"I was there."

"You were there—" I shook my head. "I'm missing something. You couldn't possibly—"

"What's the only decent hotel between here and Asheville?"

"By decent, you mean—"

"Five stars, Brat, nothing less for me."

"What's wrong with Chetola, in Blowing Rock?"

"The Sheriff invited me to stay in Beller County."

"Oh. Sure. Stupid of me."

"I was right there, having breakfast. You didn't see me?"

Meranda's breakfast meant nothing to me. I engaged the brain, found a picture in my mind of Mouse, poking at paper in the fountain. A gentle knock at the door brought Hal in, carrying one of my overnight bags. She hesitated. "I'm sorry. Matt, Lieutenant Pike is outside. Should I get rid of him?"

"I already offered," Meranda said. "My brother changed the subject." She turned to me. "We ask again: are you up to answering questions, Matts, or do we run the minions of the law off the premises?"

"No, I—I'd rather see him."

"Before the anesthesia wears off." Meranda nodded. "Good call. Do you want us to stay, or shall we go?"

I dismissed them, and Bradford leaned in as they went out. "You want some time, Matt? You okay?"

"Sure. Bring him on."

Pike shut the door on him, took over the chair. "In the first place, sir, you won't hear anything from the DA about assaulting Mr. Wyndham. If I had a kid—Anyway. I need answers."

I sat up, set my jaw. "On one condition: I want answers, too. Why would Wyndham kill Crystal? He didn't know her."

"You can talk lying down, I've seen your movies."

I subsided to the pillow, threw my good arm over my eyes. "Not all of them, I hope."

"I don't have that kind of mind. Describe seeing Ms. Beller at the ladies' room door again."

"Her robe was closed, the wig—her make-up—she behaved—Geez. Was that how he managed the alibi? It wasn't Crystal I saw, it was Nancy, wearing Crystal's robe and wig. I was right about that. Geez. But why? Did she say why?"

"As far as I know, Mrs. Wyndham's still trying to justify her husband. She came back from the Canteen and caught him with the body. He told her he found it that way. She put on the robe and wig, and trotted back to the bathroom to wait for his signal. She wanted to believe him. He was the most important thing in her life."

"That's why she smelled of 'In/Tense,' from wearing Crystal's robe—sure, she couldn't have picked it up in the ladies' room, because all the perfume had been washed off Crystal in the shower scene. I knew Nancy must have had contact with her somehow—"

"That's about it. Describe the way Mrs. Wyndham looked when you found her in the hotel?"

"In the hotel? Oh. Like any OD. The ones who overdose on purpose generally get themselves all coifed and dressed, and lay themselves out like the Lily Maid of Astolat. They want people to be sorry they're gone. It's usually done that way in films, too."

"Sure it is. And they're careful to get everything perfect, and every hair in place, right? So you wrote that her gown was mussed and her hair ruffled. Are you sure about that? Wouldn't she try and keep it all perfect?"

"But that prescription doesn't take effect right away. Nobody alive could stay that still, even when they try to."

Pike lifted his head. "Shit, sir. You wrote about that, didn't you—Ms Darcy's skirt spread across the porch swing. Quin mentioned that, but the Sheriff didn't think it was important. Damn. Okay, never mind. What about talking to Mr. Wyndham in the café, the day you went to their suite? Tell me about that."

Obediently, I rewound and let the tape roll. At the end, Pike said, "Are you sure his card was damaged?"

"No, of course not. It's what they always say, to avoid embarrassing the customers."

"You think he was over his credit limit?"

"Wyndham? He never overdrew an account in his life. He's perfect. Ask Nancy—oh. It got damaged from jimmying my dressing room door? Geez, was he the second lover? No. He wouldn't cheat on Nancy; he didn't even know Crystal—"

"She sang at Starling Resort. That place seems to be lousy with Bellers. They all knew about Mr. Wyndham's tastes, and you know what Crystal Beller was like. Making contact with him was a piece of cake for an unscrupulous girl—"

"Right." I said. "She broke into our motel room—"

"Unscrupulous and not too choosy."

"But he'd just married Nancy. How could he—"

"You said yourself, Crystal could look like anything you wanted her to be—like under-aged. He liked them young, and he liked being rough. She showed him what he wanted to see, did what he wanted her to—oh, shit. Sorry—Shit. I didn't mean—"

"Yeah—never mind. Police aren't supposed to be tactful, right? Look, I'm glad he's dead, and I didn't have to kill him, but I—actually—really wish I had."

"Yeah. It'd be a nice memory. Sir—"

"I can't believe I didn't know them, on the Starling Head. She's my little girl. I should have—"

"It was dark, sir, and you weren't looking for her. You're human. Get used to it. Did Mr. Wyndham seem surprised that his wife attempted to kill herself?"

"Rocked. Absolutely staggered. He didn't do it. Whatever else he did, he didn't poison Nancy—"

"No, she did that, and he never saw it coming. Then she called you, and you played White Knight for your ex-wife, which he'd never do. Sir, I'm the one who's supposed to be asking the questions. Can you identify any of the people who attacked you on the Starling Head?"

"Everyone asks me that. They were wearing ski masks. I'm sure they were trash-Bellers, Ken and a lot of guys he called his brothers. He said he knew everything—geez. Geez."

Pike leaned forward. "What? You got something."

"The motive," I said. "I know the law doesn't care about motive in a murder, but—"

"Motive's irrelevant. Lots of people had motives. You can't convict on motive."

"Right. Sorry." The painkillers were wearing off. "What else do you want to know?"

"No, go on. What about the motive?"

"He—Ken Beller—said he knows everything that happens at Starling Resort. And Yvan said that Crystal taunted whoever was in my dressing room—"

"Mr. Wyndham's a lawyer, his voice is trained like an actor's. You both have Northern accents."

"Right, and my sister mistook him for me at her book-signing. Anyway, Crystal said her husband told her about—if Ken Beller told Crystal about—you know—Geez. Blackmail was her favorite pastime—she couldn't miss. And Wyndham was breathing down my neck when I told Tony that Crystal would trash him. She was doomed."

"Don't blame yourself."

"Blame myself for anything those charming people do? Thanks for worrying." I shifted my weight. "Wyndham must have killed Ken Beller, but—"

"We can't prove it, but it's probable. I got to say it's a brilliant way to dispose of a weapon—report it stolen, then use it to fake a suicide. Ron Beller found Ken, and tried to get fancy, too. He—and almost everyone else in the nation—thought you killed Crystal, and you were going to get away with killing his cousin—"

"But why risk killing Ken Beller? Wyndham's too smart—"

"Don't quit your day job. You think Ken wouldn't pick up where Crystal left off? The killer got lucky when Ron Beller buried the weapon. Any evidence on it's been pretty well contaminated." Pike sat back. "We got what we need, for the moment. Thank you for your cooperation, sir. You up for more visitors? The chaplain needs to ask you something."

After Pike's urban rasp, Bradford's easy Southern swing was a pleasure to listen to. He spun the chair around to straddle it. "Hey, Matt. I got to talk to you. I've seen your ex-wife."

I shifted my shoulder. "I'd better do something about her bail. Jail's no place for Nancy. Mouse needs her mother—"

"Mrs. Wyndham has resources, Matt. She'll be out of there in a couple hours. That's not what I need to talk to you about. I spoke to her about Michaella. The child's a ward of the court now. Beller County is very aggressive when it comes to treating child abuse cases. She'll have self-defense education, therapy, counseling—and whoever she lives with will have to take family counseling, too."

"Look, I don't care how hard Nancy fights to get her—"

"Nancy won't fight."

"What?"

"Nancy won't fight for custody. She doesn't want anything more to do with Michaella."

"I don't believe that. No. Nancy lives for Mickie. She's spent three years protecting her. Mickie is Nancy's life."

"Her marriage was her life. Some people live for their children. Others, like Mrs. Wyndham, live for their mates. She spent three years punishing you for messing up her marriage, with Mr. Wyndham's help. When she married him, she got a new focus. She might have let you have visitation then, if he'd told her to. But, of course, he—didn't. I'm sorry, Matt, but those three years never did have much to do with Michaella."

For a long moment I lay there and stared. Things were happening faster than I had time to register them. "No, you don't know Nancy. Protecting her from me or punishing me—Nancy won't let me see Mickie. Not without a fight."

Bradford was patient, even indulgent. "You know her better than I do. I only know what she said. Hey. Your doctor's due
in here any minute. Is there anyone else you want to see?"

"If—If you could ask Halla —"

Hal and I came together as the door shut on him. We both
said, "Are you all right?"

We both nodded.

I sat up. "My little girl's upstairs, here. Hal, I—" And something inside me snapped. I flung off covers, swung my feet out
of bed. To hell with being brave and cooperative. "I have to see
her. Now! Before Nancy gets out of jail, I have to—"

Halla spun to the window, her face reddening. A knock at
the door and the ER doctor swept in. Her eyebrows leaped up to
her hairline. I was dressed, if that's the word I want, in one of
those wretched little hospital gowns that don't cover anything
important. Radiating from the ears, I pulled my legs into the
bed, covered up like a good patient.

The doctor's crows-feet curved wildly upward. "It's fine,
Mr. Logan, I'm a doctor, she's your fiancée. Technically, nobody saw anything they shouldn't." She turned her back to wash
her hands. "You want to let me check my repair job?"

Halla crutched herself toward the door. "I'll wait outside."

The doctor called above the running water, "Ms. McKee
can stay if she wants. Fiancées get special privileges here."

Halla looked away. I reached across and grasped her wrist.
She muttered, "I just said that so I could get in."

At the sink, the doctor noisily pulled on protective gloves.
In the last three years, I've developed a loathing of procedures
that start with a doctor pulling on protective gloves. I swallowed. "Hal. I can get through this without you. I can get through
the rest of my life without you. But I—don't want to. I—"

"You really want me to stay?"

"Yeah. As Dannal says—*duh*. Will you stay with me?
Please? I want you to."

Halla gave a tiny nod. "Then you won't get rid of me."

My life fell together. I let the doctor check the patch on my
shoulder, and then the work on my face. Halla gripped my hand
while the doctor shone her little flashlight over the burns. At

last she nodded. "You're fine. You got good-healing flesh. You want to stay here tonight?"

"I have a choice?"

"No. You're well enough to sass me, you're well enough to go home. I need your space for sick people. Get your call-back instructions and get gone."

I said to Hal, "How fast can you get me out of here?"

<><><>

It didn't take long to listen to advice, sign things, and get dressed. My Mouse was asleep when they let me into her room. I took the chair from beside the bed, moved it to the opposite wall, sat and waited. She slept hard, as she always has. Purple stains under her eyes looked like bruises, and an IV was strung into one of her hands. I'm told they did that after she was sedated for the examination and rape kit.

I want to kill him.

She stirred, sighed, opened her eyes. A sharp breath like a musical note, and she sat up and reached to me, her fingers wiggling with eagerness. She's reached for me that way since she was a baby. We held each other for a long time. When she let go, she looked my face over. It's rather different from the last time she saw it. I started to say something about it, and she grasped a piece of my shirt and shook it.

"Daddy, look, I didn't mean it. I want you to be around. He said you'd have to go to jail for coming up to the hotel, so I had to make you get away. I didn't mean it, Daddy."

"It's okay, Mousekin—I mean, Mickie—Michaella—"

And she smiled, her own smile for me. "Mouse. Say Mouse."

"Yeah. Mouse. I'm sorry, too, honey. I was a drunk daddy, and—I was too drunk to see that you were buckled in that day. I should have made you wear the seat belt, at least."

She stared at me, my shirt still grasped in her fist. "Huh? But—yes you did. I didn't want to sit in the safety seat, but you made me, because you said you weren't feeling good. And I got mad and I said I hate you and I wouldn't talk to you, and—and—" Her face began to crumple. "I'm sorry. Daddy, I never got to tell you I'm sorry—because I don't hate you—"

"Hang on—I—I made you buckle in?"

"You did it yourself. Because you were hung over and drunk at the same time. Don't you remember?"

"No—I—no. They found you unbuckled, in the front—"

"Well, *duh*, Dad. I knew how to get out of my seat. And I climbed up front, and I tried to help you, and you wouldn't wake up, and I couldn't wipe the blood away, and—"

"Okay—Mousy, don't think about it. I'm okay now."

"Mommy said you were dead."

"She—probably thought it was best for you."

"No, it wasn't. It made me sick. So, she said you forgot about me. And then, Theresa, she's my best friend, she found the *Probe*, and she bought it to show me when we got back from Paris. So that's why I knew you still love me, so I decided to go find you, and get away from—*him*. But I couldn't. So then I wrote letters—you didn't know it was me, did you?"

I shook my head. "I—I'm sorry, honey, I thought—why didn't you tell me you were you?"

"Because then you wouldn't read it, of course! *Hello*! You could go to jail, remember? It said so in the *Probe*. That's why I tried to go to you first, but I couldn't call you."

"Running away was dangerous, Mousy. You don't know what terrible things people—"

"Nothing's worse than *him*. Mommy said I had a crush on him." Her face twisted into bitterness itself. "I wish you were allowed to hate your mother. I'm going to Hell."

"No—Mousy—Sweetheart—No—"

"Theresa said that's my choice. She goes to church, so she knows. You love your mother, or you go to Hell. I'll go to Hell."

I reached for her, pulled her close. She didn't respond, but she didn't resist. I held on to her. "Mouse, Mouseling, you're— we're both—really angry with Mommy. She has her own de-mons—but I think we have a lot to be angry about. Honey, you can't go to Hell. You've already been there. Now you and I have to find the way back."

◇◇◇

Halla sneaked out a side door to bring the car around. I had to come out the main door and face a crowd of Press representa-tives. The nurses made me sit in a wheelchair and be wheeled out, so that I wouldn't faint or something. Quin finished wrapping up the case for the Press. I had to face routine questions:

"How's it feel to be a hero?"

"Didn't you ask me how it felt to be a killer the other day?"

"Oh. Yeah. So, how does it feel to be a hero?"

I escaped in time, set my mind to the fight for my Mouse. What I had to do, I did in record time—bought the house, got through paperwork. Geez. I'm her own father, and—Do you love the irony?

Next month, I'll meet Brewster Beane in New York, and we'll do some real fighting. Whatever Nancy tries to use against me, I will not give in. Not this time. Not ever again.

.Epilogue.

THE REAL BEGINNING

I came across my clipboard just now, with that last bit still on it. It's unbelievable, the amount of stuff you have to work through to get temporary custody of a ward of the court. I had to be named as a foster parent, fill out reams of paperwork, answer hundreds of questions, get permanent residence—no big problem, since I want to marry Halla and settle here. I'm in the midst of moving in, and here's my clipboard.

I was rather out of it when I wrote that last entry. Reading it brought everything back. I'll pick up from there. I can't leave the story half-finished.

◇◇◇

Dear God, I would not have put my Mouse through that for an Oscar. I didn't plan to take her with me when I went up to New York, but Halla argued with me for a day and a half over it— between takes, on the set and off. She won, with help from the kids. Halla said it wouldn't be fair to keep Mouse away from her mother, and Dannal said it wouldn't be fair to keep her mother away from Mouse. Mouse begged to come with me. I caved in.

I shouldn't have done it. I didn't need to bring her; the court said nothing about requiring her presence. But she was excited. She put aside her anger, certain that with Wyndham out of the picture, we would all live happily ever after. I didn't discourage her—didn't know I had to.

Tony growled, of course, but he agreed to shoot around me, and we made a field trip of it, taking the train from Charlotte to New York. We did whatever we felt like doing. We spent a day shopping for a special outfit for Mouse to wear when we saw her mother in court. We opened my apartment for the three days we were there, and Mouse went from room to room, exploring. The room I've kept for her all these years is too big, and she asked for the tiny room I'd been using as a study. Dannal will get the big one. We gave away all the little-girl stuff I'd decorated it with, went out and got a narrow cot and posters of horses and equestrian teams, and redid the study. It's just what you'd expect, right? My kid likes horses.

The big day came. We both got up early and took a lot of time getting ready. Brewster gave me the usual disclaimer, but he left out the we-can-always-try-again-next-year bit. I let myself hope a little. We ensconced my Mouse in an office where she wouldn't hear her parents fighting over her. Brewster gave a last-minute pep talk, I made sure I was breathing, and we went in to do battle.

And nothing happened. Sure, Nancy was there, with a new lawyer, but she never looked up. The new lawyer intoned a few lines, she assented, and suddenly I was a full-time Daddy. Full time. The judge mentioned summers, holidays and weekends, but Nancy was on her way out of the courtroom almost before he'd banged his gavel.

Mouse came out in time to see Nancy push the elevator button. She called to her mother, and Nancy didn't turn around. The doors closed an instant before our child got there. Mouse hurled herself at them, screaming for Mommy to come back.

People drew back and glared. I waded in and picked her up. No matter how Nancy felt, Mouse deserved a chance to say Good-bye to her mother. I showed her the door to the stairs, and we clattered down them together. We almost caught Nancy before she got into a taxi and let it take her away.

We chased her uptown. Nancy's doorman has standing orders to keep me out, of course, but my Mouse slipped past him and up to the apartment, still calling to her Mommy. Within minutes, the doorman approached me. She'd got in. I had to go into the apartment Nancy locked me out of three years ago, and fetch our child away.

She sat sprawl-legged against Nancy's bedroom door, wailing. When I tried to lift her up, she fought me off, calling for her mother. It took time to get her quieted down and sitting on the couch. Then I knocked on the door. "Nancy? How long can you survive in there?"

No answer.

I leaned my good shoulder on the door frame. "Make yourself comfortable, because we're not leaving until you come out and talk. We'll stay if it takes a year. Do you have enough food in there for a year, Nancy?"

No answer.

"You know what's fun, Nance? You can't call for help. You don't have a phone in there. Your husband hates phones in bedrooms, among all the other things he hates. You can't even order out for pizza. So, take your time, and we'll wait. Right here." And I went and sat beside Mouse on the couch.

It took a long few minutes. Nancy opened her door and held on to it. "Get her out."

I stood up to face my ex-wife. "What happened wasn't her fault, and you know it. Say Good-bye to her, Nancy."

"She knows what she did. She knew all the time. She's nothing but a little—"

I stepped very close to her and whispered into her face, "Don't say it."

Her eyes met mine for a split second, and I all but reeled back. Pain had shut out their light—pain, guarded by bottomless rage. Looking into her eyes was like looking into two flat, volcanic pebbles. She drew herself up. "She's just a—"

"You want us to go, Nancy. You want us out of here."

"She knew—I did everything in my power to protect her from your drunken—"

"You protected her from the wrong man, Nancy. Please."

"She deliberately—she—"

"Look at her—she's ten years old! Get a grip."

"Get out."

"Not until you say Good-bye. Nicely. We'll wait."

I thought she was about to fight back. Maybe she did, too. Then she looked away, far away, through the opposite wall. "Good-bye," she enunciated clearly. "Go to—"

I stepped between them. "We have plenty of time."

She amended, "Go home with your father. Don't ever—
Good-bye. Enjoy yourselves."

Mouse wiped her soaked face. "Bye, Mom. I love you."

Nancy may have wanted to say something about that, but I
raised an eyebrow, and she wheeled around and slammed into her
bedroom.

The trip to North Carolina was mostly silent. I lifted my
little girl on and off the train, let her stare out the window, kept
her supplied with tissues. As we drove up the mountain to the
new house, Mouse pressed her face against the glass and peered
out into the night. The house was dark and empty-looking when
we got there, even with the lights on.

◇◇◇

Dannal's the one who saved everything. As we stepped onto the
porch, he rose from the swing. Beside him was a pet carrier,
and a couple of grocery bags. The carrier emitted some high-
pitched profanities. Dannal claimed, "Ma says it's okay with
her if it's okay with you."

He lifted the carrier to the porch floor. "It's Corrigan. He's
supposed to help you get adjusted, sort of. I brought food and
litter and stuff."

It worked. Mouse cuddled down on her knees to get a good
look at the furious, cream-colored fluff in the carrier. In love at
first sight, she pleaded to be allowed to keep it.

◇◇◇

Dear Mouse,

*You have a long, hard road ahead of you. We all do. We'll
get through it, though. We're a tough bunch. What was it
your Aunt Meranda said? "Logans breed strength; Logans
marry strength." I've been doing pretty well in that
department, haven't I, Mousy?*

◇◇

◇

ACKNOWLEDGEMENTS

Writers like me need advice from people who know more than we do, and support from those close to us.

Without the help of my extraordinary circle of friends, advisors, and colleagues, I could never have finished this book . . .

I owe a huge debt of gratitude to members of High Country Writers, who read, advised, critiqued, and then read again, my frequent revisions of this novel . . .

For advice, especially concerning my younger characters, I thank Jessica Leigh Black . . .

My sharpest literary critic is Russell Kaufman-Pace, who prevented some egregious errors. . . .

I am profoundly grateful to all those anonymous people who never allowed me to get too hungry, angry, lonely, or tired . . .

For help with my depictions of law-enforcement personnel in the pursuit of their duties, I owe a solid chunk of gratitude to:

Detective (now Sergeant) Charles Danner of the Watauga County Sheriff's Office, who showed me the workings of law enforcement at the county level in North Carolina . . .

Sergeant Robert Henson and his partner Charlie, who gave me background on the lives and duties of K-9 officers. Charlie, who, sadly, succumbed to cancer before this book was finished, really *did* move like a helium balloon . . .

Lieutenant William Watson of the Boone, NC, police, who gave me background on the operations of a town police department; also, his chair inspired Inspector Quin's office furniture . . .

Attorney Scott Casey, who graciously answered my sometimes rather odd questions about criminal law . . .

Attorney Ed Blair, who gave me excellent general background help regarding North Carolina domestic law . . .

For valuable feedback and help with formatting, I thank:

Parkway Publishers . . .

High Country Publishers' incomparable managing editor, Judy Geary, who guided me through the final edits and rewrites with true insight and respect for my story . . .

AND

Perhaps more than all, I thank
Bob and Barbara Ingalls,
publishers who routinely
make dreams come true

With the publication of this book, my profoundest gratitude goes out to these remarkable people . . .

ALL OF THEM.

ABOUT THE AUTHOR:

Dear Mouse . . . is a culmination of schuyler kaufman's experience with writing in a variety of genres; acting in film, on stage, and in children's theater; and teaching writing, communication, and mathematics on the local university campus. She is currently at work on her next book.

Also from *High Country Publishers*:

ALL ROADS LEAD TO MURDER
By Albert A. Bell

Makes the ancient world a living, breathing entity but never fails to remind us on every page that a vast chasm separates us from them, 200 years ago. . . . a *real* historical novel! . . . the *best* of them – I do hope that it is the first book in a long series.
– Rachel A Hyde, MyShelf.com

Masterful blend of history and mystery.
– Barbary D'Amato, award-winning author of
the *Cat Marsala* series

An absolutely wonderful, engaging story, which breathes life into the Roman Empire of the first century.
–N.S. Gill, host Ancient and Classical History About.com

Bell captures the essence of what it is to be a Roman citizen as he crafts the nuances of early Christianity and the burden of slavery.
– Lynda S. Robinson, author of the *Lord Meren* series

ISBN: 097130453X
October 2002
Hardcover, 246 pages, $21.95

HCP books are available through Biblio Distribution, a division of NBN Books to bookstores, wholesalers, and online retailers.

Also from *High Country Publishers*:

Magdalena's Song

By Pat Mestern

Pat Mestern's deeply evocative historical novels are among the most rewarding, and the most pleasing, being published today. While they conjure a time long gone and imagine characters long dead, they never fail to embrace the sorts of scandals, dreams and secrets that can haunt nearly every family in every walk of life for many tomorrows.
— J. **Marshall Craig**, film director, author of the *Eric Burdon memoir Don't Let Me Be Misunderstood*

(M)arvelous. Congratulations. That is just what any writer hopes to do with writing, and yet so few of us achieve it.
— **Ryan Taylor**, author: *Across the Water, Routes to Roots*, radio show host, Fort Wayne IN

A combination of plot and Mestern's proven talents is bound to produce another first-rate novel with a strong local character and appeal.
— **Jim Rohman**, radio journalist: CBC, CKWR

ISBN: 097130453X
March 2003
Trade paperback, 276 pages, $16.95

Also from *High Country Publishers*:

Monteith's Mountains

by Skip Brooks

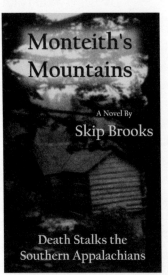

. . . a suspense thriller set in 1900 . . . as real as today."
– *Publishers Weekly*

. . . extraordinary work. . . . the Smokies and its people come to life. . . . creative, profound and interesting.
– Dr. Bob Hieronimus, Co-Founder of 21st Century Radio

. . . suspenseful, powerful and arousing read, holding you by plot, character, and the inspiring beauty of its southern Appalachian settings.
– Howard Dorgan, Past President of the Appalachian Studies Association and author of four books on Appalachian Culture.

. . . dramatic portrait of the Great Smoky Mountains and their people. . . captures both the voices of mountain people and the dramatic landscape of their beloved Smokies in a haunting tale.
– Dr. William Ferris, Public Policy Scholar The Woodrow Wilson International Center for Scholars and Former Director; National Endowment for The Humanities

ISBN: 0971304548
October 2002
Hardcover, 288 pages, $21.95

HCP books are available through Biblio Distribution, a division of NBN Books to bookstores, wholesalers, and online retailers.

Also from *High Country Publishers*:

Where the Water-Dogs Laughed
or
The Sacred Dream of the Great Bear

By Charles F. Price

Tusquittee Bald, known in Cherokee legend as the place where the water-dogs laughed, frames this the latest in Charles F. Price's saga of the Southern Appalachians at the close of the 19th century. Hamby McFee seeks out Yan-e'gwa, the great bear that has terrorized and excited loggers and hunters, and finds his own fate in the process.

ISBN: 1932158502
October 2003

Visit our website to learn more about High Country Publishers books and authors
www.highcountrypublishers.com

HCP books are available through Biblio Distribution, a division of NBN Books to bookstores, wholesalers, and online retailers.